The Preacher's Daughter

 Horseshoe Home Ranch

LIZ ISAACSON

"Lead me in thy truth, and teach me: for thou art the God of my salvation; on thee do I wait all the day."

— PSALMS 25:5

CHAPTER 1

*L*andon Edmunds woke to the sound of his phone vibrating against the decades-old dresser. For a moment, he wasn't sure where he was. The sun slanted through the window in the wrong spot.

He sat up, the familiar gray walls of his cabin coming into focus. "Not in Peach Valley anymore," he muttered as he reached for his cell. He'd taken a couple of weeks to get out of Montana before the summer planting started.

Sure, Jace needed him here all the time, as evidenced by the text on Landon's phone. *Need you at my place in fifteen minutes. Doable?*

Of course it was doable, whether Landon wanted to show his face around the ranch or not. He hadn't been able to escape his best friend's all-seeing eye, though he supposed he wouldn't want any less from the foreman at Horseshoe Home.

But Landon didn't want Jace's scrutiny any more than he

wanted his sister—and Jace's wife—to set him up with every able-bodied person with an X-chromosome. He was done with women, and his trip to Peach Valley had only solidified that decision.

Doable, he sent back to Jace and heaved himself out of bed. He wasn't supposed to work today either, but when Jace called, Landon answered. That road went both ways, as Landon had leaned on Jace's strength for most of this past year. And before that, Landon had helped Jace through a hard time after his fiancé abandoned him on his wedding day.

Grateful for good friends, Landon splashed water on his face and brushed his teeth. His phone chimed again, and he recoiled from a text from another cowboy about the first dance of the summer.

Landon used to lead the boys down the canyon to the valley dances. Cowboys were popular and he'd never had to scrounge for a partner. But he didn't want partners anymore. Not after Lauren had chosen him three years ago. Not after they dated for a year. Not after she decided another cowboy intrigued her more. Not after he found them kissing behind the barn.

They'd both left Montana now, thank goodness. For a while there, Landon had considered leaving the ranching business altogether. But he didn't have much else to do in his life. He loved ranching the same way he'd loved the rodeo. But he couldn't return to that career. The injury to his left leg prevented him from riding bulls ever again.

He had been considering leaving Horseshoe Home. He

and Jace had been looking at ranches all over the western United States, researching the cost to buy one, the time needed to move, to prepare the ranch, to get the best cowhands. Not that Jace was going to leave, but he'd done everything to support Landon.

Not going to the dance, Landon texted back to his friend. No reason. No excuse. Just not going. Hopefully Caleb wouldn't press the issue. Landon combed his hair and threw on a pair of jeans and a short-sleeved shirt in black-and-white plaid. He'd gotten a new hat from his friend in Peach Valley, and he mashed the black hat over his blond hair and headed out the door.

The first week of June in Montana sported an endless blue sky and temperatures Landon wished would stick for the whole year. He took a deep breath of the fresh mountain air, glad to be back in Big Sky Country.

His jaunt to Wyoming had been welcome, cleansing, but he'd realized he didn't want to move there. Sure, Jackson and Maya were wonderful and accommodating. It had been good to see his old friend from the rodeo, Jackson's brother, Blaze.

But Landon had realized on his two-week hiatus that he loved Montana. Had been born and raised here. But as he climbed the steps to Jace's front door, he still wasn't quite sure what he wanted.

He knocked at the same time he opened the door. "Mornin'," he called, closing the door behind him. Jace rose from an armchair at the same time Belle and a dark-haired woman twisted from their position on the couch to look at him.

Belle sprang to her feet, her face showing much more emotion than Jace's. Landon catalogued the fear, the nerves, and the hope in his sister's face before turning his attention to his best friend and boss.

"What's goin' on?" Landon glanced back to Belle, and then the second woman stood and faced him. A smile graced her familiar face, but Landon worked to recall who she was. Her beauty was obvious in the bones of her face, the depth of her dark eyes. She radiated an air that soothed Landon's soul, and his anxiety dropped a notch. Something about her called to him, made him want to get closer to her.

He worked hard to keep himself in place, looking to Jace and Belle for an explanation. He couldn't believe the attraction he felt; he'd sworn off dating and women. Completely. Totally. He'd been female-free for two years now.

But maybe this beautiful woman would break his—

"You remember Megan Palmer, don't you?" Belle wrung her hands, but put a smile on her face and in her voice.

All at once, recognition hit Landon full in the chest. "Megan Palmer." He settled his weight on his back foot and folded his arms. "Of course. The preacher's daughter."

She flinched, her smile folding for half a second before hitching back into place.

"She's helping out her dad for a while," Jace said. "Her father's retiring."

"That right?" Landon tore his eyes from the raven-haired beauty to flick his eyes to Jace for a moment. "That's great. What have you been up to?"

A shadow crossed her eyes, but when she said, "This and that," she sounded perfectly pleasant. Landon could read people, and he could tell she was hiding something. For some reason, he wanted to talk to her until he figured out what it was.

That's just because she's pretty, he told himself, strengthening his resolve not to let a familiar, gorgeous face persuade him from his bachelor life. Still, he had expected her to say she'd achieved something grand. She seemed like the type who would, the type Landon usually gravitated toward.

"She's just moved back from Wyoming," Belle said.

"Oh, I've just returned from a vacation in Wyoming."

"So Jace was telling me." Megan gave him that warm smile, and Landon basked in it. When he realized what was happening, he shut down his emotions.

"So what did you need, Jace?"

Jace settled back into the armchair, a sign that sent every alarm inside of Landon into red alert. He glanced at his sister, but she sat too, leaving his gaze to migrate to Megan. Still stunned by her beauty, and remembering her now from high school, he didn't quite understand when she said, "I'm afraid they got you over here so I could ask you for a favor."

Megan felt breathless. She'd prepared herself to be in the same room as her high school crush, Landon Edmunds. Or at least she'd thought she had. But facing him now, she knew she was ill-equipped to deal with his male magnetism, his stunning good looks, his wide shoulders. And her defenses against that sexy cowboy hat?

Nada.

She attempted to school her thoughts into something more godly, something that would represent a preacher's daughter. She hated the label that came with her name. She'd endured it growing up, and it really rubbed her the wrong way as an adult.

Of course, Landon didn't know that. Megan had never told her high school best friend, Belle, about her schoolgirl crush on her older brother. And he'd left for the rodeo circuit before she'd graduated from high school.

She'd always chalked up their separate lives as simply fate. But here she was, back in town, and Landon was nothing but available—if Belle was to be believed.

"Come on over and sit for a second," Jace said.

Landon obeyed him, and Megan fell heavily back to the couch beside Belle, her emotions spiraling up and then down. Had she really asked her best friend to set up a meeting with her brother? Like Megan was in junior high and couldn't use a phone to call the man herself.

Landon did not sit, but leaned against the kitchen counter and faced the living room. "Favor?" he asked, his attention on Megan singular.

She could barely breathe under the weight of it, and she

commanded herself to stop finding him so attractive. *Speak, Megan! Speak now.*

Belle elbowed her, and Megan cleared her throat. "That's right," she said, making her voice as smooth as she could. Thankfully, it flowed like honey. Dad had always said she had a soothing voice—something he'd used against her when he'd asked her to start teaching Bible Study classes.

"I'm helping my father get ready to retire, and I'm trying to get the church into shape before then." She exhaled, turning it into a laugh. "Well, before winter, really." Her eyes flitted all over the place, finally landing back on Landon. "That's where you come in."

He crossed his arms, making his biceps bigger and his presence fill the cabin. "Me?"

She swallowed and glanced at Jace, who nodded. "Yes, Jace says you've been looking for something different."

Though he made no sound, Megan could hear the internal growl Landon made as he swung his gaze to Jace. "He did, did he?" His voice sounded sharp, and cold, but Jace didn't so much as flinch.

"Don't look at me like that. You *have* been thinking about doing something different," he said. "This is carpentry work. You're the best cowhand when it comes to building repair."

"I have a job." One eyebrow rose. "At least I thought I did."

"You do," Jace said. "But I don't see why we can't loan you out to Miss Palmer for a few months."

"It's summer planting season," Landon said as if Megan and Belle weren't even in the room anymore. "You expressly told me I had to be back from Wyoming to start on Monday."

"And you're back a whole weekend early." Jace's steady gaze never left Landon's. The men seemed stuck in a battle of wills, and whoever looked away first would lose.

Jace sighed and glanced at Megan. "I can probably send out Ty. He's good with a hammer too."

"But Landon's the best," Belle piped up. Megan could feel her friend's nerves, and she smoothed her palms down her thighs.

"It's fine, guys," she said. "I can ask around town too." She stood and stepped over to Landon, her heart galloping, thundering, in her chest. She stretched up and kissed him on the cheek, startled at the spark of electricity that leapt from him to her. Or from her to him, she wasn't sure. "Good to see you again." She hastily stepped away and made for the front door.

She had to get out of there. *Get out. Get out quick.* She couldn't stand to be in Landon's presence for another second, though the twelve years since she'd seen him in person hadn't diminished her attraction to him at all.

She was surprised by that. Time should've been able to dim some of those feelings. Heck, her broken past with her recent ex should've been able to tame those emotions. But no, here she was, acting like a sixteen-year-old again, all infatuated with the gorgeous, strong cowboy.

She escaped and pressed her back to the closed front door. She finally managed to take a breath that wasn't filled with the scent of Landon's cologne, and reason infused her senses.

She did need help at the church. Her father hadn't been able to keep it up like he used to, not with his hip replacement five years ago. She'd hired Belle to do some interior design work, but she needed a handyman to really complete her vision for the project.

Voices behind the door filtered to her, and she hurried away, not wanting to eavesdrop on Landon as he questioned his family. Once in the safety of her car, Megan mentally recited the things she needed to accomplish before her father gave the congregation of Gold Valley to another pastor.

Fix up the building.

Repair the grounds.

Start community outreach programs.

Figure out how to teach the gospel.

Sure, she'd grown up listening to her dad preach. She loved going to church, and hearing the lectures, and reading the scriptures. But she hadn't gone to school, had never taken a theology class. Dad said the people wouldn't mind her lack of credentials just for Bible Study, but it bothered Megan.

She'd enrolled in several theology classes through the local college, and a couple online through the university in Missoula. With only seven months to get herself worthy to teach, the physical facilities were the least of her concerns.

She felt certain people would care if they found out her last boyfriend had stolen from her. They'd want their instructor to be smarter, know more, be more street-savvy, than that. She hadn't even told her father Eric's theft was the deciding factor in her return to Gold Valley.

Her dad had been asking her for a year to come home and help him teach, but she'd resisted. Eric lived and worked in Wyoming, and she'd been in love with him. As she turned back onto the highway and drove out of the canyon, she wondered if she still was.

Six months wasn't a very long time, and though he'd swindled dozens of people out of a lot of money—and taken thousands from Megan herself—she knew she needed more time to come to terms with how she felt about him, about herself, about everything, before she'd be ready to move forward.

"Maybe Landon can help you with that," she said. With her words came the fantasy of holding his hand, laughing with him, maybe even kissing him.

Annoyed with herself for even thinking such things about a man she no longer knew, Megan reached over and turned on the radio. Loud. She needed to use something to drive Landon from her mind.

CHAPTER 2

$\mathcal{M}$egan arrived at the church with a box of doughnuts and two mugs of coffee. She entered her father's office and found him seated behind the desk, bent over his notes. "Just how you like it, with sugar and cream," she said as she set the coffee next to him. "And I got you one of those apple fritters you like."

She put the box of baked goods next to him. He glanced up and smiled, though Megan saw the burdens he carried. That line of pain between his eyes from the hip that never stopped hurting. That edge of weariness in his eyes that had appeared when her mother had died four years ago. The pinch of his mouth because of the love he had for the people in Gold Valley. He prayed for them, thought of them often, served them when he could. The vein that pulsed in his neck with worry about someone else taking over the congregation.

"What are you studying this morning?" She reached for a long bar doughnut covered in whipped maple frosting.

"The Savior's teachings about charity."

"Deep." Megan bit into her doughnut, unsure of where the chapters on charity were located in the Bible. She had a ton of her own studying to do, but she couldn't seem to focus on it until late at night. Even then, Megan didn't have many scriptures memorized.

"A lifetime pursuit," he agreed. "Did you get a handyman?" His voice strayed a bit higher than she would've liked, his apology for the church needing a handyman.

"Not yet," she said. "But I will." She wanted it to be Landon, simply to be in his company. She may or may not have imagined confessing to him that she'd crushed on him for two years, that she'd followed his rodeo career online and on television for much longer than that.

She tucked her curly hair behind her ear and kept her thoughts silent. No one wanted to be told they'd been stalked, even through a screen. That wasn't romantic. As she polished off her doughnut, Megan was relieved Landon hadn't jumped at the chance to work for the church this summer. He didn't need to know what kind of pedestal she had him on, and she suddenly didn't want anyone to find out.

Yes, Megan had a lot to keep under wraps now that she was back in Gold Valley.

"Well, I'm gonna…." She hooked her thumb over her shoulder like that would convey to her father what she was going to go accomplish. He waved, his attention back on his scriptures, and she moved down the hall, noting the need for new paint on the walls, the crooked doorway on the men's restroom.

She definitely needed a handyman—and a boost of confidence that she could get the church and herself ready by January.

———

Landon had to practically fold himself in half to fit in the back of his sister's sedan. He hadn't seen or spoken to Jace or Belle since their "intervention" on Friday morning. After Megan had delicately removed herself from the conversation, he'd demanded to know what they'd been thinking.

His sister's words hadn't left his mind. *You can't be alone forever, Landon.*

When he'd challenged her and asked her why not, she'd looked to Jace for help. "Because that's not what people do," he'd said. "They get past hard things. They move on."

Landon had tried to tell them that he *was* past Lauren, but Jace—who'd been through a much more difficult experience when it came to women—hadn't believed him for a second. And he shouldn't. Landon knew he wasn't past Lauren. But he also knew that he'd spoken true when he'd told Belle and Jace that, "I'm just not interested in dating right now."

The miles passed as they continued toward the church. Landon had spent his Saturday wondering what it would take to get him interested in dating again. Flashes of Megan's face, her calming influence, had plagued him all day.

"You think Megan will be there?" he asked as they passed the horseshoe-shaped falls where Jace and Belle had gotten engaged.

"'Course," Jace said.

His gut pinched, and he stared out the window without seeing much.

"You think any more about workin' for her?" Jace asked.

Landon checked his watch. "Twenty-four minutes," he said. "Which one of you wins the bet?"

"I do," Belle said at the same time Jace said, "There was no bet."

Landon laughed, the sound starting deep in his chest. While they frustrated him sometimes, Landon was grateful to have Belle and Jace in his life. They'd seen him at his worst and still wanted him around.

Jace pulled into the parking lot at the church. "All I'm sayin' is the church needs a handyman, and he could do it."

"I said you'd bring it up before church," Belle said. "I win."

"If I hadn't brought it up before church, you would've after. Then *I* would've won." He grinned at her, the love between them obvious and a tad infectious. Landon thought of Megan as he climbed out of the car, as Belle and Jace continued to bicker about who'd really won the bet. He followed them into the building and paused at the entrance into the chapel.

He kept his gaze forward though he wanted to scan for dark, curly hair. His fingers balled into fists and his jaw ground together with the effort it took not to examine everyone who walked by. He spotted his parents and had a fleeting thought that he should just go sit by them, but Jace beckoned to him from a row in the middle of the chapel, and Landon stepped into the flow of people to take his place on the bench.

Landon didn't see Megan before the meeting started, and she didn't sit up front, and Landon's nerves felt raw and strained. As the closing prayer ended, relief poured through him. Relief he didn't quite understand. He thought he wanted to see her, maybe explain why he couldn't come work at the church.

But now that he didn't have to see her, talk to her, the relief combined with a sense of disappointment he didn't understand.

He stood and turned to leave, seizing when he found Megan only a foot from him. She startled too, her gaze flying up his chest to his face. "Landon," she said, his name almost a gasp.

He couldn't quite get his voice to work, so he swallowed and stepped back—right into Belle. "Sorry," he mumbled as he tried to figure out where to put himself that wouldn't be in someone's personal space.

Belle looped her arm through Landon's. "Hey, Megan." She released Landon and swept toward Megan for a hug. As Megan came closer to Landon, he caught a whiff of something floral.

She moved back and Landon found himself leaning forward, still trying to identify that scent. He became very aware of Jace's gaze on the side of his face, and Landon put more distance between him and the very exotic smelling Megan.

He wasn't sure who said what, but he suddenly found himself alone, face-to-face with Megan. His boots made loud scuffing noises as he tried to find his center. The memory of her lips on his cheek—an innocent gesture from an old friend—now burned like a brand as he thought about her as a woman, not his little sister's best friend he used to know.

"Did you like the sermon?" she asked.

Landon blinked, his mind blank as to what the pastor had even said. "Uh, yeah. Sure. Great sermon." The lie seemed to echo around the near-empty chapel.

Megan cocked her head and grinned. "What did my father talk about?"

Landon rubbed the back of his neck. "I don't remember," he admitted with a soft chuckle. "I have a lot on my mind."

"Is working for the church one of them?" Megan asked, her eyes sparkling like dark, dangerous fireworks.

"You're a persistent little thing, aren't you?" Landon grinned at her.

"Let me take you on a tour of the building." She nodded toward the back of the chapel, a half smile on her full lips. "Do you have time?"

Landon's phone vibrated in his pocket. As if her question had reached Jace's ears, he'd texted to say they'd go up to the falls and he could text when he was ready to go.

With his mind whirling, and a ready excuse gone, he met Megan's eye. "I suppose I do."

"Great," she said. "Let's actually start right here in the chapel."

CHAPTER 3

Landon moved behind Megan, and not only because she was the tour guide. He basked in the scent she left behind—jasmine, he'd finally identified. And if he were being honest, he enjoyed the view from the back as the woman walked.

His senses on overdrive, from her sensual smell to the curves of her body, Landon couldn't quite get his ears to work. But his eyes seemed to, and he found all the dings in the stairs leading to the stand, the chips in the podium where the pastor stood, the way some of the choir seats wouldn't go back up.

He nodded, nothing he'd seen so far outside his wheelhouse that he couldn't figure it out. Some sanding, some staining, some replacement parts.

"I want to figure out how to clean that stained glass window too." Megan turned to him as if he'd restored a thousand stained glass windows.

"It is beautiful," he said though most of the panes had clouded. Montana weather could be brutal, even in the summer. "I bet I can figure out how to clear it up."

Her eyebrows rose. "So you'll come clean it?" Her interest seemed a little strong, but maybe she was just being passionate about her father's church.

"I didn't say that." He smiled to soften the blow, and because he was truly considering the offer. He could plant in his sleep—in fact, come tomorrow morning when he rose at five a.m. to get up to the prepared fields, he probably would plant while asleep. "But show me the rest of the church."

By the time he texted Jace to come on back and pick him up, he'd spent almost an hour with the centered and sexy Megan Palmer, his interest and curiosity piqued. He'd seen some challenges at the church—an entire section of the balcony needed to be rebuilt, not to mention that stained glass window—and some things that wouldn't take much brainpower, like painting and installing new light fixtures.

He hadn't committed to Megan that he'd help her. He'd said he'd talk to Jace and the ranch owner and see if they could spare him.

"So?" Belle asked, twisting in her seat to look at Landon.

"I win," Jace whispered under his breath as he turned to head up the canyon toward the ranch.

"So, what?" Landon enjoyed teasing his sister.

"So, are you going to go help Megan at the church?"

Landon watched the scenery pass by. "It wouldn't be to help Megan."

"No, of course not," Belle said. "To help the church."

Landon couldn't think about it any other way. Couldn't think about it in an emotional way. He'd done that before and been burned.

"I'm thinking about it." He caught Jace and Belle exchange a glance, but he didn't know what it meant. He listened to his sister talk about Megan, how kind she was, how successful she'd been in Wyoming, how Belle was so happy to have her back in town.

Her enthusiasm seeped into Landon—or maybe he'd already started to feel things for Megan that went beyond just seeing someone he'd known in high school. He wasn't sure. She dominated his thoughts. Her voice crowded its way into his ears. The touch of her lips against his cheek made him wonder what she'd feel like pressed up against him as he kissed her for real.

"You gettin' out?" Jace was bent over and peering into the backseat. "Belle threw something in the crockpot before church. Lunch should only take a few more minutes. Tom and his family are comin'."

Landon scrambled to get out of the car, straightening and looking toward the horse barn. "I think I might take Crossfire up the mountain."

"Come to lunch first." Jace clapped his hand on Landon's shoulder. "Belle and I have something to tell you." He moved away before Landon could decipher the look in his eyes.

And he did need to eat. He went back to his cabin and changed out of his white shirt and tie, his mind churning about what Belle and Jace needed to tell him. If they laid into him again about his girl problems, he wasn't sure what he'd do. He knew they meant well, but he didn't need their help.

Tom and his family, complete with a new baby girl, had already arrived when Landon stepped through the front door. He said hello, sat next to Mari on the couch, and asked her about Olivia.

"She likes me best," Mari said. "She cries, and I help her."

Landon chuckled as Rose passed the baby to Mari. The little girl sat up, her bright blue eyes trained on Landon. Mari bounced her. "See?"

"Oh, I see, Miss Mari. You're the best big sister in Montana."

"That's what Tom says." She beamed at Tom and then Olivia.

"Okay," Jace said. "So we asked you to come to lunch today because we have some news of our own." He drew Belle into his side. "You want me to tell them?"

"Yes." Her eyes seemed glassy to Landon.

"Okay, so—"

"Wait," Belle interrupted. "I want to tell them."

Jace waved for her to go on then. Landon had watched Belle and Jace work through issues of their own, both before and after they got married. He knew things with them weren't perfect. He wasn't even sure if perfection existed.

Yet he still yearned for someone perfect for him. Someone who could put up with his intensity, his muddy boots, his inability to have long conversations.

Is there anyone out there like that? He tossed the question toward heaven while Belle wrung her hands. *And not just out there, but right here, in Gold Valley?*

Landon didn't get off the ranch much. Maybe working down in town would be good for him. Certainly a lot of women came and went at the church.

"Jace and I are going to have a baby," Belle said, drawing Landon's attention away from his circular thoughts.

Rose squealed, and as Landon stood, he realized for the first time in two years that he didn't want to be alone. As he looked at the absolute joy on his sister's face, he knew he didn't really want the bachelor life. As he hugged Jace and felt his happiness, Landon wanted it for himself.

And maybe it was time to start doing something different if he expected a different result.

Megan stayed up late on Sunday evening, studying. She'd always been at her best after ten p.m., though it made for a slow start the following day. After she'd crammed as many scriptures as she could into her brain, she drafted a help wanted ad for the online classifieds. Near two a.m., she fell into bed, utterly exhausted.

She hadn't posted the ad. Wanted Landon to call and say he'd take the job. Spending an hour with him that afternoon had been the sweetest kind of torture Megan could experience. At the same time, she'd spent the rest of the afternoon and evening second-guessing how she felt.

She'd been doing that a lot since she'd discovered that Eric had taken her bank account and put his name on it. She couldn't withdraw her money, transfer it to another account, nothing. And he'd cleaned out the account the following day, then disappeared from town only to be arrested and brought back a few days later.

She'd gotten her money back, even though so many others hadn't. He'd apologized, but not to her directly. He'd written a statement to all those he'd hurt. For several months, Megan hadn't even realized how deep her wounds had been.

When her alarm woke her in the morning, she immediately swiped it to snooze. She'd just drifted back into a quiet, rocking slumber when she remembered she had an appointment with her therapist that morning.

She couldn't miss it, so she heaved herself out of bed and into the shower. An hour later found her in Daisy Turner's office, seated on a blue flowered chair Megan wanted for her own apartment. Megan had liked the psychiatrist from the first moment they'd met, because Daisy didn't want to be called Doctor Turner.

"Morning," Daisy said as she entered the room, a folder in her hand. "How are you today, Megan?"

"Good." Megan didn't believe in keeping things bottled up. She never had. She liked holistic healing, but she relied on modern medicine too. "I brought you some lavender." She leaned forward and put a small bottle of clear liquid on Daisy's desk. "You said your husband's headaches were getting worse. That should help."

Daisy looked at the bottle for a long moment, and then switched her gaze to Megan. "Thank you." She took the bottle with a smile and tucked it out of sight. "Did you find a handyman for the church?"

How does she do that? Megan wondered. She'd mentioned the need for a handyman once, three weeks ago. How did Daisy know to bring it up at this moment?

A sigh escaped Megan's mouth. "Not yet. I have someone in mind, but he hasn't committed yet."

"Who is it?"

Megan wasn't sure why that mattered, but Daisy often asked questions Megan wasn't sure about—until the doctor hit on the one that really made Megan dig down deep and examine how she felt.

"Landon Edmunds."

Daisy always looked at Megan while they talked, but now her eyes rounded. "Landon is—" She cleared her throat. "Doesn't he work at the ranch?"

"Yes." Megan squinted like that would help her see past Daisy's stumble. "Do you know him?"

"He's about my twins' age," Daisy said. "My son followed his rodeo career. You know how boys are. Bryson wanted to be a bull rider, and he spent years watching Landon on TV."

"Me too," Megan said without thinking.

Daisy blinked, blinked again. "And my daughter, well, he dated my daughter for a while before things didn't work out between them." She opened the folder and picked up a pen. "Landon is a good man. I'm sure he'd do a great job at the church."

A flash of jealousy stole through Megan at the mention of Landon dating someone else. She considered it miraculous he hadn't been snatched off the market years ago, and intellectually she knew he'd dated. But actually knowing someone who'd done it was a completely new feeling Megan didn't know how to deal with.

"So you watched Landon in the bull riding on TV?" Daisy's tone had settled into professionalism, but Megan's neck heated.

She tried for a carefree giggle and got a strangled, choking sound instead. "Who didn't? I mean, Gold Valley is a small town. Anyone who leaves and does anything remotely public is going to have a lot of fans." She tucked her hands under her legs, and Daisy catalogued the movement. "I mean, look at Sterling Maughan."

"Mm." Daisy's pen scratched and her eyes moved to follow what she wrote. "Sterling is doing well, isn't he?"

"And he didn't even grow up here," Megan said. "Summering at a cabin doesn't count. And yet we'll have 'Good luck Sterling!' on the marquee at the movie theater come winter."

Daisy laughed, and to keep the attention off of her obsession with Landon, Megan joined her. "I may only have been back in town for a month, but I already know who he is, where he lives, *and* that he has a pool in his backyard for conditioning."

"Having a swimming pool in Montana is pretty strange," Daisy said. She asked another question, this time about Megan's sleeping habits. As their conversation continued,

Megan kept her focus on the topics Daisy wanted her to explore. She couldn't afford another slip about her stalkerish habits with Landon.

In a town the size of Gold Valley, it would only take one comment from one person to another before he heard she'd had a ginormous crush on him twelve years ago. Heck, Daisy could mention something to her daughter, who could say something in the grocery store, and before Megan knew it, Landon would know she'd watched him win the National Championship on a bull named Catfish John, only a few months before his career-ending injury.

CHAPTER 4

On Wednesday afternoon, Megan listed her help wanted ad on Gold Valley's classified website. She'd been holding out for almost three days now, hoping and praying Landon would call and say he was outside with a tool belt and a plan.

She'd resisted the urge to text Belle and ask her, deciding to act like the twenty-eight-year old woman she was. She rubbed jasmine oil on her temples in an attempt to soothe her anxiety and closed her laptop so she wouldn't get the instant notifications when someone looked at her ad.

But that didn't help. She'd put her cell phone number on the ad, and it began chiming faster than she could check the messages.

Four men wanted to know more about the job—and Belle had asked her to come out to the ranch in the morning so they could go over carpet samples.

I can come to you, too. Let me know.

I'll come out there, Megan typed out. She needed a break from the church anyhow. *How long will it take?*

A couple of hours probably.

Megan confirmed and she sent texts back to the job applicants, asking them to come by the church in the afternoon for interviews. With that done, she packed up her lunchbox, grabbed her purse, and headed home.

Her apartment sat near downtown, and she liked the bustle of the shops, the deli, the restaurants in the early evening. She parked, took her books and purse upstairs, and changed into a comfortable pair of shoes and a dark pair of jeans. She tucked her driver's license and her debit card in her back pocket and headed back downstairs.

The summer evening breeze played with her curls, and a carefree smile danced across her face. So what that Landon hadn't called about the job? She was planning to be in town for a while, and if he hadn't left Gold Valley yet, he probably wouldn't.

And your schoolgirl crush is pretty ridiculous, she told herself as she entered the coffee shop. She stepped up to the counter. "Maple waffle and a cappuccino," she said. After paying, she settled with her dinner on the patio to watch the townspeople go about their lives.

A sense of contentment washed over her as she sipped her drink and ripped off pieces of the maple-infused waffle. Sure, she'd left Gold Valley for college, but she'd never earned her degree. She'd worked as an elementary school secretary for a few years, then took those skills and moved into the corporate world.

She'd met Eric through her job for a social media marketing firm, and his good looks, easy way with conversation, and polished personality had won her over in just a few short months. They'd been together for three years before he asked her to marry him, and if she hadn't found out about her bank account only a few minutes after he'd been fired for laundering money that wasn't his, she'd have married him last April.

Her smile had faded into nothing and she downed the last of her coffee. As she meandered through the park, past the courthouse, and back to her apartment, she solidified her determination not to go all gaga over Landon again.

———

Thursday morning, Landon rose only a hair past the time he would've to go planting. Jace had insisted he take the day to work closer to the ranch. He liked to rotate people out to the fields and back to the homestead, and though Landon didn't need to be up at five-thirty to feed chickens, he was.

He finished with the small animal feeding and came out of the barn, clapping his hands together to rid them of the dust. He froze as his eyes landed on a blue sedan in front of Jace's cabin.

No, not the sedan. The curvy, dark-haired woman currently moving away from the car and toward the porch.

"Megan," he called without thinking.

She turned, seeking for the source of her name. When

her gaze landed on Landon, she lifted her hand in a friendly gesture. He expected a smile but didn't get one.

Something snaked through him, but he couldn't identify how he felt. Disappointment cut through him when she turned away from him and continued toward the cabin. Disappointment he didn't understand.

"Shoulda called her," he muttered as he put his head down and walked to the administration lodge. He'd been toying with the idea of taking the job at the church. Thankfully, neither Jace nor Belle had brought it up again, and though he'd followed Megan around the church for an hour, he hadn't committed.

He tried to put his indecision from his mind, but he only succeeded in getting the church to fade behind the ranch he'd found in Utah on Monday evening.

It featured one of the fanciest homesteads Landon had ever seen. He'd been in touch with the real estate agent. She'd told him about the sellers—a family that had lived on the land for over a century. Their father had passed away, and none of the children wanted the ranch. So the family was selling the land, the homestead, everything.

It wasn't a cattle ranch, and that appealed to Landon. He could finally focus on what he really wanted to do: train horses for the rodeo circuit.

True, he was a cowboy, but at heart, he loved the rodeo. He loved horses more than cows. Loved summer more than winter. A half-smile quirked his lips. It would still be cold in Utah, but he also knew nowhere had snowdrifts as high as rooftops the way Montana did.

And the fact remained that Landon needed a change.

He pivoted on the bottom stair leading to the administration lodge and faced Belle's cabin.

"You need a change," he said aloud, and he strode back the way he'd come. He marched right up the steps and knocked on the door. Long seconds passed before Belle opened it, and she fell back, surprised.

"Landon."

"Is Megan here?"

"Yes, we're looking at carpet samples."

"I need to talk to her."

Belle stepped all the way back and swept her hand toward the kitchen, where Megan watched him with a pile of carpet samples stacked behind her on the table.

Landon didn't second-guess himself, didn't rehearse what he should say. "Hey." He crossed the room and stopped only a few feet from Megan. She blinked up at him, her long lashes framing her dark-as-night eyes. Eyes he could fall into if he wasn't careful.

Landon was tired of being careful too. "Do you still need a handyman?"

A smile slowly spread her lips, and Landon thought he could lose himself to that mouth too. He shook his head to clear it as she said, "I just put up an ad yesterday afternoon for it."

"Oh."

"I'm interviewing everyone this afternoon."

A shockwave traveled through Landon, and new determination filled him. "What time should I come down to interview?"

His sister's giggle behind him made a flush of heat rise through his face.

Megan stood and dug her phone out of her pocket. "Let's see…." She thumbed through something. "How about you come by the church tomorrow morning, ready to start?" She grinned up at him. "The job's yours if you want it."

Landon stared at her for a few seconds, not quite comprehending. "What—?"

"She said you could have the job," Belle said, her laughter filling the empty spaces in Landon's mind. "You'll probably need to let Jace know." She sounded all innocent as she moved into her kitchen to refill her coffee mug.

"Yeah, Jace." Landon focused back on Megan, and he kicked a grin in her direction. That electricity he'd felt when she'd kissed his cheek last week leapt again. He thought he'd imagined the attraction between them, even went so far as to think her shoes had accumulated static electricity, but now, standing only a few feet from her and caught in a shared smile with her, he felt a connection with her that went beyond old friendships.

"So we'll start fresh tomorrow?" Megan asked.

"Yeah," Landon said slowly. "We'll start fresh." And for the first time in two years, Landon wanted a new friendship with a woman. And not just any woman—with Megan. The thought unsettled him as much as it excited him.

CHAPTER 5

$\mathscr{L}$andon pulled into the church parking lot the next morning, surprised to see half a dozen cars already there. He wasn't sure why someone besides the pastor would be at the church on a weekday. He wasn't entirely sure why he was there.

But he'd spoken with Jace while Belle kept throwing him knowing smiles from the kitchen. He'd stayed for dinner, unsure of why he didn't want to be alone with himself. Once he'd gone back to his cabin, his mind had spun out of control.

Like it was now.

He took a deep breath and centered his thoughts. He was just going to be sanding and staining and straightening. Megan probably wouldn't even be around most of the time. She didn't seem like the micromanaging type.

After dinner last night, Belle had thrown around details about Megan while Jace scooped ice cream. Landon had listened to about three—"she's detailed, and so kind, and she deserves to be happy"—before he'd tuned out his sister's voice.

He didn't need the pressure of making Megan happy. He hadn't quite figured out how to do that for himself yet.

He pushed his way into the church and turned down the hall toward the offices. The pastor's door was closed, and Landon continued on toward the meeting room where Megan had texted she'd be.

Peering through the open doorway, he found Megan surrounded by four other women. Notebooks and textbooks and pens covered the table between them. One woman, probably a decade older than Megan, spoke and pointed to something on a paper in front of another woman. "We'd need to have more classrooms than that in the evening."

"Do you really think we can get that many people to come?" she asked, peering over the top of her glasses.

"In the evening, yes."

Landon leaned against the doorjamb and listened to the group talk about the possibilities for having more than one class. After a few minutes, he'd learned that the church—Megan, really—was organizing a class to teach English as a Second Language for the community.

He lifted his hand to adjust his cowboy hat, and that caught Megan's attention. Her chair scraped loudly against the floor as she hastily stood. "Hey," she said, tossing a look to the rest of the group, who had paused in their conversation. "Can you guys give me a second?"

She came out into the hall, and Landon fell back a few steps to give her room when he really wanted to stay and inhale the scent of her skin. As it was, he could barely detect any of her usual jasmine.

Tucking a lock of hair behind her ear, she said, "Sorry, our meeting got started late."

"That's okay."

She glanced toward the room and back to him. He drank in the slim cut of her black skirt, the height of her shiny heels, the way her bright green sweater complimented her dark eyes and hair. He swallowed hard.

"We'll probably be at least another thirty minutes."

"The church is doing ESL classes?"

A glow entered Megan's face, and Landon glanced down at his boots as a smile curved his lips. "Yes," she said. "I'm starting several programs this summer, and ESL is one of them."

"What else you doin'?"

"A sewing club and a recipe exchange," she said. "A couple of other things."

"And you're going to do them?"

She laughed, and he lifted his eyes to hers, drowning in the joyous sound of her voice. "Heavens, no," she said. "I'm using volunteers from the church. The more you get members involved, the more they feel like they belong to the church." She shuffle-stepped toward him. "You want to get involved?"

Fear bolted through him with the speed of a raging bull. "No, ma'am."

Her laughter bounced around the hall again. "Too late, Landon. You're my handyman, so you're already involved." She flashed him an irresistible smile, and Landon returned it.

"That I am."

She sobered. "I really do need to finish this meeting. Poor Mrs. Brooks doesn't get out of the house that often, and I'd hate to make her come back another day."

Landon waved his hand. "No problem," he said. "Take your time." His phone sounded as he finished speaking, but he didn't reach into his pocket for it. Whoever it was could wait until he wasn't with Megan, because she required his undivided attention. "I'll wait outside."

"You can sit in the chapel too," she said, giving him a grateful glance. "I'll come find you just as soon as I'm done."

He nodded and she ducked back into the room. He stared after her, like she might come back and give him another one of those cheek-kisses. His hand drifted to his face and he turned away. That had been an innocent gesture, nothing more.

You just want it to be more, he thought as he moved swiftly down the hall. He burst back into the summer sunshine, arguing with himself about what he wanted with Megan. He parked himself on the bench under a tall pine tree, still trying to puzzle it through.

This indecision was new for Landon. He'd always known what he wanted. He'd grown up around the rodeo, and when his father had gotten him into bull riding, it had fit like a glove. The professional rodeo circuit had always been in his future, and he'd done it without question. Even when he'd gotten injured and he couldn't continue in the rodeo, he'd known he'd come back to Montana and get a job at Horseshoe Home Ranch.

He'd never questioned that—until Lauren left. Then, he'd seriously called into question what he should be doing with his life. He felt like he'd been stumbling in the dark for two full years—until this past winter when he'd told Jace he thought he might like to buy a ranch of his own.

Money wasn't an issue for Landon. Winning bull riding championships for seven straight years and investing wisely meant he didn't really have to work at all. But he loved the feel of fresh country air in his lungs. Loved being up before the sun. Loved working with a horse until it trusted him completely.

He pulled out his phone and checked it. The real estate agent for the ranch in Utah had texted him back. *Sorry to take so long to get back to you. We'd love to show you the ranch. When can you come to Brush Creek?*

He looked up from the phone and stared at the horizon. When he'd texted three days ago, he could've gone this weekend. Could he still go tomorrow? Would Megan mind if he delayed his work on the church until next week?

His gut pinched with uncertainty. Focusing back on his phone, he typed, *Is Monday too soon?*

Monday is fine. The answer came back quickly. *I'll send you an email with a pin for the address. Is that okay?*

Landon confirmed that yes, Shelly could send him an email and he'd see her on Monday at ten a.m. Peace filled him from top to bottom, and he hoped Brush Creek Ranch turned out to be as magical as it looked online.

But one glance toward the church door as it opened and the ladies spilled out made Landon wonder what going to Utah would impact here in Montana.

———

Gertrude Brooks could barely walk, and she shuffled a few inches forward so slowly, Megan thought she'd lose her mind before they made it through the exit. She hitched a smile in place and kept a firm grip on the elderly woman's elbow. A fierce love for her overwhelmed Megan, and the patience she needed suddenly flowed through her.

So Landon was waiting. Big deal. Megan wanted to make the church the hub of activity in Gold Valley, and she wouldn't be able to do that by rushing anyone. She helped Gertrude all the way to her car and stood in the parking lot and waved as the woman drove away.

Only then did she allow herself to relax, a huge sigh escaping her lips.

"Tough meeting?"

She twisted at the deep sound of Landon's voice and found him loitering on the sidewalk several paces away. Heat rushed into her face at the glorious sight of him wearing that dark cowboy hat, his legs long and lean in those jeans, the sun haloing him like he was divine.

"Just long," she managed to say. She walked over to him and stepped up onto the curb, but he still towered several inches over her. "And I've got another one this afternoon with a couple of gentlemen who want to talk about gardening classes. One of them is your dad."

"Sounds fascinating." He clipped a grin in her direction, but it came and went so fast she didn't get to truly enjoy it. "Listen, something's come up. I have to go out of town tomorrow. I'll be gone…." He gazed over her shoulder, his expression almost haunted. Definitely lost.

"You'll be gone…?" she prompted.

He gave himself a little shake. "Yeah, I'll be gone for a few days. Don't really know how long."

She wrapped her arms around herself as if cold. "Where are you going?" Eric had often disappeared for a "few days." He'd told her he was going on business trips, or to a marketing conference, but he really went to Grand Cayman to check on his accounts, make withdrawals, and who knew what else.

She'd asked him repeatedly if he had another girlfriend in his life, but he'd insisted he didn't. Megan still wasn't sure she believed him. After all, the rest of his life had been a sham.

"Utah," Landon said. "There's a horse ranch there I'm interested in buying."

Her heart fell to her shoes and rebounded like the cement was a trampoline. "A ranch? In Utah?" She wished her voice didn't sound like Alvin the Chipmunk.

Way to be obvious, she chastised herself. But when he said, "I can still do the repairs this summer. I wouldn't move there for a few months, at least," she realized she could've been squeaky and surprised by his purchasing of a ranch because she didn't want to lose her handyman.

Which was also true. But she could replace Landon in that capacity. No, she didn't want him to buy a ranch and up and move to Utah, because she genuinely wanted to see if they could make something between them work.

Ridiculous, maybe. But by the spark in his eye and the electric pulse she'd felt between them, Megan didn't think a relationship with him was impossible, the way she once had.

"Yeah." Landon scuffed his feet, his pine-tree-colored eyes hidden by that delicious hat. "I've been thinkin' about makin' a change for a while now."

"Right. I remember that now." Megan didn't quite know what else to say. "Where in Utah?"

"Brush Creek?" He brought his eyes to hers. "It's in the Uinta Mountains. Northeastern Utah."

"Yeah, sure," she said.

His eyes crinkled and he chuckled. "You have no idea what's in Northeastern Utah, do you?"

"Do you?"

His chuckle morphed into a laugh and it was the most delicious sound Megan had ever heard. She realized, standing there with him, that Landon didn't do a lot of laughing.

"No," he admitted. "I don't know what's in Utah." He turned his phone toward her. "But this property is there, and I thought I'd go check it out."

She peered at the pictures on his screen. They showed a

gorgeous blue sky—though nothing like the wide open area in Montana—and snow-capped mountains, and miles and miles of green grass. "Wow, it has a pond," she said, taking the phone fully from him. "And a riverfront view." She glanced up, not really interested in seeing more. Somehow though, her eyes got pulled down again.

"It's gorgeous country," she said, flipping through the pictures and reading the description. "Water rights, ten-thousand square-foot horse arena, three barns…." She gasped, and her gaze flew to his. "Two-point-three million dollars?"

He reached for the phone and she released it to him. "Has a swimming pool and everything." He stared at the screen, a definitive look of longing on his face. He wiped it away when he looked at her. "It's been in their family for generations. The father died. I'm just looking right now, and the price is a bit high."

"The place has sentimental value," she said.

"To them," he said.

"You have two million dollars to buy a place like that?" She immediately regretted asking. Every wall and shutter Landon possessed flew into place, and his eyes disappeared under his hat's brim again.

"Should we get started?" he asked, which meant, *yes, I have two million dollars.*

And of course he did. He'd won tons of rodeos. Had only been out of the circuit for five years.

"If you want," she said, a dose of poison in her tone.

"What does that mean?"

"It means you probably have a flight to book, and laundry to do, and bags to pack if you're going out of town tomorrow." Megan drew her shoulders back and took a deep breath for strength. She was tired of feeling weak around Landon. Sure, she liked him, but she didn't want to forever be cowed by his presence. "And since you can't really start today anyway, what's the point?"

She stared right back and him when he leveled his gaze at her. "So if you'll excuse—"

"I'm starving," he blurted. "Want to go to lunch?"

She blinked. *Blink, blink, ba-blink.* "It's ten-thirty."

"Yeah, well, I get up at five-thirty and eat breakfast by six. Lunch comes early for me." The way he watched her undid every nerve ending in her body.

"Okay," she said. "But you have to tell me something."

"What's that?"

"Why are you buying a horse ranch in the middle of Utah?" She stepped past him and his stormy expression. "You can tell me anytime before you drop me back here. I just need my purse."

And she walked away from him, something she thought she'd never do. She may have even added an extra swish to her hips, hoping he was watching. Hoping he'd still be in the parking lot when she came back out.

CHAPTER 6

Megan took precious seconds to apply a fresh layer of lip gloss and make sure her curls were cooperating before clicking her way back down the hall and out of the church. She had time for a meal with Landon; she was only going to try to find an excuse to stay with him while he worked today anyway. At least until three o'clock when George Milner came by about the gardening club.

Thankfully, and with a whoosh of relief, Megan found Landon leaning against the passenger door of his huge, gray truck. He'd moved it right up to the curb where they'd been talking, and he pushed to standing as she approached.

"Ready?" she asked, cocking one hip and putting her hand on it.

He raked his eyes from the top of her head to her heels and back. "I'm not entirely sure if I'm ready, but let's go." He stepped to open her door for her, leaving her to wonder what that meant.

"You don't want to go to lunch?" she asked as she squeezed past him. "You're the one who suggested it."

"I want to go to lunch." His voice sounded like he'd swallowed cotton and a couple of pieces had gotten lodged in his throat.

She turned back to him and found herself trapped in the narrow alley between his body, the door, and the truck itself. "Then what—?"

"I'm not sure I'm ready for you." The intensity in his words sent surprise through her, and if she were being honest, a little bit of fear too.

Employing that brave side, drawing out that woman who walked away from Landon Edmunds, Megan said, "I guess we'll find out, won't we?" She tossed him a bright smile and climbed onto the leather seat in his truck—which for Megan, wearing a pencil skirt and heels, was quite the feat. Heat licked her cheeks as she pulled her skirt into place, hoping he hadn't seen too much skin. A quick look in his direction revealed his smile—and a hint of redness in his face. So he'd seen. And he wasn't entirely upset about it.

Satisfaction sang through her as he hurried around the front of the truck and climbed in the driver's seat.

"Where do you wanna go?" he asked as he stuffed the key in the ignition. The engine roared to life and settled into a purr. Megan had never ridden in such a nice vehicle. Most cowboys drove semi-broken down trucks. Mister Two Million clearly had enough money to pay for cars too.

"It's ten-thirty," she repeated. "I have no opinion." She giggled and adjusted the air conditioning so it blew on her. "You choose."

"What do you like?"

She exhaled as she thought. "Well, I am a sucker for a burger…."

"A woman after my own heart." He buckled his seat belt and flipped the truck into drive. "So, Megan. What have you been up to since high school?"

Oh, how she wanted to tell him. Tell him everything and see if he'd still want to take her to lunch at ten-thirty every morning. At the same time, she wanted to bottle up everything that had happened over the past twelve years and keep them to herself.

She didn't quite trust herself to tell him the right things. She didn't quite trust herself to even be in the truck with him. She hadn't quite gotten over Eric, but she knew she needed to.

"Wow, that's a hard question," she said with a light laugh. Her mind raced as she tried to figure out where to start, what to say, what *not* to say.

Her brain landed on one thought: *If you want to have a real relationship with him, tell him the truth.*

"I went to college for a while," she said. "Didn't graduate. Started working a lot. Time passes, and here I am." She didn't have to start with the biggest item to be telling the truth.

"That's it?"

"My life is pretty vanilla."

He slid her a glance. "I don't believe that." He turned away before she could determine the emotion in his eyes. "I remember you being fun and popular. The real life of the party."

"Well, that party ended a long time ago." Megan wasn't upset about it. She had always been positive, upbeat, a glass-half-full type of girl. So Eric had darkened that glass a little. Didn't mean she still didn't see the good in people, in herself.

But she certainly wasn't exciting enough for a rodeo champion.

"Ever been married?" he asked, his voice guarded.

Megan's stomach twisted but settled quickly. "No."

"Are you seeing anyone right now?"

She twisted and stared at him. "Landon Edmunds. Do you think I'd go to lunch with you if I had a boyfriend?" She huffed and faced the front. "What kind of *preacher's daughter* do you think I am?"

His knuckles tightened on the wheel. "I sense you don't like bein' called the preacher's daughter."

"It's not my favorite, no."

"Noted," he said, like they'd be spending a lot more time together. But a four-letter-word that started with *U* and ended with *-tah* said differently. "What else did you do?"

She told herself that he might hate the ranch in Utah. Just because he was going to look didn't mean he'd drop a cool two-mill on the place tomorrow. Heck, she'd done tons of looking at shoes, at furniture, at houses, without buying.

"Watched you ride bulls for a few years." She tossed him

what she hoped was a flirtatious smile. She'd been with Eric for so long, she wasn't even sure she remembered how to flirt.

"Oh yeah?" He didn't seem like it was strange she'd followed his rodeo career. At the same time, she didn't want to be one of *those* women.

She shrugged. "Yeah, you know. If I happened to be flipping through the channels."

Landon didn't answer, and Megan's nerves rioted at her to *say something!* But she didn't know what. She knew what he'd done with his life, but as they approached downtown Gold Valley, she realized she knew very little about him personally.

"What do you like?" she asked. "If I was driving and I asked you where to go, what would be your favorite?"

"I like anything I can put between two slices of bread."

"Ah, a sandwich king."

"I just need a crown." He tapped the brim of his cowboy hat with a chuckle.

She found him regal enough, but she clamped her lips around the words and asked him another question.

———

Lunch with Megan became Landon's favorite event of the week. She was easy to talk to, easy to look at, easy to consider starting something with. He had a tri-tip sandwich while she stuck to her request and ordered a bacon cheeseburger—no onions.

He liked the lilt of her voice. He liked the way she kept smoothing down her curls, like she was trying to iron them out. He liked the way her left eye crinkled more than her right when she smiled and laughed. He liked making her smile and laugh.

They lingered over coffee, and Landon wished he didn't need to get back to his place and book a flight, but that he could follow her back to the church, strap on his tool belt, and ask her to stay nearby as he sanded something.

Eventually, though, he stretched and said, "Well, should we go?"

She flipped her phone over and checked the screen. "Oh, wow, it's almost two o'clock."

Landon grinned as he stood and threw some bills on the table. "We had fun, right?"

"Landon." She stared at the money. "That's too much."

He looked at the three twenties. "It's fine."

"You already paid with your card." Her round eyes met his. "You can't leave a sixty-dollar tip." She whispered the last part, and Landon lifted his arm and tucked her into his side. A powerful zing shot down his spine and jolted out his boot tips.

"Sure I can," he said. "We sat here for almost four hours. He could've probably had three tables in that time." He glanced over his shoulder as he steered her toward the exit, but he didn't see the waiter. "Besides, I like to tip well. Someone who's working the lunch shift in a restaurant isn't there for fun."

They stepped into the heat. "Landon—"

He dropped his arm, though he'd like to keep her close, maybe bring her closer. "Look, Megan, this isn't going to be a thing, is it?"

She blinked those long lashes at him, and he had a mental fantasy about them tickling his face just before he kissed her. He shook himself and reminded himself that he was annoyed at her obvious preoccupation with his money.

So he had money. Big deal. She said she'd watched him bull ride on TV. Surely she knew he'd won. A lot.

"Is it?" he asked again. "Because if so, maybe you should find someone else to help you with the church."

She shook her head. "No, of course not," she said. "I won't bring it up again."

Landon stepped toward his truck so he wouldn't reach for her again. "Thanks."

"Okay." Megan darted in front of him, causing him to pause in his stride. "I'm sorry, okay? I'm just—" She glanced over her shoulder. "I just have to get used to that. My last—I mean—my ex—" She pressed her eyes closed, but curiosity burned through Landon.

He held his questions though. He didn't need to ask her everything on the first date. His shoulders jumped when he realized he'd just considered himself dating Megan.

No, he told himself. *You just went to lunch with an old friend.*

But the thought of another man asking her out, taking her to dinner, holding her hand, made his gut writhe in a way that spoke of jealousy. He definitely wouldn't like that.

"I'm going to Utah to look at a horse ranch, because I've been thinking about training horses for the rodeo," he said.

Her eyes popped open, and she searched his for more. He wasn't sure if she found it, and she'd examined him a few times over their meal too. He didn't necessarily dislike it, but he wondered what she was thinking, what she was looking for.

"That's the kind of change you need?" she asked.

He sighed, reached for her hand, and threaded his fingers through hers. "I don't really know. That's the problem." He tugged her gently toward the truck and helped her up. He didn't mind waiting and watching her climb into his truck in that tight skirt, and he once again wondered what he was doing.

Holding her hand? Putting his arm around her? Thinking about kissing her?

And going to Utah.

He dropped her off at the church with the promise that he'd call her from Utah and drove back to the ranch. He couldn't make sense of how he felt. Couldn't figure out what holes existed in his life and how he could fill them. Couldn't see the light at the end of the tunnel.

Help me have a clear mind, he prayed as he entered his cabin and settled in front of his laptop. He really wanted to saddle up Crossfire and get out under the sky that always cleared his head.

But first, he needed to book a flight to Utah and start a load of laundry. Then he could ride his horse and find a way through this mist in his mind.

CHAPTER 7

Landon clicked his tongue and pulled on the reins to get Crossfire to enter the stream. For some reason, the horse always balked at water, despite Landon's training. The animal shuffled sideways, and Landon said, "C'mon."

Finally, in Crossfire went, and water splashed onto Landon's chaps. The leather protected him from the wetness, and he kept the reins tight as Crossfire continued through the stream to the other side.

The ponderosa pines brought him comfort. He loved the way they stood sentinel over the savannah, how they grew straight and tall into the expansive sky above. Landon kept his focus on the ground, scanning for rattlesnakes. They loved to come out onto the dirt and sun themselves at this time of year, and the last thing he needed was Crossfire getting spooked by a snake.

He could watch and think at the same time. He felt like

the Lord had answered his prayer, because everything seemed clearer than it had before. Maybe because he wasn't being influenced by the scent of jasmine and the beautiful smile of a kind soul.

Landon felt more like himself in the saddle than anywhere else. He took a deep breath, expanding his lungs until he thought they'd burst. As he slowly exhaled, he decided that yes, he wanted to go to Utah. He needed to explore all the options available to him.

At the same time, he wanted to work on the church—and see if he could have something meaningful with Megan. He didn't need to move to Utah right away. The horse ranch was already vacant. It could sit until he was ready to move. And he might not even like it. He might hate the weather in Utah, or the homestead, or the fact that the mountains there weren't the same. He didn't know, and that was why he needed to go.

Crossfire stutter-stepped, and Landon pulled him up short. "What is it, boy?" He searched for the source of the horse's agitation but couldn't see anything. Faintly, as though blown to him on the wind, the distinct sound of a rattle reached Landon's ears. He swung the horse around and they retraced their steps at a much faster clip. He noticed the moment Crossfire settled down, because the horse slowed back to his lazy clop-clop, his head bobbing with each step. He entered the stream with only a slight hiccup this time, and Landon pointed him toward the upper fields he'd planted earlier this week.

The wind brought welcome relief to the blazing sun,

and with every step closer to the ranch, Crossfire moved faster. The dinner bell was ringing as Landon came within range of Horseshoe Home's homestead. Gloria, the matron of the ranch, didn't make supper every evening, but tonight she stood on the deck, chiming the bell for all she was worth.

Cowboys streamed from the barns and their cabins, and the unique scent of grilled hamburgers lifted into the air and met Landon's nose. He pulled Crossfire to a stop so he could watch the activity on the ranch.

A sense of contentment swept over him. He'd been at Horseshoe Home for five years. He loved it here—well, maybe not in the winter. He had friends here, men he could count on. He felt like if he left, he'd miss Montana, miss the ranch, miss the other cowboys.

Doesn't mean there's not something better for you out there. He urged Crossfire back into a walk and hurried through brushing him down so he could go eat with his ranch family.

***

The next day, his plane touched down in Rock Springs, Wyoming, just after noon. He rented an SUV and got on the road. He had a two-hour drive ahead of him, if he could find his way through all the small towns and forests to the right spot.

By hour three, he wondered if he should've just booked a flight to Salt Lake City. He'd thought Rock Springs would be closer to Brush Creek, but as he navigated himself into Vernal, he wasn't so sure.

The horse ranch sat northwest from Vernal, and he'd have to make the forty-five-minute drive every time he needed groceries or gas or anything. After he'd retired from the rodeo circuit, he'd thought a thirty-minute drive from Horseshoe Home Ranch to Gold Valley was torture. And by the time he climbed from the SUV in his hotel parking lot, he wasn't sure he could stomach such a long drive just to get to civilization.

At the same time, being so far from everything and everyone sounded heavenly.

By the time he showed up at Brush Creek Ranch, Utah had charmed him. It was hotter than Montana, but he loved the old town feel of Vernal, and he didn't mind the drive up into the Uinta Mountains to the quaint town of Brush Creek.

He'd passed a grocery store and a gas station in town, and that had soothed his worries about driving so far just to get staples.

He got out of the SUV and looked around at the gorgeous mountains. He'd arrived before Shelly, the real estate agent he was meeting.

The house looked like a log cabin. An upscale log cabin. The yard boasted of professional landscaping, with grass so green he wondered if the water rights had all been used on the lawn.

Generational trees offered shade, and as Landon wandered the perimeter of the property, he appreciated that the ad had been accurate when it said that the buildings were immaculate. Tires crunched over gravel, and he turned back to where he'd parked.

A bright red sports car pulled in next to his rental, and a leggy blonde woman emerged from the car. "You must be Landon Edmunds."

"And you must be Shelly Harvey." They shook hands, and she handed him a folder. "That has the square footage, the water rights, a map of the property—there are thirty-four additional acres to the south that are available, if you're interested."

"I'm interested in it all," Landon said.

"Perfect," Shelly said. "Let's start in the house."

Two hours later, Landon buckled himself into a burning hot car and set the air conditioner to blow, hard. He waited while Shelly drove away, while the deluxe horse ranch sat before him in all its glory.

"It's beautiful," he said to himself. Megan tumbled through his mind, and Landon's thoughts scattered. He hated this new feeling. This feeling of not knowing what to do.

He imagined her in the car with him. "So what do you think?" He wasn't sure if Megan would enjoy living so far from a city, but he wanted to find out.

He imagined her dark eyes as they searched his, and he pulled out his phone and called her.

"Hey, you," she said.

"Hey yourself."

She laughed. "How's the horse ranch?"

He exhaled. "It's really nice, actually."

"It looked beautiful in the pictures."

He couldn't tell her mood or her emotion through the phone. He'd lost some of his bravery when his leg had been injured. He'd lost a lot of his confidence when Lauren ran off with someone else. But now, he needed both of those things.

"Megan," he started. "I want to buy it. I really like it."

"Well, that's—"

"But I'm not going to move down here until...well, I'm wondering if maybe you want to go to dinner when I get back in town."

She remained silent for so long, Landon pulled the phone from his ear to make sure the call was still connected. It was.

"Megan?"

She inhaled. "I eat dinner, yes."

Relief speared the tension in Landon. "Great."

"Don't be all 'great' yet."

He wished she'd tack a giggle onto the end of such a serious statement. But she didn't. "What do you mean?" he asked.

"I want you to finish the sentence, 'I'm not going to move down here until....'"

Landon looked out the window. "Are you always this pushy?"

She laughed. "Usually."

At least she was honest too. And Landon appreciated honesty, as well as someone who seemed as intense as he was. "I like you," he said simply. "I don't want to leave Gold Valley until I help you fix up the church...until I have a chance to get to know you better."

"When will you be back?" she asked.

"Tomorrow night."

"Can't wait."

After Landon hung up and started the journey back to Rock Springs, where he was staying until his flight home the next day, he realized he couldn't wait to see Megan either.

———

Megan's stomach felt like someone had released a herd of hungry caterpillars. So many feet moving in a thousand different directions.

"Calm down, calm down," she coached herself. Her own legs paced her from one end of the living room to the other, completely uncalm.

Landon would be at her apartment any minute, and she couldn't remember the last time she felt this nervous. She pressed her palms together and sent up a prayer that she wouldn't say something about how much money he had, wouldn't ask him a question that would drive him away.

"Be natural," she muttered. "Be cool." Problem was, she'd never really been able to act cool. When something got her worked up, she addressed it.

Before she could give herself another pep talk, knocking

sounded on her door. She spun toward it, her heart skipping a beat and then pumping out two.

A man hadn't come knocking at her door for years. After she and Eric had settled into their relationship, they'd leave work together, or he'd text her when he was outside her house, or they'd meet somewhere.

To actually have Landon come to the door and knock made Megan's throat dry and her pulse pound. Somehow she got her feet to move toward the door, her fingers to curl around the knob, her arm muscles to pull.

The sight of him standing on her landing made her weak, and she sagged into the door for support. "Hey," she said breathlessly. He wore jeans and a black polo, his cowboy boots, and a charcoal-colored cowboy hat. She could just see his blond sideburns, and her fingers itched to touch them.

He gripped the doorframe like the sight of her rendered him weak too. "Hey, yourself." He kicked a smile in her direction, his eyes traveling from her head to her feet and back. "Don't you look nice?"

She glanced down at her black-and-white flowered blouse, her dark skinny jeans, and her jeweled sandals. She wondered if she'd be too warm on this summer evening and briefly considered running to change into shorts.

"I don't know," she said, dismissing the idea of leaving him in her living room while she changed. "Do I?" Megan glanced up at him in time to see the spark of desire in his eyes.

"Mm hm." He swept into her apartment, his presence

powerful and welcome, and took her in his arms. He squeezed her tight and said, "It's good to see you," before he stepped back.

Every cell in her body started to hum. "I want to hear all about your trip to Utah." Megan half-stumbled, half-stepped to the couch, where she'd set her purse in anticipation of his arrival. "But first, I want a plate of French fries and the biggest diet soda I can get."

"I know just the place for that." Landon extended his hand to her, a hopeful, vulnerable edge in his eyes. She held his gaze for a few moments, basking in that look, wondering why he wasn't the all-powerful, super-confident rodeo star she'd seen tame the wildest of bulls.

As she willingly slipped her hand into his, she realized that all her fantasies about Landon were just that—fantasies. He was a *person*. Someone with successes, sure. But also someone with failures.

And she wanted to know the good, the bad, and the ugly.

"You been to Fizz & Fries yet?" he asked. "I mean, I know you said you've been back in Gold Valley for several weeks, but well…." His head dipped as he scanned her again. "You don't look like the type to eat a plate of French fries every day."

She tipped her head to the sky and offered a carefree laugh. The sound of joy it contained surprised her. As she sobered, she realized the heavy cloud of fear and shame she'd been hiding under. And she didn't like it. She wanted to feel and sound as joyful as that laugh had been.

"You're right," she managed to say through the fog of her

self-realization. "I haven't eaten a plate of French fries once since I came home." She looked up at him. "What else do they have there? Or are French fries between two pieces of bread acceptable?"

He beamed down at her, and time seemed to slow. If he'd stop walking, and just lower his head, his lips could find hers. She'd arch up to meet him.

"They have all kinds of toppings," he said instead, shattering her singular thought of kissing him. "I like the fries with pulled pork, cheese, and ranch dressing."

"Oh, so it's like a meal."

"Yeah. You can get just a plate of plain ol' French fries too." He opened the door of his truck for her, his hand sliding out of hers to her waist as he helped her into the monstrosity. "But they have garlic fries, sweet potato fries, spicy sriracha fries. Pretty much everything you can imagine."

While he circled the truck, she took a deep breath of its Landon-scented interior, committing the masculine smell of leather, horse, and aftershave to memory. On the way across town—the Fizz & Fries had smartly opened up next to the college campus—Landon told her about his trip to Utah, the horse ranch, everything.

"Sounds amazing," she said, thankful she'd been able to keep the strangled note out of her voice.

"It's really far from anything," he said, glancing at her. "You more of a city girl, Megan?"

"Not big cities, no." She turned toward him. "I lived in Jackson Hole before coming back here. It wasn't huge, but there were a lot of people. Tourists all the time. Busy." She'd worked in a tall building downtown, preparing marketing agendas for her bosses. "We did a lot of work with rafting companies, tour groups, that kind of thing." She switched her attention out the windshield and watched a couple make their way into the restaurant. "I don't really miss it."

"The place? Or the job?" He opened his door and slid out of the truck, stalling on his side and waving her across the bench seat.

She slid over and down into his arms. "Both," she murmured, feeling swimmy and safe in the circle of his arms. "Jackson did have a small, country feel," she said. "I liked that."

"Gold Valley has that," Landon said. "Brush Creek does too, though I'll admit it's a bit smaller. There's maybe five thousand people, and the horse ranch is outside of town, surrounded by acres of land."

"Well, that's what a cowboy loves, right?" She peered up at him, getting lost in the depth of his eyes beneath the brim of his hat. "Lots of land and a good horse to explore it with." She smiled.

He returned it and moved away from her. He caught her hand in one of his and pushed the truck door closed with the other. "A man gets awfully lonely with only a horse for company. Believe me, I would know."

"You would?" A thrill pulsed through her, originating at the place where his palm pressed against hers. His hands were so big, so warm, so calloused. They spoke of his work ethic. She sensed a gentle soul in the rough cowboy.

"Sure," he said. "Traveling on the rodeo circuit isn't a picnic. You have no permanent home. Livin' out of a trailer doesn't count. People come and go every weekend." They stepped into the restaurant, which buzzed with activity and laughter, even on a Tuesday night.

"How long have you been at Horseshoe Home?" She stepped into line, very aware of everyone who glanced their way. She wasn't a celebrity, and Landon had been off the rodeo circuit for a while, but she still felt self-conscious standing there holding hands with him.

"Oh, almost six years now. Six years in January, to be precise."

"That's got to be stable."

"It is, sure."

"But you're still lonely." She wasn't really asking, because he wore the loneliness in the lines on his face.

"I—" He leaned closer to her as he cleared his throat. "I used to date all the time, but I went on a female fast a couple years ago." He stepped forward when the line moved, turned toward her, and looked her straight in the eye. "Until you."

Fear combined with shock and traveled through her bloodstream with the strength of a tsunami. "Did something happen?"

"Yeah," he said darkly. "My girlfriend decided she liked cowboys."

Megan squinted, trying to see what he really meant. "And you're a cowboy."

"She decided she'd try us all out."

Megan squeezed his hand. "I'm sorry." She wanted to tell him about Eric, but she bit the words back.

"I loved her," Landon said, his voice quiet among the louder voices of the college-age crowd around them. "It took me a long time to get over her."

"But you're over her?" Hope lifted Megan's spirits.

"Most days," he said, and Megan's insides iced. "I still have some hard moments." He stepped up to the counter and ordered the "Big Foot Fries," and looked at her expectantly. She hadn't even looked at the menu. She scanned it quickly while he ordered her diet soda.

"Garlic fries," she said. "As many as I can get."

The cashier smiled and punched a button. "What kind of sauce?"

"What kind do you have?" She was thinking ketchup—the classic for dipping fries.

Landon handed her a half sheet of laminated paper. "They have gourmet dipping sauces. My favorite is the mustard aioli, but I like the barbeque ketchup and the lemon pepper too." He pointed to the paper. "Oh, and the honey butter."

She scanned the list, her mind whirling through the two dozen choices. "Honey butter on fries?"

"It's good." He turned back to the cashier. "We want the mustard aioli, the barbeque ketchup, the lemon pepper, and some honey butter."

"And some wasabi mayo," Megan added, putting the sauce menu on the counter.

"Wasabi?" Landon asked. "That's spicy, you know."

"I like spicy."

He drew her into his side but not before she caught a glimpse of the heat running through his expression. She smiled to herself, glad the feelings she had for him seemed to be mutual, and accepted a massive cup of diet soda. After she drew a long drink of liquid heaven, she sighed.

"Thank you," she said, to Landon who smiled, and to the Lord, who had brought her back to Gold Valley. She hadn't wanted to come. Had almost hired someone else to help her father get ready for retirement.

But now, standing with Landon as they waited for their gourmet French fries, she realized God had brought her home to heal.

And to fall in love? she wondered, but she quickly dismissed the thought. She needed to know more about Landon before she could even approach the subject of being with him for longer than it took to have a meal.

Sure, she loved the idea of him. She had since her teen years. But she was smarter now. Older. And no matter how much she tried to tell herself she was over Eric, she knew deep down she wasn't.

CHAPTER 8

Megan didn't pull herself from bed until almost ten o'clock the next morning. She'd been up until almost three a.m. so she wasn't really just lying in bed, doing nothing. She did stay under the fluffy comforter for a few extra minutes, her thoughts rotating around Landon, and holding Landon's hand, and seeing Landon later that morning.

She sat straight up, her heart thumping against her ribcage. She was supposed to meet Landon at the church that morning.

At nine o'clock.

Scrambling for her phone, she almost fell out of bed. She caught herself in time but stubbed her right big toe against her nightstand. A sharp hiss escaped her mouth, lengthening when she saw the flashing blue light on her phone.

He'd called—how had she not heard it?

Her panic reached epic proportions as she scanned the three texts Landon had sent.

At the church.

Tried to call you.

Coming over.

She yanked her head toward her bedroom window, which faced the parking lot. She hadn't heard him knock. The doorbell hadn't rung that she was aware of. Had she really been so tired she'd heard nothing?

The timestamp on his last text was forty minutes old. She launched herself toward the window and peered through the blinds. Sure enough, his truck waited in the parking lot. She couldn't tell if he sat inside or not. She raked her fingers through her hair, and they got stuck in the tangles.

A moan rose through her throat. Her phone fell to the floor as her fingers turned numb. The resulting crash thawed her, and she flew into action. Her thumbs had never moved so fast.

I'm so sorry. I just woke up. Where are you?

It's fine. I went to grab lunch. I'm downstairs.

At his lunch comment, a choked laugh shook her shoulders. *I just need to shower. Can you give me another half hour?*

Take your time.

But time she didn't take. She flew through her shower, threw on clothes she hoped matched, and ran down the stairs with still-damp curls.

Sure enough, he sat in his truck and she caught him lowering half a breakfast sandwich from his mouth when she wrenched open the passenger door. "I am so sorry." She climbed into the truck, the fleeting thought that she'd slide all the way over next to him and place a quick kiss on his cheek before he gave her the meal he'd bought for her.

"No problem." He flashed her a smile and nudged a paper sack toward her. "Stay up too late?"

"No." She opened the bag and found a bag of tater tots. "Well, yes. But I was studying and then I needed to get a sourdough starter going. Time got away from me."

"Do you commonly stay up late?"

"I think best late at night. I can't seem to focus until ten p.m."

"I'm dead at ten p.m." He chuckled. "In fact, I just put up black-out curtains because the dang sun doesn't set soon enough."

"I have them for the morning sun." She slid him a glance. "Thank you for breakfast."

He extended his hand toward her, and she slid close enough to feel his body heat. She ducked her head and popped another tater tot into her mouth. The silence settled between them easily as he drove over to the church.

By the time they arrived, she'd finished her orange juice and tater tots—but she'd never tire of holding his hand. He slid from the truck, taking her with him. He paused a few steps away and took a deep, deep breath. "It's a good day to fix something." He moved toward the back of the truck and lowered the tailgate.

By the time she turned toward him, he'd slung a tool belt around his waist. Standing there, Megan thought sure she'd faint. A man shouldn't be allowed out in public looking so delicious. He made jeans look like an Italian suit and cowboy boots seemed like the finest footwear in the world.

And that tool belt hugging his waist?

She pulled her gaze away from him before she lost consciousness. Thankfully, breathing was an involuntary bodily function or he'd be peeling her off the pavement.

"Where do you want me to start?" Landon approached her, kicking her heart rate into overdrive.

Right here, with me, Megan thought. Ice spread through her insides, making every breath feel like it would crack her lungs. She'd never felt like this before, even with Eric. With a jolt, she realized she hadn't thought of Eric for several days.

"Megan?"

"Hmm?" She swung her gaze toward him in slow motion, like she'd been caught in quicksand. Her muscles felt encased in the stuff, and when he locked his eyes on hers, everything in the world turned brighter. Moved swifter. Seemed better.

"Where do you want me?"

Again, her mind misfired. "Um, the church?"

"Right, the church." His husky voice carried a playful note. His pinky hooked hers; he shuffled closer. "Maybe I should start by making a list of supplies I'll need to get started."

Megan startled, her brain finally sending messages to the rest of her body. "A list! I have a list of supplies." She twisted toward the church building. "I'll go grab it. Can we go today?"

"I don't see why not." He dropped her hand and stepped back a bit.

"Be right back." Megan cursed herself for turning stupid in front of Landon just because he added a tool belt to his ensemble. But she'd never been so happy to need some repair work done, and she wondered if she could "accidentally" break something while she got the supply list to keep him here longer.

———

Landon ignored his phone while he was with Megan. He'd made an offer on the horse ranch in Utah, and Shelly had come back with a counteroffer while he'd sat in his truck, waiting to hear from Megan.

Two million was still too much for Brush Creek, even if Landon did agree that the barns and training facilities were immaculate. He wanted her to come down at least another two hundred thousand dollars. He'd have to buy equipment, and horses, and find a way to pay a small staff of cowhands.

His stomach had tightened and released every time he'd felt his phone vibrate, so he'd finally set it to completely silent. He wanted to throw it in the river as he drove back to the ranch. As Megan walked away, he let his gaze linger on her until she disappeared into the church.

Then he checked his phone. Shelly had said she'd check

with the owners. She wanted to know what his absolute highest price was.

He sent off his original offer, along with *I'm sorry. That's as high as I can go. It's cash.*

Megan returned, a piece of paper flapping in the breeze and a beautiful smile on her face.

"Ready?" he asked.

"I guess we'll see."

He unlocked the truck and she climbed in his side, scooting over only barely far enough to leave him room to drive. A tickle started in the back of his throat, and a flush worked its way up his neck. Happiness that tasted very similar to how he'd felt with Lauren filled him as he settled next to her.

"Do you have an idea of what project you want me to begin with?"

"I'm thinking the cosmetic things in the chapel. The dings, the scratches, the painting, the stained glass window." She glanced at the paper as a sense of unease swept through him with the strength of a swift river. "So we'll need brushes and stain and sandpaper…."

"And manpower," he said.

"Manpower?"

"Maybe we can organize a community service project to come help clean that window," he mused. "I've been reading about it online, and it seems like it's a job that has to be done by hand."

"You've been reading about it online?"

"Yeah."

She didn't respond, and he cut a glance in her direction. He found a small smile on her face as she tucked her curls behind her ear. "I guess you like that I've been reading about it online." He chuckled as he put his hand in hers. "I'm gonna get that church lookin' like new."

And if he had to spend the next several weeks with Megan to do it? Even better, in Landon's opinion.

———

Sunday morning dawned hot, though the warmer temperatures in Montana usually didn't happen until July. Or maybe Landon was the only one sweating through his sheets. Either way, he rose about the same time as the sun, already wishing for a cold shower and he hadn't even seen Megan yet.

Working with her these past few days had been a sweet experience. He'd learned about her younger sister, the death of her mother, the depth of her patience as she worked with several elderly groups of men and women helping her to organize her community outreach programs.

He'd watched her enthusiasm for the people and programs blossom, and he'd gotten joy from simply listening to her talk about what she was doing while he nailed new planks in place, or sanded out scratches, or swiped new stain onto the pulpit.

He'd gotten a lot done in only a few days, and he couldn't wait to see the chapel in all its new glory. Megan had asked her father to put out a call to the congregation today for next Saturday's stained glass window cleaning, and Landon couldn't wait to see how that would transform their Sunday worship services.

With church still several hours off, he headed out to do the early morning chores. He found Jace in the barn, brushing down his horse.

"Mornin'," the foreman said. "What're you doin' up? You're not on chores this morning."

"Yeah, I traded with Caleb for next Saturday."

"Oh, 'cause you're going to see your new girlfriend."

Landon jerked his head toward Jace. "She isn't my girlfriend."

He grinned. "Yet."

Landon sighed, the sound half annoyed and half defeated. "I don't think she's ready for that yet."

"Are you?" Jace didn't look up from Flint's legs.

"Most days I think I am."

"Today?"

"Sure, today's a great day." He started pitching out the old hay in Crossfire's stall. "Found another ranch in Utah."

"Sorry about Brush Creek."

Landon shrugged, but Jace didn't see it. "Wasn't meant to be."

"Megan should be happy about that."

Landon pressed his lips into a thin line and kept quiet. He hadn't told her about the failed offer on the horse ranch. He wasn't sure why. He didn't want to admit that he wasn't as ready for a new girlfriend as he claimed to be. Didn't want to see the joyful light in her eyes. Didn't want to think that maybe he should just stay in Montana.

The unsettled feeling he'd had for months remained. "Did you ever consider leavin' Horseshoe Home?" he asked. "You know, after what happened with Wendy?"

"Not really," Jace said. "She'd left, you know? And I grew up on this ranch."

"There's just so much more to the world," Landon said. "Maybe I should try Texas."

"You've always said you'd rather die than go to Texas. The heat, remember?"

"Yeah, but Tom says it's not so bad."

Jace draped his arms over the fence line between them. "Tom did love Texas. But he came home to Montana."

Landon quirked one eyebrow and got back to work. "I'll keep lookin'."

"Trust your gut," Jace said as he finished up and placed the currycomb on the shelf outside the stall. "She's been with you for thirty years, and she won't let you down."

Landon lifted the pitchfork to show he'd heard, and Jace left the barn. Left Landon to wonder how exactly, his gut would let him know what to do.

Hours later, he sat in the pew next to his sister and Jace, his right knee bouncing like he'd put jumping beans in his boots.

"Calm down," Belle hissed. "What's got you all riled up?"

"Megan's sittin' with him today." Jace leaned forward on the other side of Belle.

"Sh." Landon sent a glare in Jace's direction.

"Oh yeah?" His sister's eyes held equal parts curiosity and hope.

"Don't act like you don't know," Landon whispered to his sister. "Surely she's called you and told you all about how I've been holdin' her hand."

Belle's smile appeared instantly. "She has not." She swiveled toward Jace and back to Landon, pure joy on her face. "You've been holding her hand?" She leaned closer. "Kissy wissy?"

"Stop it," he said almost out loud. The fact that Megan hadn't been gossiping with his sister about her new relationship with Landon made comfort thread through him, the way the lilting breeze wove through the ponderosas.

Megan slid onto the pew next to him. "Good morning."

He tucked her into his side by quickly lifting his arm and settling it over her shoulders. She crossed her legs, further leaning into his chest—right where he wanted her—and tugged at the bottom of her skirt to keep it from riding too high. He'd learned she favored classic colors—black, navy, brown—and floral prints to match her jasminy scent. She'd brought him a bottle of lemon oil to infuse in his kitchen and a vial of lavender oil to rub on his temples before he went to bed at night.

He'd mentioned casually that he had a hard time falling asleep, and she said the lavender would help. He'd never paid much attention to anything outside the traditional health care system, and essential oils were, well, non-essential.

Thankfully, she'd never asked if he'd used the oils. He

was glad he hadn't had to lie. The bottles sat on his dresser; maybe one day he'd use them. But the reason he'd been having trouble falling asleep wasn't because he needed lavender oil on his temples. It was because Megan starred in his thoughts and it wasn't until he tamed them into submission that he could settle to sleep.

Her fingers landed on his thigh, and he darn near jumped out of his seat. A current zipped through his body, lighting every muscle on fire. He'd often wondered how a forest fire spread so quickly, but now he knew. All it took was one little spark, one touch, and everything combusted.

"Dad said he'd announce about the stained glass window service project." Her breath wafted across his neck, and Landon pressed her closer to him.

"Great." His lips skimmed her temple just as the pastor stood to begin the services. Good thing, too, because Landon wasn't sure if he could contain the waterfall of desire tumbling through him without a distraction.

CHAPTER 9

The sermon wasn't a suitable distraction. Landon didn't hear a word the preacher said, consumed with Megan as he was. Several things gnawed at him. First, the horse ranch in Utah that had fallen through. She deserved to know. Second, the new ranch he wanted to go look at that next weekend—the same Saturday as the stained glass window service project. Third, the rapid way his heart beat every time he thought about kissing Megan.

At this point, he wasn't worried about his affections being reciprocated. No, what plagued him was how to kiss her without it coming too soon, or too late, or too sloppy, or too rushed.

Despite what most women thought about him, Landon wasn't terribly experienced when it came to girls. He'd spent seven years wooing bulls, not females. And in the five years since he'd quit, he'd only dated a handful of women, especially since he'd lost three years of that time to Lauren.

Pastor Palmer finished and Landon stood with everyone else to sing the closing hymn. Megan tucked her arm into his and affection rushed through him. Before the song ended, he leaned over and whispered, "You want to come to lunch out on the ranch?"

She tilted her head back to look at him, and her mouth came within kissing distance. All he had to do was close the gap. Six tiny inches….

"You can cook?"

"Heavens, no." He grinned as her shock melted into something softer. "Belle feeds me on Sundays. She'll feed you too."

"Are you sure?"

"Sure I'm sure." He knew Belle wouldn't mind. In fact, he was probably setting himself up for a world of hurt by inviting Megan to lunch. But the thought of leaving her already made his lungs seize.

The service ended, and Landon turned toward Belle. "Megan can come to lunch, right?"

Belle's smile could only be categorized as one the Mad Hatter might wear. "Sure she can."

"Who's comin' to lunch?" Jace practically yelled.

"No one. Sh." Belle tossed him a disgruntled look while Landon tried to usher Megan out of the pew and into the aisle. Yeah, maybe taking her to the ranch for lunch had been a very bad idea.

———

Landon took Megan to his cabin instead of following Jace and Belle into theirs. The ride out to the ranch had been charged, with somewhat stilted conversation between Megan and the others. Landon found he didn't have much to contribute to the conversation about a sermon he hadn't actually heard.

"I've got a bench out back," he said, moving through the space quickly. He wasn't entirely sure when he'd last cleaned anything, and he didn't want to stay in the house on such a pretty summer day anyway.

Megan tucked her feet under her body as she tucked herself into his side. He spread his arm around her, the feel of her next to him comforting and peaceful.

"The ranch in Utah is a no-go," he said to break the silence.

She stiffened, straightened to look up at him. "Oh, no. What happened?"

"They wouldn't come down on the price." The weight of her gaze on the side of his face made his insides writhe. "What?" He finally trained his eyes on her.

"You loved that place."

He cocked his head at her. "How did you know I loved that place?"

"I could hear it in your voice. See it in your face."

Great. So he was emotionally transparent. He took a deep breath to steady himself. "I'll find something else."

"So you're still going to look?"

He gazed into the Montana wilderness behind his cabin. How many times had he sat here on a warm summer night?

How many times had he brought his coffee to this exact spot and watched the sun rise? Had the view ever gotten tiresome?

He'd lost count years ago, and he loved Montana as much now as he always had. And yet....

It was that *and yet* that kept his soul in constant turmoil. "There's something else out there for me, Megan. I can feel it." He hadn't meant to hush his voice, but it came out soft and somber anyway.

She settled back into him, her own eyes on the horizon now. He let her have the silence, because he needed it too.

All he could come up with was: *Well, there might be someone right here for you.*

And he didn't know how to reconcile the need he'd felt to find his own ranch somewhere else with his growing feelings for Megan. She was here; he felt like he should leave.

But she's left Montana before.... Landon let the thought hang there, because Jace texted and said lunch was ready.

———

Megan hadn't felt at home—truly at home—in Gold Valley until she went out to the ranch with Landon. Eating lunch with Belle and Jace had been so enjoyable that Megan dreaded the following Sunday when she'd surely have to go to her father's house and make her usual grilled cheese sandwiches and tomato soup.

"Thanks for inviting me," she told Landon as he drove her down the canyon. "That was really fun."

His fingers on hers tightened. "Glad you liked it. My sister can be…."

"She's Belle," Megan said. "I know her." She leaned her cheek against Landon's bicep, her heart suddenly pumping twice as fast. Would he walk her up to her apartment? Kiss her? Call her later?

Her phone broke into her thoughts with the shrill ring of an old-fashioned phone. "That's a client," she murmured as she dug the phone out of her purse and checked it. "It's Sterling Maughan." She swiped open the call. "Good evening, Sterling."

A smile poured onto her face as he started speaking about his upcoming wedding. He and his fiancé, Norah, were getting married at the church at the end of the month. "Yes," she assured him. "My father's planning on it. We have you on the schedule, and your florist has already been in touch with me."

She answered his few questions, asked him some of her own about the rooms he needed prepped, who the photographer would be and if he wanted her to reach out to them for a tour, and then she said, "And we're getting that stained glass window cleaned this week, so your ceremony should be just beautiful."

Next to her, Landon's muscles bunched. She glanced at him but he kept his eyes on the winding road. Still, his fingers flexed and re-gripped the steering wheel a bit too aggressively.

"Talk to you soon," she told Sterling and hung up, a heavy exhale leaving her lips. "Weddings are stressful."

"I have to talk to you about the stained glass window," Landon said.

"What about it?" She slid her fingertips down his forearm, an obvious invitation for him to release the steering wheel and hold her hand instead. He didn't.

"I found another ranch I want to go see." He blipped his eyes to her and back to the road, not long enough to even see her. "They want me to come this weekend."

Everything inside her crashed to the ground, as if her hopes, fantasies, and dreams had been flying on a jet that had suddenly lost all its engines. "Oh." She sat back and let her hands fall into her lap. In situations like these, her mind usually sped a mile every second. Now, though, only numbness spread through her, turning her dumb again.

"I'll go next weekend," he said.

"No—"

"Yes." He dropped his hand to hers and cupped her fingers. "I can go anytime. It doesn't have to be this weekend. I was just thinking about it."

Megan didn't quite know what to say. A sick feeling churned in her stomach when she thought about competing with a ranch.

"So I'll go next weekend?" he asked.

"Yes, if you can," she answered. "I would appreciate it."

His lips pressed against her forehead, a sweet gesture he'd done a couple of times lately. The gentle way he made her feel cherished caused her anxiety to settle a few notches, but it didn't disappear completely. And she wanted those lips on hers, not her temple.

"Tell me about this new place," she said to keep herself preoccupied and thinking about the right things.

"It's in central Utah," he said. "Near the Capitol Reef National Park area. Seems to be closer to civilization than Brush Creek."

"What's it called?"

"Island Park."

"And?"

"And it's more land. Comes with some equipment. In my price range. It looks promising."

Megan let her frustrations slip away as he spoke. He didn't usually entertain her with long stories or even have much to say about things he was passionate about. She didn't mind his sparse communication. If anything, it only endeared him to her more.

"Maybe you'd like to come with me," he said, and her heart exploded toward the back of her throat.

"To Utah?"

"To Utah," he confirmed. "We'll fly into Salt Lake. There's got to be something to tour there. Drive down south the next day. Check things out." He turned toward her, making eye contact this time. "Yeah?"

She blinked, trying to decide if she really could go with him for a weekend trip to Utah. Her father would be fine. She'd make sure she didn't schedule any meetings with her community groups. Theoretically, she could go.

Emotionally, though, her heart quaked near an eight on

the Richter scale. She somehow managed to get her voice to say, "Yeah."

———

Megan assigned Landon to finish the repairs in the chapel and then she set him to work on the bride's room. A fresh coat of soft pink paint and a new set of alabaster baseboards really did make a huge difference. She hung a new curtain rod and a new set of curtains while he prepped the hallways for their facelift.

By the end of the week, he'd made everything in the church look shiny and new. There were still a couple of doorways that needed fixing, and the carpet in the basement classrooms needed to be ripped out and replaced. And Megan didn't even want to think about the balcony.

She'd confirmed with Sterling that their wedding guests wouldn't exceed the capacity of the main chapel, and Landon said he'd get everything else done and tackle the rebuild on the balcony last.

"Don't forget about the landscaping," she'd told him.

He'd groaned and gone back to painting. Apparently, he didn't like yard work. Megan couldn't blame him. She'd moved into a second-floor apartment to avoid taking care of property. She spent every moment with him that she could spare. He didn't seem to mind, and in fact, she learned that he was deathly afraid of snakes and spiders, that his childhood horse, Brownie, was buried in the backyard under his bedroom window, and that he'd never conquered a bull named Semper Fi.

"Came up against him six times," Landon said on Friday afternoon as he finished up. "Never made it to the eight-second bell."

"You don't sound happy about that."

"I'm not."

"You won like, a million dollars, that year."

"Yeah, something like that." He kicked a grin in her direction. "So we're going over to the hardware store to pick up the cleaning supplies tonight, right?"

"Right."

"Want to go to dinner?" He focused on the paintbrush in his hand.

Megan's insides turned warm and gooey, like she'd put a package of M&M's in the microwave before popping them into her mouth. She loved the treat that way, because then when she bit through the outer shell, the warm, oozy chocolate would burst out.

"Sure," she said.

"You think I can clean up at your place?"

The thought of him in her apartment, looking at her photos, using her bathroom, made her skin tingle. "Yeah, sure."

"Great," he said. "Because I feel like I have a film on my skin I can't wash off here."

Fear sliced through her. "Do you think we have a problem with the plumbing?"

"No, I think I need something stronger than that pink soap to wash with. That stuff does nothing."

"It's cheap," she said. "Comes in a huge bottle."

"I know why you buy it," he said. "I just don't think it does much against paint and grime and sweat."

She liked him painty and grimy and sweaty, but she kept that thought to herself. Watching him work had only added to her desire to have his large, capable hands on her, and she'd spent a fair number of hours this week imagining what it would be like when he finally kissed her.

At her apartment, he disappeared into the bathroom for several minutes. He came out with clean hands and freshly combed hair. She whistled at him, and he laughed as he drew her into an embrace.

She tensed; her heart raced; her breath caught. The moment she'd longed for had finally arrived: Landon Edmunds was going to kiss her.

But he chuckled, ran his hands up and down her bare arms a couple of times, and stepped back. "I'm starving. Can we get pizza tonight?"

Megan put her hands where his had just been, suddenly feeling cold without his touch. "Sure. You want to order in or go out?" She wasn't sure what they'd do in her tiny living room, and her gaze gravitated toward the loveseat and then the television, nerves skipping through her veins all the while.

"We can go out. We have to go to the hardware store anyway."

She went with him out to his truck and to the pizza

parlor. He ordered spinach Alfredo with ham and pineapple while Megan opted for a margarita pizza. "In Jackson, there were tons of gourmet pizza parlors." She leaned her elbows on the table and rested her chin in her hands.

"Yeah?" He lifted his soda glass to his lips, and she followed every movement. "What else did you like to do there? Did you do the white water rafting?"

"No." Her mind flew back to her life in Jackson Hole. "I did some hiking in the Tetons. Jenny Lake is gorgeous, and the walk to Phelps Lake is one of my favorites." She didn't mention that she'd escape civilization in favor of the National Park when she needed a break from work, from life, from Eric.

"Huh." He leaned back in his chair and folded his arms across his chest. "I didn't peg you for an outdoorsy woman."

"I'm not, not really. But I like the boat ride across the lake, and the hike to the hidden falls is only half a mile. Even I can do that."

"I think you can do anything you want to do, Megan."

"Thank you, Landon." She beamed across the table at him, wishing he didn't sit so far away, wishing the pizza stand didn't fill the space between them, wishing she could hold his hand as he smiled at her.

"So." He exhaled. "What's our budget for tonight?"

Her eyebrows crinkled downward. "Budget?"

"Yeah, for the cleaning supplies. You said the church doesn't have a ladder either, so we'll need that." He took another drink. "And I want to price carpet. I just need to know the budget."

Megan blinked. They'd bought a bunch of stuff last week, and she'd tucked the receipt…somewhere.

"I'll ask my father," she said.

"You don't know?"

A surge of fear hit her at the same time the waiter set their pizza on the table. "Spinach Alfredo. Margarita. Anything else I can get for you?"

"No," Landon said, his gaze never leaving Megan's. He seemed…curious, if not a little bit confused.

The waiter left, and Megan suddenly wanted to call him back. Ask for a lemon wedge for her diet soda, a shaker of red pepper, something.

"How can you not know what the budget is to remodel the church?" Landon asked. He didn't so much as twitch toward his pizza. "What if we go over?"

Megan picked up her slice of pizza, but the thought of putting it in her mouth made her stomach revolt. "My father said there's plenty of money."

"But you don't know how much."

"Why does it matter?" Tears burned hot against the back of her eyes. The smell of marinara rushed her; the world narrowed and collapsed, transporting her back to that bank in Jackson Hole. It hadn't smelled basil-y and tomato-y and cheesy. But the horror pulling through her felt the same. The disbelief shredding her confidence.

"Excuse me," she managed to say before practically falling off the counter-height stool and striding toward the restroom.

CHAPTER 10

 $\mathcal{M}$ egan wasn't sure how long she'd been hiding in the bathroom, but she felt sure at least ten minutes had passed. And yet, she couldn't get herself to leave the safety of the women's restroom and go face Landon's questions, his curious looks.

Because then she'd have to tell him. Tell him about Eric. Tell him about her failed engagement. Tell him about her inadequacies when it came to budgeting and keeping track of her finances.

She didn't think someone as accomplished as Landon would understand. The man probably had a financial advisor and knew where every penny of his money was spent.

"As he should," she murmured to her reflection. After all, when dealing with millions, accounting was important. She'd managed to keep the tears dormant, but simple thoughts brought them roaring to the corners of her eyes.

"How can I go back out there?"

The restroom door opened and an elderly woman came in. Their eyes met in the mirror, and recognition lit up the older woman's face. "Megan, sweetie, how are you?"

Lois Garland swept toward Megan, and she let her mother's old friend hold her and comfort her. "What's the matter?"

Megan stepped back and shook her head, her focus on the bathroom tiles. "I—I don't know."

"Must have to do with that tall, gorgeous man keeping vigil outside the door."

Megan yanked her gaze up. "He's right outside?"

"I think he was about to come in when I walked down the hall." Lois gave her a motherly smile, and Megan's heart twisted with longing to see her own mother again. Talk to her. Get some advice about men and what to do about Landon. What to tell him.

"You want me to send him on his way?" Lois asked. "Because I will."

"No," Megan said. "I just need to tell him something."

"Of course." Lois stepped toward the bathroom stall. "Bathrooms aren't really conversation hot spots, are they?" She locked the door behind her, and Megan faced the exit.

Drawing a deep breath, she pushed her way into the hall, where sure enough, Landon stood waiting.

———

Landon wasn't sure why Megan had bolted, but he knew he wanted to fix it. He'd sat at that table like a fool for several minutes before heading down the hall to the bathrooms. He'd even gone so far as to ask someone if there was a dark haired woman still in the bathroom.

From the look of horror and panic on Megan's face, he wouldn't have put it past her to leave the restaurant completely. Thankfully, he'd been reassured that she was still inside.

As every second had passed, his mind had raced. He was just about to go in the women's restroom when an elderly woman came down the hall. She'd given him a look that said she was watching him before pushing into the bathroom.

Now, faced with Megan, his brain went on vacation again. Thankfully, his muscle memory took over. He stepped forward and ran his fingers up Megan's arms to her shoulders. "Hey, what did I say?" Because he knew he'd said something. Her distress was his fault.

She caved into his chest, pressing her cheek right against his pulse. He held her, right there in the hallway outside the women's restroom, his heart tripping over itself and his worry that she'd never talk to him again evaporating at the feel of her body next to his.

Her shoulders came up as she inhaled. "I have to tell you something."

"Okay, sure." He stepped back to give her space and so he could see her face.

"Can we eat first?"

"We can do whatever you want, sweetheart." He smiled at her, a gentle, timid smile—one where he hoped she could recognize his adoration. He offered her his hand, and she slipped her fingers in his without looking at him.

Their table waited, their soda getting less fizzy by the minute. He wondered if he could send his pizza back to be warmed, but he determined not to ask. He didn't need Megan to feel any more self-conscious than she already did.

He waited while she situated herself on her barstool, and then he sat across from her. As if sent from heaven above, their waiter appeared. "Let me take those slices back to be reheated," he said. Without waiting for confirmation, he swept their plates away, leaving Megan without anywhere to look but at Landon.

Sure, she tried her napkin, then her soda. Finally, she managed to glance at him and their eyes locked.

"Might as well just tell me now." He made his voice as nonchalant as possible.

She swallowed, the movement visibly difficult for her. "So I had a boyfriend in Jackson Hole."

Everything in Landon roared in protest. His fingers curled, and the restaurant suddenly seemed twenty degrees too hot. "Okay," he managed to say without sounding like he'd swallowed glass.

Megan tucked her curls behind her ear. "He was more than a boyfriend, actually. A fiancé."

Landon schooled his features into a blank slate, determined to let her finish before he showed any emotion, any reaction. Besides, he wasn't sure how to feel or what to say, so the blank look came pretty easily.

"We should've been married in April," Megan said, her voice lowering in pitch and volume. "Eric worked for the same company as I did. Then they found out he was stealing money and stashing it off-shore. I found out he'd been stealing from me when I went to the bank because my debit card wouldn't work and I was told I didn't have access to my own money." Her gorgeous, deep eyes found his, and he almost lost himself in them.

He blinked, opened his mouth to speak, and waited as the server returned with their food. Landon acknowledged him but ignored his pizza. "So that's why you...why my comment about finances upset you."

"I don't have millions," she said. "But I have enough that I'm not living paycheck to paycheck. I rarely balance my checkbook or worry about if I have enough to buy groceries." She picked up her pizza and took a bite. Thankfully, she didn't look like she'd throw up this time.

He ignored her comment about having millions and focused on his own food. "I didn't mean to stir up old pots."

"I know you didn't." She sighed, and Landon hated the weight of it. "I should've learned something from what happened with Eric. I should pay more attention to my accounts—and to my father's. It just never occurred to me that you'd need to know a budget." Her embarrassment and shame filtered across the table to him. "I'm not good at those kinds of details."

"Well, you can't be perfect at everything." He bit, chewed,

and swallowed. "It's actually kind of nice to know you're not." He chanced giving her a smirk, and though she looked like he'd thrown icy water in her face, after a moment, her features softened into a smile.

"And I would like to hurt Eric." Landon curled his fingers around his soda glass, squeezing like it was Eric's neck.

"He's not worth your time." Megan sounded dismissive, but Landon caught something in her tone that sent a shiver through him.

"Megan, when did you break up with him?"

"Eight months ago."

Landon fell back against the chair, the wind knocked right out of him. She wasn't ready for another relationship. How could she be after only eight months? He couldn't remember anything that had happened for a year following Lauren's departure. And now he understood why everything about money was a big deal to Megan.

"I can see you thinking about something," she said.

Landon ducked his head, cursing himself for not using his cowboy hat to his best advantage. At the same time, he wasn't one to play games. "You sure you're ready for this?"

"Ready for what?"

He lifted his chin and looked her straight in the face. His heart raced like he'd just encountered a dozen rattlesnakes and couldn't keep them from biting Crossfire. "Ready for me to be holdin' your hand. Ready to go to Utah next weekend." He waved his hand like whatever else their future might hold would be included. "Ready for *this.*"

"I'm trying to be." She reached across the table and put both of her hands on one of his. "I like you, Landon. I like being with you."

Though she'd said what he wanted to hear, he wasn't sure he believed her. "We don't have to go to Utah together next weekend." He squeezed her fingers. "I can go myself. I don't want—"

"Did I say I didn't want to go?" She pulled her hands back. "I don't have to decide our entire future right now, do I?"

"No," he said. And she didn't have to decide if she was ready for a relationship with him right this second. He honestly didn't want her to. But he did wonder if she'd grow tired of him the way Lauren had. If she'd want to explore the dating pool now that she was back in it. If another cowboy would catch—

"Great," she said, a smile blooming on her face and causing heat to rise in Landon's.

Give me patience, he prayed as they finished their dinner with lighter conversation about the upcoming town celebrations, the trip to Utah, and if they could really clean the stained glass window with cotton balls and distilled water. *I need patience for everything. For Megan, for finding a ranch in Utah, and for getting that window done in time for the wedding.*

———

Landon hadn't anticipated Megan's power in rallying people together. He witnessed it first hand as he pulled into the church parking lot the next morning. It seemed like every space had already been taken, and people milled about on the lawn beneath the stained glass window.

He parked and pulled the ladder they'd bought the previous evening from the back of his truck. Several men appeared at his tailgate. "Miss Megan said you had buckets, water, and cloths," one said.

"Right there." Landon pointed further up in the truck bed. "Bring 'em all over." Armed with the supplies they needed, the men returned to the grass. Landon set up the ladder while Megan gave the instructions they'd found together online.

Water got poured, and another ladder got brought in, and before Landon knew it, he found himself at the top of the steps, gently wiping with a cotton wand Megan had asked a group of women to make.

Much to his surprise, the grime came off, brightening the color of the glass. The water evaporated quickly, and he passed the cotton swabs to the man waiting a few steps from him. It moved from person to person down to the bottom, and a fresh one was wetted and passed up to him.

After twenty minutes, a whistle sounded. Landon nearly fell off the ladder, focused as he was on cleaning a section of green glass. Adrenaline spiked through his chest like lightning had struck his heart.

"Time to rotate!" Megan called from her position on the ground. "Everyone down. Everyone drinks."

For someone who didn't think she paid attention to details, Megan had organized this event to the minute.

Landon obeyed her, descending the ladder and collecting a plastic cup of ice water.

People mingled and laughed, but Landon stood on the outskirts of the conversations. Megan migrated to his side. "How's it going?"

"It's working," he said. "It's just slow."

"Slow I can handle." She flashed him a smile. "You're on cotton wand transfer," she said before moving away as someone called her name. Landon watched her go, wondering if she meant more than she'd said. He'd been thinking about kissing her. He'd been thinking about it a lot, even after she'd told him about her ex-fiancé.

If things had gone according to her plan, he might have been reunited with her while she was home visiting with her new husband.

Husband.

The word caused a tremor to vibrate his muscles. He lifted his cowboy hat and wiped the sweat from his forehead. Carter North topped the ladder, and Landon took up his new duty. Hours later, the crowd dwindled as the window cleared. Eventually, the buckets found a home in the outdoor shed on the edge of the church's property. The distilled water jugs got thrown away. The ladder folded and leaned against the shed.

Landon lingered on the lawn with Megan while she spoke to his parents. He approached them and caught, "Well, I'll be going to Utah next weekend," from Megan. "So I'll need to reschedule the gardener's meeting. Perhaps Monday would work?"

Landon froze as he realized what she'd just said. His mother's gaze swept his way, but she didn't say anything as his dad confirmed that Monday would work for their meeting. With the knowing look his mother gave him as she followed his father toward their car, Landon fully expected a phone call from her later.

"You ready?" he asked Megan as he pulled his phone from his back pocket. He silenced it so he wouldn't have to ignore his mom when she called. He could simply claim he hadn't heard the phone ring. Not a lie if his cell was silenced.

Megan turned toward him. "I'm beat. It's been a long day."

Disappointment knifed through Landon. "I'll take you home."

"I drove here." She leaned into him, and he gathered her into his arms. "But maybe I'll let you take me home anyway."

"Can I stay?" Landon wasn't sure where the question came from, only that he'd spoken from the barest place inside him. "You can fall asleep on the couch." He touched his lips to her forehead, skated his lips to her ear.

She giggled and pulled away. "Will you buy me some Chinese takeout from that place over by Silver Creek?"

"All the way over there? Why can't we go to The Shrimp Palace? It's like, four seconds from your apartment."

"The Shrimp Palace?" Megan wrinkled her nose and folded her arms. "That place should be shut down by the Health Department."

"What're you talkin' about? They have fantastic coconut shrimp."

"I don't like seafood."

Landon gaped at her, a smile tugging at the corners of his mouth. "You don't like seafood? I think that's criminal."

"I want the string bean chicken from Pan's."

"Pan's?" He lunged toward her, but she seemed to be able to anticipate his movement, because she danced out of the way. Her laughter floated back to him. "Pan's!"

He caught her easily as she reached the sidewalk, and he tucked her into his side. "Fine, we can go to Pan's." He'd do almost anything for her, anything to make her happy. As he realized that, a thin skin of fear coated his euphoria. Thankfully, the warmth from the sun and from Megan's skin as she stayed close to him warmed him.

Like she'd said, he didn't have to decide their future right this second.

CHAPTER 11

"Finished," Landon declared late the following Thursday. "And I'm not comin' in tomorrow, remember?"

Megan sat several paces away, her tablet on her lap. "I remember," she said without looking up. "You're getting ready for the trip to Utah."

"*Our* trip to Utah." Landon tossed the paintbrush in a can of cleaning liquid, which sat on the covered desk, and reached for a blue cloth to wipe his hands. "I'm pickin' you up at six-thirty on Saturday morning." He walked toward her and stopped when she finally tore her gaze from her device.

She tipped her head back to look up at him. "It should be illegal to be up that early on a Saturday."

He chuckled. "You'll have to go to bed at a decent hour."

"Even when I try to do that, I can't sleep."

He crouched in front of her. "I know, sweetheart." The

smile he gave her felt wonderful on his face. Like everything between them could be contained by a simple smile. Last weekend, after they'd spent the day cleaning the stained glass window, she'd laid her head in his lap while he put on a movie. She hadn't been able to fall asleep, and the next day at church she confessed she'd been awake until two o'clock in the morning.

He'd fielded a phone call from his mother, where he hadn't bothered to hide anything. He was thirty years old, and responsible, and independent. His mother had asked three questions before running out, a new record for her. Probably because Landon had been so straightforward with her.

Her gaze drifted to his mouth, and Landon's pulse picked up its pace. But he didn't want to kiss her in the church's basement. Or the chapel. Or her dad's office, which he had just finished painting.

No, Landon wanted his first kiss with Megan to be magical. He felt himself falling for her with every passing day, and he hadn't dared to hope that this next first kiss could actually be his last, but he wanted to do it right if it was.

"I'm assuming you'll want to swing by the gas station for a soda," he said, standing and putting distance between them.

"Of course."

His stomach roared. "And I need to clean up, so we better get this show on the road before I starve to death."

———

Megan had a particularly hard time sleeping that night. Not only because Landon stayed until midnight, and not because he left the intoxicating scent that belonged uniquely to him behind. Well, maybe partly because of those two things. But mostly because she'd be going on her first ever weekend trip with a man. Eric had claimed to loathe traveling, only doing it "for business" when he had to. Yeah, she now knew what his travels had been about.

She hummed to soothe herself as one a.m. approached and she still didn't feel the slightest bit sleepy. She tossed her pajamas into her suitcase and topped them with her toiletries. No way she could get up in the morning and shower. She'd pile her hair on top of her head and swipe on extra deodorant and call it good.

Landon claimed to have a "fun-filled" day planned for them on Saturday in Salt Lake City. On Sunday morning, they'd drive south to meet the realtor at the ranch by two p.m. She hoped he'd scheduled a time and place to finally kiss her. For a moment there, when he finally rose from her couch, rubbing his eyes, she thought he'd give her what she wanted so badly. He held her hand. Held her close. But he hadn't kissed her yet.

Bees buzzed in Megan's blood. Ants crawled over her skin. Bats swarmed in her stomach. She wasn't sure what she was supposed to contribute to this trip. Did Landon want her opinion on the ranch? Or just company for the trip?

If it was up to her, she'd keep him right here in Montana. But he seemed called somewhere else, and she didn't know what to do about that. She'd prayed morning and night for a solution, for a clear head, and no answer had presented itself yet.

So she zipped her suitcase closed and went down the hall to make herself a cup of hot chocolate. As she waited for the milk to warm, she sent a similar prayer up again.

Please help me to know what's right. Guide my feet. Make the path with Landon Edmunds clear.

The microwave beeped, and Megan's eyes snapped open. No revelations had come, so she stirred the chocolate powder into her hot milk and took her steaming mug back to her bedroom, where she turned on the TV and settled against her padded headboard.

Her alarm woke her before the sun claimed the day. She groaned as she realized she'd fallen asleep sitting up in bed. The TV still flickered, and her empty hot chocolate mug lay on its side halfway across the bed.

She stretched her back and neck before standing. Taking the mug with her, she hurried to the kitchen and put it in the dishwasher. She was ready when six-thirty came, and she opened her apartment door with her carryon rolling behind her.

Landon stood there, and she collided with him. He grunted as her shoulder hit him in the chest, and his hands came up and landed on her waist to keep her from falling back. "Whoa, there."

Heart hammering from surprise as much as desire, Megan peered up at him. "Sorry."

"Yeah, I don't think you are." He chuckled, released her—much to her disappointment—and reached for her suitcase. "This is it?"

"We're going for two days. How much do you think I need?"

Darkness crossed his face, and he twisted toward the stairwell. "My last girlfriend would've brought a suitcase for each day."

My last girlfriend.

The words sliced through Megan's cheerfulness. Well, as cheerful as she could be at six-thirty on a Saturday morning. Landon lifted the luggage and took it down the steps, Megan following in his wake. She waited until they'd both settled in the truck before asking, "Did you take a lot of weekend trips with your last girlfriend?"

Landon flinched but recovered quickly. "Not a one."

"Then how do you know she'd take a suitcase for each day of the trip?"

"That's just who she was."

Megan pressed her lips together, wondering how quickly he'd grow tired of her questions. "And who was she?"

He made a show of backing out of the parking stall, like it required his utmost attention and he couldn't even spare the brain power to speak. Once he'd set the truck on the deserted road toward Missoula, he said, "Lauren Tuttle. We dated for a year before she ran off with another cowboy from the ranch."

He delivered the words with precision, without emotion. His fingers remained relaxed on the wheel, and the only indication that he felt anything at all was the slight shift of his body against the seat.

"She didn't grow up here." Megan couldn't remember a Tuttle family.

"She moved here with her mother after her father's death a few years ago. Her mom lives in Monkeytown."

"Oh, so north of the elementary school."

"Right."

"How long ago did she…leave?"

"Couple of years."

Relief rushed through Megan, mostly because she didn't feel the undying urge to ask him another question. Definitely because he didn't seem haunted by the broken relationship. "One more question," she said as it occurred to her.

"You can ask me whatever you want." His hand dropped from the steering wheel and found hers.

"Have you dated anyone since Lauren?"

"You'd be the first."

"So we're dating?"

"That's your second question." He tossed her a grin. "And yeah, I think—I mean, I'm not seeing anyone but you."

"*And* you hold my hand whenever you feel like it," she teased.

"And you let me."

"And you buy me dinner."

"And—" He cleared his throat; his fingers tightened around hers. "And we're goin' on a trip together."

"If that's not dating, I don't know what is."

"Right."

"So can I call you my boyfriend?"

"Third question."

She laughed, snuggling in closer to him. But he wasn't soft; his strong-as-steel muscles didn't bend against her touch. He was kind, though, and gentle, and she thought sure if he would just kiss her, she could fall in love with him.

This weekend, she thought as the miles passed beneath his truck's tires. If he didn't kiss her this weekend, she'd kiss him before they came back to Montana.

———

Once on the ground in Salt Lake, excitement made Megan bounce off the plane. "We're here. We're here."

"I thought for a minute there we weren't gonna make it."

"That was just turbulence."

"Didn't happen on my other trip." Landon paused to wipe his face, and he still looked a bit gray. "I need something to drink." They stopped at a fast food joint in the terminal so he could buy orange juice and water. He found an empty seat and guzzled the orange juice while impatience ate a hole in Megan's stomach. She didn't want to spend her weekend in an airport, but Landon *was* airsick and she wanted to be as attentive and patient with him as he was with her. So she sat beside him and laced her fingers in his free ones. Color returned to his face soon after he finished the juice, and he stood.

"For the record, that's never happened before."

"How often do you fly?"

"Not often."

"Even for the rodeo?"

"I drove," he said. "Big truck and a horse trailer. My manager drove the trailer we lived in. No airplanes."

"And you didn't get sick a couple of weeks ago?"

"I'm telling you, that plane we were just on was about to go down."

Megan giggled and stepped closer to him. "So, what are we doing today?"

"I thought we'd check out some of the country here. There's a pretty easy hike to a waterfall up Provo Canyon."

She groaned and stepped beside him as he got in the line to get a rental car. "I shouldn't have told you about hiking to Phelps Lake."

"This is a walk," he said, a chuckle close behind his words. "It's on a paved path and everything."

"Oh, well, okay."

Provo Canyon turned out to be about an hour south of Salt Lake City, and Megan enjoyed the ride—though she wished she could sit right next to Landon in the SUV the way she did in his truck. It felt awkward to hold his hand across the console, and a sense of weariness pressed her back into her seat.

"Time to wake up, sleepy head."

Megan woke with a start, her heart leaping to the back of her tongue. Sunlight assaulted her at the same time she realized she'd fallen asleep. She turned her attention to the handsome man sitting next to her. Landon gave her a gentle smile, his adoration for her evident in his expression.

Everything inside her softened, and she leaned her cheek against the headrest to return the smile—and the feelings. "Sorry," she said. "I got up early."

"You still wanna…." He nodded out the windshield.

"Yeah." She unbuckled her seatbelt. "Yeah, I want to go see the waterfall."

He joined her outside the truck, taking her hand in his as they moved toward the trailhead. "This is called Bridal Veil Falls. Then we can go to dinner, and I hope you brought your swimming suit." He bumped into her in a playful gesture.

"I did *not* bring my swimming suit." The very idea of donning spandex in front of him brought more horror than she'd felt in months. "You never said anything about swimming."

"The hotel has a pool. It's a given to bring a swimming suit."

"Maybe for you." The very thought of sharing a wall with him brought more butterflies than she knew what to do with. Which was ridiculous. Just because he'd be sleeping in the room next door didn't mean anything. She certainly wasn't going to do anything improper with him, unless kissing was considered improper—and it wasn't.

Too many people loitered nearby to stop him and kiss him right now. Her lips tingled in anticipation of when she could finally be alone with him. At the same time, fear struck her right behind her breastbone. What if Landon didn't want to kiss her? Maybe that was why he hadn't done it yet.

She fell silent as she lost herself inside her worries. Landon let her go, his quiet nature sometimes a curse. They reached the falls, and Megan pulled herself from her introspection. If Landon was going to move to Utah, she wanted to live in the moment with him while she had moments to spare.

The drive to the horse ranch took forever, in Megan's opinion. And they'd left the last town of any decent size about thirty minutes ago. *That's not so bad,* she told herself, especially because Landon turned onto a dirt road in the very next moment. Just like Horseshoe Home Ranch.

"Should be just down here," he muttered. He'd turned mute for the past hour, but Megan didn't mind so much. She felt near the edge of a cliff herself. She still wasn't sure what he expected from her, and she wanted to give him the right reaction to the ranch.

The red and white striped rocks on the buttes surrounding them rendered her breathless, and she seized onto them for a conversation topic. "This is gorgeous country."

Landon peered up and out the windshield. "It is."

"I bet it's super green in the spring."

"Still pretty green right now."

Megan nodded, ashamed of herself for bringing up the landscape. Though it was pretty, surely she and Landon could do better. The fact that he couldn't spoke of his anxiety.

He pulled up to an all-brick house that sported three full-size garage doors. The grass along the front of the house practically shone like emeralds. The gravel driveway obviously had a dedicated caretaker.

Megan's sandals crunched on the rocks as she stood. "This place is nice, Landon."

He closed the car door, shattering the silence and stillness out this far. "It is nice." His tone suggested he wasn't going to judge or commit until he'd seen everything. He wandered along a chest-high fence made of the same gray brick as the house. "Nice backyard."

She wondered how many times he'd say "nice" today. How many times she should say it. The sound of another car approaching drew her attention. She watched as a man wearing a navy blue suit climbed out of his luxury SUV. "You must be Landon." The man barely spared Megan a glance, even when Landon stretched his hand toward her and slid his fingers in hers.

"Yes. This is my girlfriend, Megan."

The man gave her a cursory glance, but Megan suddenly didn't mind. Sure, she and Landon had had the boyfriend/girlfriend talk, but the label certainly rang nicely in her ears. She moved with her *boyfriend*, catching the name Rick as they went up the front steps.

"Now turn and check out that view," Rick said. "Can't beat it anywhere."

She twisted with Landon and found the beautiful red rocks only about a mile away. She sucked in her breath, grateful to be with Landon as he toured this ranch. Grateful he'd included her. Grateful for whatever time with him she had.

———

Landon liked Island Park just fine. The only barn was half as big as the smallest one on the ranch at Brush Creek, and the homestead paled in comparison though it boasted twice as much square footage. The previous owners had obviously decorated for the last time in the eighties.

He didn't mind the cosmetic issues so much. The place came with forty-two acres at half the price of Brush Creek. The tack rooms were functional and heated, which was more than he could say for Horseshoe Home. No swimming pool, no hot tub. Still, he imagined himself at Island Park, with horses and a couple of dogs—and Megan.

He'd glanced at her several times during the walk-through, but he couldn't get a read on her. Everything about the place seemed to mesmerize her. She let him take the lead on asking questions and examining areas first, seemingly happy to follow in his wake.

God existed out here, and Landon liked that. He could get out of his reality just by escaping the yard. Crossfire would love the fields here, but Landon couldn't make a seven-hundred-thousand dollar decision on what he thought his horse would think. That would be ridiculous.

Rick handed him a business card at the conclusion of the tour, quite the difference from the folder of information he'd gotten from the other real estate agent. "Let me know what you think."

"I like it," Landon said as he slid the card in his back pocket. "How many people are looking at it?"

Rick glanced away and when his eyes came back, Landon could see the hint of a lie in the man's eyes. "I have a lot of interest in it."

For some reason, the fib bothered Landon. Something about Island Park wasn't quite right. Maybe *he* was the one out of place here. He held onto the door as Megan got into the SUV, leaning in after her. "What did you think?"

Her startled gaze flew to meet his. "It's nice."

"You don't even mean that." He turned toward the house again. It was nice.

"I don't know what you want me to say," Megan admitted, drawing his attention back to her.

"Say what you want."

"This is a beautiful place." She sighed and cast her eyes around. "It's peaceful here. I have no doubt you and your horse would be happy here. But...it's in Utah."

Landon heard everything she didn't say—as well as everything she did. Though the sun sat at its zenith, he stepped away from the car. "I don't want to head back yet." He nodded toward the wilderness. "You want to walk with me?"

She didn't hesitate but joined him at his side. "This doesn't look that flat." She frowned, but it wasn't one of her real ones. "And it's definitely not paved." She grinned up at him, and everything in his world lightened. Everything finally made sense.

"I don't want this ranch," he said, sobering the moment. He sighed and glanced at the horizon, his mind everywhere but on the red rocks.

Megan slid her arms around his waist and stepped into his arms. She gazed up at him, and she looked like she wanted to say something. Instead, she tipped up on her toes, her eyes drifting closed a moment before her lips touched his.

He molded his mouth to hers, every cell in his body firing. He pulled her closer, held her tighter, kissed her deeper.

Landon wanted to kiss her forever under the clear blue sky. Hold her everyday of his life. Breathe in her floral scent and call her his.

She broke the kiss with a giggle and snuggled into him. "Sorry, that probably doesn't solve your problem."

"Maybe I don't have a problem." Landon wished he could figure out what to do, where to live, why he felt he needed a change when one of the greatest things that had happened to him stood in his arms.

Her fingers trailed across the back of his neck, causing a shiver of desire to spiral down his spine. "Landon—"

"Will you help me figure things out?" He grazed his lips

along her temple, pleased when she pressed further into him.

"I can try." She tilted her head back and Landon pushed his worries to the back of his mind so he could enjoy kissing Megan.

———

Monday afternoon, Landon towed Megan's suitcase to her front door. "Sorry the trip was a bust."

She smiled up at him, leaning into him. "Oh, I think it was quite productive."

He kissed her, something that thrilled him every time—and he'd been doing it as much as possible since yesterday. She rendered him breathless, and he pulled back. "Let's go inside."

She laughed and unlocked her door. He barely waited for her to enter the apartment before he pushed the door closed and pressed Megan against it. He traced his lips along her jawline, his skin prickling as her hands ran across his shoulders and dislodged his cowboy hat. The thud of it hitting the floor was drowned out by the growl grinding through his throat. He brought his mouth to hers, heat engulfing his entire body at the touch of such a good woman.

He wanted to abandon everything, tell Megan he loved her, and ask her to move into a place with him on the northwest edge of town so his commute to the ranch wouldn't be too bad. At the same time, he knew a couple of things. One, he wasn't in love with Megan—yet. Two, he didn't want to stay at Horseshoe Home.

Though he loved it there, he'd felt unsettled and he couldn't ignore that feeling. But when he was kissing Megan, it was a lot easier to wonder why he couldn't just be satisfied with his life here in Montana.

He ended the kiss and stepped away, suddenly feeling foolish. He ran one hand through his hair and then down his face. "Want me to make us something to eat?"

"I thought you said you didn't cook." Megan hadn't moved from her position at the front door. Landon liked the sight of her leaning there, like maybe he'd rendered her so weak she couldn't move quite yet.

"I live thirty minutes from civilization," he said. "I can put together a sandwich or something." He turned in a circle, his mind forgetting what even constituted a sandwich at the moment. He took a deep breath and released it, trying to get his brain to work. "Okay, so what have you got here?"

Megan darted in front of him as he tried to step into the kitchen. "So...I live right downtown and actually don't cook."

"Another flaw." He smirked at her so she'd know he was kidding.

"Ha ha." She crossed her arms. "It would be nice if you had a flaw or two."

"Oh, I've got plenty." Landon took a slow step toward her.

"Name one."

Landon's mouth turned dry. "I'm indecisive."

She rolled her eyes. "Who isn't?"

"I like seafood."

"I'll give you that one. But it's pretty lame. What else have you got?" She turned toward her fridge like maybe she'd open it and produce something edible to eat. She jerked away from the appliance.

"I'm not a great conversationalist," Landon said.

Megan tipped her head back and laughed. "Sometimes that's a good thing."

"What about when it's not?"

"I've only felt like that once."

Landon's stomach tightened but not from hunger. "When?"

"So we'll have to go out," she said, her voice turning airy and high-pitched. "What do you feel like?"

"Megan."

"I have a lot of flaws too," she said. "And one of them is when I don't want to talk about something, I don't." She gave him a half-crooked smile that really said, *Drop it, Landon.*

So he dropped it. Said, "I feel like pasta."

CHAPTER 13

Two weeks passed while Landon painted and laid carpet and replaced light fixtures. He took Megan to the Fourth of July parade, and kissed her whenever he could do so without prying eyes.

And this particular Sunday, his mother had invited the pair of them to dinner at his childhood home. He sat in the pew, Jace and Belle between him and his parents. Landon had been driving himself down to Gold Valley so he could loiter in Megan's parking lot until she came out. He'd been spending mornings with her. Days with her. Evenings with her.

In the quiet moments where he drove back up the canyon in the dark, he wanted to spend his life with her. Whenever that thought came—and it had been coming more and more often—he turned on the radio as loud as it would go, grateful for the pricey satellite service in his truck.

And he hadn't admitted it to anyone, least of all Megan, but he missed ranching. Sure, it had been nice to have a break, to build and repair things instead of feed and haul things. But he missed the fresh air, the wide open sky, the sound of men talking and his horse snuffling.

Megan spoke to him pretty much all day, if she wasn't busy with her community programs, and the cacophony of hammer blows added to the conversation. Thankfully, because Landon didn't have a whole lot to add to the stories Megan told.

He *had* kissed her in the basement classrooms—all of them. She was just too pretty sitting there to keep his hands to himself. He'd kissed her in the chapel, her office, the conference room, against the side of the building, every-where he could.

"You're not listening," Megan whispered, her cool breath sending a tremor through his shoulders.

Landon jerked himself from his fantasies and focused on the preacher at the front of the congregation. "Yes, I am," he said out of the side of his mouth. "Besides, there won't be a quiz later."

"No?" She leaned into him. "Your dad seems like the kind to discuss religious topics for hours on end." She fell silent as Mrs. Fletcher turned and shot her a look. "You know, like at lunch."

Landon let several seconds go by. "Oh, so that's what you're worried about." He admired the cut of her navy skirt, the way her bright pink blouse accentuated her dark curls. "You've met my parents loads of times."

"Never as your girlfriend."

Landon's hand tightened around hers. "I haven't kept you a secret."

"I know."

Landon glanced toward Jace when he detected movement on his right. "What?"

"What're you guys talkin' about?"

"Nothing."

"Maybe do it quieter then, before Mrs. Fletcher loses her mind."

Landon clamped his lips shut, though they tried to twitch up into a smile. Finally, Megan's dad finished his sermon—no, Landon didn't know what he'd spoken about —and the people stood. Chatter broke out, but Landon stayed sitting, his gaze on the clear, colored glass in the window. A sense of safety filled him, a feeling he'd only experienced a couple of times before.

Once, just before his first National Championship. Again, when he'd returned to Montana after the injury that had ended his rodeo career. He could still ride a horse, and walk, and do almost anything. But his hip and knee couldn't handle the high velocity of a bucking bull.

Confusion riddled his mind. Why did he feel like this now, here? Was he supposed to stay in Montana after all? And if so, what did the restless feelings and urge to find a horse ranch of his own mean?

"You comin'?"

Landon glanced up into his father's face. He had the same green eyes as Landon and Belle, the same square jaw as his son. Landon found comfort in his father's kind face. "Yeah, I'm comin'."

"Good. I think Megan was starting to wonder if she'd have to eat with us alone." He cracked a smile, and Landon shot to his feet. He found Megan at the rear of the near-empty chapel, his mother standing next to her. They both wore an anxious expression, and Landon hurried down the aisle toward them.

"Hey." He swept an arm around Megan's waist. "Sorry, that stained glass window is so beautiful, I got lost for a minute." He glanced at his family. "Who's hungry?" His stomach rioted at the thought of spending the next couple of hours trying to make conversation. Not that he didn't enjoy his parents, but he didn't feel like discussing his job, his hopes, his unrealized dreams to have his own horse ranch. Not today.

Megan fed off Landon's unease. She hadn't realized she knew him so well, but she could see the tension in the set of his mouth, read the anxiety in the stride of his step, feel the unrest in the grip of his fingers.

He got in the cab and closed the door. When he didn't start the ignition right away, Megan said, "We'll die in here if you don't turn on the air conditioner."

He stuck the key in and turned it. Megan adjusted the vents so they blew right into her face, because a gray truck in the middle of the summer trapped enough heat to bake cookies.

"You okay?" she asked when he simply stared out the windshield.

"Do you think God's plan for you can change?" He turned and looked at her, his expression vulnerable and curious.

Megan blinked. Nothing in her theology classes had prepared her for questions, especially deep ones. She'd been so focused on re-learning the Bible stories, really digging deep to be able to understand the doctrine behind them, that she didn't have time for questions of her own. Sometimes she thought she didn't have any, that she just believed because she'd been blessed with faith.

"Sure, I suppose," she forced through her dry throat. "Different choices will bring different results."

Landon nodded, returning his attention out the windshield. He heaved a sigh. "Well, I suppose we better get to lunch. My mom might freak out if we're any later than we already are." He put the truck in gear and pointed it toward an older section of town, one named Battle Creek. A pioneer park with the same name sat in the center of the community, as well as a small stream where kids and grandparents fished for crawdads.

He pulled up in front of a sprawling brick home, and nerves assaulted her. She reminded herself that she had met his parents before, that this was just another meal. She hitched a smile into place and flashed it at Landon.

He didn't return it. "This is where my awful conversation skills will be a real problem." He hung his head. "I'm sorry, Megan."

"No need to apologize." She tucked her arm in his. "We shouldn't have to apologize for who we are." She glanced at the house and caught a flicker of movement behind the gauzy curtains on the front windows. "Besides, your parents know you're...the quiet type."

He gaped at her for several seconds before a chuckle filled the truck. "The quiet type. I think those men are usually classified as dangerous."

"Just how I like 'em." She pushed against his solid shoulders with a giggle. "Now get out. Your mom's watching us through the windows."

He laughed as he spilled from the truck, and Megan joined her voice to his. But really, she kept a prayer going that she'd be able to enjoy lunch, impress Landon's parents, and maintain her sanity. It was asking a lot, but she believed God could deliver.

Please, just help me say the right things, she prayed as she ascended the steps and his mother pulled open the front door.

"Megan, dear." Landon's mother swept Megan into a hug. "Thanks for coming. I was beginning to think Landon would never share you with us." She gave her son a mother-knows-all look and took Megan into the house. She glanced back at Landon, who wore a half-scowl on his handsome face as he trailed in her wake.

She took a deep breath and got a noseful of roast and potatoes. "Sister Edmunds, it smells delicious."

"Oh, none of that Sister Edmunds stuff. Call me Karen."

Megan let herself get ushered into the kitchen, where Landon's father stood using a hand mixer to whip potatoes.

"Jerry, how are you?" Megan stepped up to him and patted his forearm. "Does Landon get his culinary skills from you?"

"I don't cook," Landon said. "And remember how you didn't have any groceries in your apartment?"

She shot him a glare. "I…cook."

"Heating things up doesn't count."

"Landon, be nice to the girl." Karen handed Megan a bowl of salad. "Will you take that out to the picnic table, dear?"

Despite the fact that she despised being called "girl," Megan took the bowl and headed toward the sliding glass door that led to the deck. Four place settings had already been laid out, complete with two pitchers of lemonade, napkins, and salt and pepper shakers. Megan placed the bowl in the middle of the table and returned to the kitchen.

Before she could, Landon pointed back toward the yard with a bag of rolls. "We're bringin' everything out." She turned, and he came up beside her. "My mother already lectured me for bein' late."

"I was gone for fifteen seconds."

"She has the art of lecturing down to a science."

Megan nudged him, thrilled at the growl he emitted. She loved that playful sound, adored the strength in the way he barely moved, delighted that he swept a kiss along her jaw just before his parents joined them on the deck.

"So, Landon, what did you think of the sermon today?" His father set the mashed potatoes on the table and folded himself onto a bench.

Megan snorted to cover the laugh threatening to escape and blinked at Landon.

"It was fine," Landon said. "What about you, Megan?"

Miraculously, his father didn't question him further. Maybe Landon had always gotten away with saying things were "fine" and the conversation moved on. Megan tried to watch him out of the corner of her eye, a sudden gnawing in her gut she didn't like.

Would he cover their hard conversations with "It's fine," or "I feel fine."? She wanted more than that. She *deserved* more than that, especially after the non-relationship she'd endured with Eric. Eric, who she hadn't really known at all. And if Landon said things were fine when they weren't, she wouldn't be able to get to know him either.

Even though the summer sun shone, and a brisk breeze kept them cool, and the food was so delicious Megan actually wished she could cook, her spirits had been dampened by Landon's "fine."

She made it through the meal, never letting on that anything was wrong. As she said good-bye to his parents and settled by his side in the truck, she wondered if she'd just done the same thing. After all, she'd pretended everything was fine when it wasn't.

CHAPTER 14

"I don't want to go home," Megan said. "Can we...I don't know. Go for a walk or something?"

Landon eased up on the accelerator. "Can't be too hard," he said. "What with your heels and all."

"Maybe just around the park."

He put on his blinker and pulled into the parking lot. "Your wish is my command."

"Landon."

He must have sensed or heard something in her voice, because he trained his full attention on her. She squirmed under the weight of it, but she couldn't look away.

"What's wrong?" He put two fingers under her chin when she tried to duck away from his penetrating green eyes.

"I'm trying to figure out when you've told me things were fine when they weren't."

He frowned. "I haven't done that." He tilted his head to the side. "Why would you think I had?"

"You told your dad the sermon was fine when you didn't hear a word of it."

"I'm sure it was fine."

"I don't want fine." Megan drew herself up, the realization striking like lightning. "I had fine, and I—I—" Her voice broke. Numbness spread through her, and she felt wobbly inside and out. "I want more than fine."

He took her face in both his hands, his eyes kind and though he was strong and tough, he handled her with such gentleness. "I am not Eric." He touched his lips to her forehead. "Tell me what you need." He skated his mouth down the side of her face, causing a ripple to cascade through her. Safety and warmth flowed through her. If she could trust herself, she'd say *love* poured through her. "And I will give it to you," Landon finished, his voice husky and hushed.

"Just you," she whispered against his lips. "I just need you." And though Megan couldn't exactly pinpoint how she felt about Landon, or if she'd unconsciously projected some of her issues with Eric onto him, she kissed him. Kissed him like she was falling in love with him.

———

Megan stuffed her debit card and driver's license in her back shorts pocket and hurried out of her apartment. After Landon had come in and they'd somehow cobbled together homemade ice cream, she'd puttered around the house, waiting for sleep to claim her.

She'd studied. Cleaned. Thrown out the sourdough starter she'd been planning to use for the cooking class at the church. Made a list of who she needed to call the next day. Painted her toenails.

By the time she woke in the morning, she had a text from Belle, inviting her to lunch. She'd answered it with a *Yes! What time?* before she realized it was practically lunchtime already.

Thankfully, Belle was already in town, and she'd given Megan fifteen minutes to get over to the deli. The scent of fresh bread hit Megan half a block away, and she increased her pace. She'd always been motivated by carbs, and a lunch with her best friend—who happened to be her boyfriend's sister—would definitely need a lot of bread and butter.

She entered the deli and found Belle waiting just inside the door. She stood and drew Megan into a hug. "Hey." She held her by the shoulders and stepped back. "You look great." A knowing smile touched her lips. "No wonder my brother is smitten by you."

Megan scoffed. "He's not smitten," she said, though some small part of her hoped he was. "And you're looking good. How are you feeling?" She moved toward the ordering line, her thoughts jumping to if she should get a double-fudge brownie or a German chocolate one.

"I'm halfway through the second trimester," Belle said. "So I'm feeling a lot better than I was a couple of months ago."

"When do you find out if it's a boy or a girl?"

"In a couple of weeks." Belle practically glowed, her smile lighting the entire place. The happiness of it infused Megan, and she longed to be that happy. She thought she had been, once. But what she'd believed to be true and what turned out to actually be fact had been two very different things.

Her familiar friend, fear, crept into her mind. Was she doing the same thing with Landon? Everything with him had been easy—maybe too easy. She sighed before turning to order the biggest chef salad on the menu.

"And a German chocolate brownie," she added. She could have a treat if she ate lettuce for lunch. She and Belle went through the line and settled into a booth in the corner, making idle chit chat about life, the church, the ranch, and Belle's pregnancy.

Soon enough though, Belle put an end to the small talk. "So, Landon said he might not be buying a place now."

"Oh?" Megan's eyebrows shot up, and she tried to cover her surprise by taking a big bite of cucumber and ranch.

"Yeah, he stopped by to grab Jace before he went up to the higher fields. I heard him tell Jace he wasn't sure he should buy a ranch of his own. Said he couldn't find anything he really liked."

"He's only looked at two places," Megan said. "And he did really like the first one. It was just too expensive."

"Do you want him to buy a ranch?"

"No." Megan blinked and attempted to think through the situation. "I mean, yes. I mean…I want him to be happy."

Belle peered at her, her green eyes as intense as her brother's. "What if he moves?"

"We haven't talked about it."

"I'm asking *you*," Belle said. "What will *you* do if he buys a horse ranch in Utah or Nevada and moves away?"

Everything inside Megan recoiled at the very thought. "I…don't know." She wished Belle would look somewhere else, but her best friend didn't usually back down from anything or anyone.

"What's keeping you here?" Belle asked, finally turning her attention to her wiser dessert choice—a fruit tart.

"My father. The church…."

"He's going to retire in a few months, right?"

"Right."

"And he's still relatively healthy."

"His hip just bothers him in the winter."

Belle nodded, her expression turning innocent. Megan had seen this tactic before. "So you could go with Landon."

Megan almost choked. "I wouldn't go with him. Not if we were just dating. If we were engaged—" She gasped the word out. She lifted one shoulder like they were discussing whether or not they'd have a winning football team this year. "Then I'd go."

"So you'd need to be engaged to go with him."

"I didn't say that. We've been dating for a few weeks."

"More than a few."

"Several. It hasn't even been two months." Megan had only been back in town for two and a half months, and

Landon didn't come along until the beginning of the summer. "Six weeks," she said. "He's not going to fall in love with me and ask me to marry him in six weeks."

Belle plucked the strawberry off her tart and popped it into her mouth. Her eyes were wide and innocent as she licked her fingers and said, "You never know."

———

Landon wasn't sure why everything anyone said or did made annoyance burn through him. He'd brought a crew to the church on Monday morning to get the weak and damaged area of the balcony demolished, but he couldn't stand their conversation, their endless questions.

He'd expected to see Megan at some point. Sure, she liked to sleep in, especially when she was up late. And she had been, because she'd sent him a text at two-forty-seven that morning.

But she hadn't shown up yet, and lunchtime was almost over. He sat against the trunk of a tree on the far side of the church where no one could see him. He knew himself well enough to get away from people when he got in a foul mood.

Distantly, he heard someone say his name. He ignored them and tried to reposition himself so his wide shoulders didn't poke out the sides of the tree trunk. Didn't work. Whoever was looking for him came closer, their footsteps strong and sure.

Landon turned when he realized Jace had come into town. Alarm raced through him as he stood and dusted off his jeans. "What's goin' on? What are you doin' here?" Landon glanced over his shoulder, like the reason for Jace's visit would be standing there.

"Belle wanted me to come baby furniture shopping with her." Jace didn't roll his eyes, but his tone conveyed his desire to do so. "Don't know why. It's not like my opinion matters."

Landon laughed. "Belle has her eye on somethin'."

"Yeah, a changing table that costs six hundred dollars," Jace grumbled. "I don't even know why a baby needs a changing table. Why can't we just lay him on the floor to change his diaper?"

Landon shrugged. "Don't ask me." He shoved his hands in his pockets. "So it's a boy?"

Jace shook his head. "Don't know yet." He gestured back the way he'd come. "Carlos said I'd find you over here. Just thought I'd hang out while Belle's at lunch."

"Why didn't you go to lunch with her?"

"She wanted to meet a friend."

Sirens and bells went off in Landon's head. "Who?"

Jace's boots scraped the cement as he shuffled them. He swiped his hat off his head and wiped his hand down his face, tugging on the end of his beard, which he only did when he was nervous. Landon had witnessed the habit enough to know.

"Megan, right? I mean, it's not like my sister has a lot of friends in town."

"Of course she does," Jace said.

"But it's Megan, right?"

"I didn't really ask."

Landon tipped his head back and gazed into the blue sky. "What're they talkin' about?"

"I imagine they'll talk about you. Belle loves a good love story."

Landon inhaled, but air seemed to be the wrong thing to breathe and he choked. "Love story?"

"Yeah." Jace folded his arms and settled his weight away from Landon. "I mean, you're holding her hand and kissin' her. What do you call that?"

"Dating." Landon's mood darkened by several shades. "And it's still brand new at that. I'm not in love with her."

"Of course you aren't." Jace snorted like Landon being in love was the stupidest thing ever.

Fear seized Landon's muscles. "Jace, do you...do you think I could love her?"

"Of course you could." He cocked his head as if that would help him see Landon clearer. "Why couldn't you? She's pretty, she's kind, she's fun to be with. Right? You like being with her? Talking and...whatever?"

"Yeah." Landon's voice sounded so wispy. "I like being with her. I just...I loved Lauren too, and that was a fiasco."

"I thought you were over Lauren."

"I am," Landon said firmly. "But maybe I don't know how to—I don't know." He exhaled and his eyes flitted everywhere but at Jace. "Maybe I don't know how to love someone the right way."

Jace chuckled. "There is no 'right way' to love someone. I mean, look at me and Belle. No one would ever put us together. We argue constantly. She riles me up. I make her see red. But we love each other in our own special way."

"You didn't get there easily, though." A flash of horror hit him. "Maybe this is too easy. That's why it doesn't feel right."

Jace started laughing, and the sound grated against Landon's nerves. "What? What's so funny?" He rolled his eyes as Jace continued chuckling. Finally he sobered.

"Look, Landon. Falling in love is the easy part. That's good if it's easy. But." His eyes sparked. "If something doesn't feel right, you can't ignore that." He took a step closer, and Landon felt smothered by it, though plenty of space existed between them.

"So what doesn't feel right?" Jace asked.

Landon sighed, his frustration skyrocketing. "I don't know." An idea occurred to him. "Maybe because she's so... good, and I'm just, you know, starting back to church."

"You've been going for two years, Landon."

"Yeah." He exhaled again, the weight of the world seemingly pressing down on his shoulders. "She's still the preacher's daughter."

"You think she judges you?"

"No, it's not that."

"Well, you should probably figure it out before you, you know, go falling in love." He said the last part of his sentence over his shoulder as he walked away. Landon watched him round the church, everything inside him jumbled.

His mind spun from one side of the spectrum to the other. Was he falling in love with Megan?

Yes, his mind whispered.

Why did that terrify him to the very core?

Because of Lauren.

Why did he feel like something was wrong? Was it him? Megan? Them together? Something else?

As if the heavens had opened and lightning had struck his mind, he knew. "The horse ranch." He'd been frustrated that Island Park hadn't panned out, but he still had a bad feeling about that place. He wasn't supposed to be there.

"But Horseshoe Home isn't where you're supposed to be either." He kicked at the ground, more annoyed and frustrated than ever. He strode toward the church, his anger a scent on the air. Carlos even lifted his head long before he should've been able to hear Landon coming.

"I'm done for today," Landon barked in his direction. "Can you bring your guys back tomorrow?"

"Done?" Carlos called.

"I—" Landon nodded. "If you can't get your crew together again tomorrow, I understand. I'll call you later." He practically sprinted to his truck and he wanted to peel out of the parking lot. But he showed some restraint by only gunning the engine once he was on the road and headed for the canyon.

When he should've turned right to go up to Horseshoe Home, he kept going straight. He didn't want to face Jace, because his friend was right. He needed to get things figured out before he continued down the current road he was on. It wouldn't be fair to Megan if he didn't.

He slapped the steering wheel and pressed on the accelerator. He'd escaped to Bear Mountain when he'd learned about Lauren. He always made sure the cabin was well-stocked before he left each time. He'd have enough to get through the next couple of days, until he could clear his head and make an informed decision.

When he turned onto Tibble Fork Road, he wouldn't have cell service. So he pulled over at the intersection and called Megan. Sure, he needed time to get his thoughts together, but that didn't mean she should be ignored.

The call went to her voicemail, and he assumed she was still lunching with Belle, talking about him. Annoyance reared once more.

He took a steeling breath to tame his voice into something placid before he spoke. "Hey, Megan, I won't be back to the church for a few days. I just—" He paused, his emotions starting to bleed into his voice. "I'm headed up to my cabin on Bear Mountain. I just need some time alone to get my head on straight. I'll call you when I get back, probably on Thursday." He wasn't sure how to end the call. "I'm sorry if this doesn't make sense. It has nothing to do with you, and everything to do with me." He pulled the phone from his ear and looked at it, hoping a proper salutation would appear on the screen. It didn't.

"Okay, talk to you soon." He said before thumbing off the call. He called Carlos and rescheduled to work on the church the following week. And then he dialed Jace, expecting another emotionally exhausting conversation.

Instead, Jace said, "Be safe. Work things out. We'll manage without your help on the morning chores," and hung up. With all his loose ends tied up, Landon faced Tibble Fork Road, took a deep breath, and started up the mountain.

CHAPTER 15

*L*andon's frustrations, worries, and bad mood lifted as soon as he pulled up to the remote cabin. A sense of peace existed here he couldn't find anywhere else. A feeling he'd been trying to find in Utah.

"Because you can't live in a two-room cabin on the top of a mountain," he muttered to himself. But the truth was, he could. He didn't need to work, he just liked the feel of calluses on his hands, the smell of horses, the tired ache in his muscles that testified that he'd put in a good, honest day's work.

Sure, there was plenty of work to do around the cabin. He could wash windows, repair the front steps, clear the land in the back and plant a garden. Build a paddock and keep horses. Erect a barn and raise cows and pigs and chickens. If he got all that going, he probably wouldn't even have to go down the mountain for groceries.

The thought was as attractive as it was horrifying. He

twisted the knob and entered the cabin. He didn't keep the door locked, though he often thought he should. The interior looked the same as it had the last time he was here, if not a little dustier.

A sigh leaked from his lips. He flipped on the lights and opened the fridge. Bottles of water stood like soldiers and he took one out. The cupboards housed enough syrup and pancake mix to last a couple of months, and he opened the one above the stove to find a bag of his favorite spicy nacho chips.

With those in hand, he retreated to the bedroom where he piled the pillows against the headrest he'd bought in Butte after his last National Championship win. He selected a documentary on the science behind training horses—something he'd watched a couple dozen times—and stuck it in the DVD player. With the sound of wind blowing from the TV and his snacks nearby, Landon slipped off his hat and set it on the dresser. He got out a pair of gym shorts and a T-shirt, changed his clothes, and settled against the pillows.

He didn't even try to think. He just stared at the screen, his attention on the horses, and munched on his chips. Once he was fully relaxed, he'd figure out what God wanted him to do.

The following morning, Landon felt more like himself. He pulled on a sweatshirt and laced his hiking boots. In the backpack he kept on a hook by the backdoor, he packed granola bars, bottled water, and fruit cups. He wasn't planning to hike very far, but he knew better than anyone how the trees just beyond the cabin could blend, blur, multiply, move if he didn't pay attention.

The pack also carried a flashlight, an emergency blanket, a first aid kit, and pain medication. He never left the cabin without it, and he checked its contents to ensure he could survive if he got stuck outside after dark.

Because he'd risen so early, the sun hadn't quite claimed the day yet. Landon's favorite time to be alive. He loved being awake when seemingly nothing else on the earth was. He felt like he could ask the Lord questions and He'd actually have time to answer.

He kept his thoughts dormant as he walked along the path he'd marked through the trees. About a half-mile from his cabin sat a fresh water spring, and the bubbling, bright sound of the water always soothed him.

After reaching the spring, he sat on a boulder and pulled out his packaged breakfast of a peach cup and a semi-stale chocolate chip granola bar. He let his mind wander, and it landed on Megan.

Oh, how he liked Megan. His fingers twitched at the memory of holding hers. His lips curved, almost able to taste her mint and maple flavor. He took a breath, and he could've sworn he smelled jasmine.

"You're in deep with her," he murmured as he lifted the water bottle to his lips. He recognized the feelings—he'd experienced them before. The more time he spent with Megan, the more he trusted himself, the more likely it was he'd fall in love with her.

He felt nothing but restful. No fear. No panic. Being with Megan was easy, and that wasn't a bad thing.

Landon cast his eyes toward the top of the trees. "Why do I feel unsettled then?"

The answer didn't come in a voice like thunder, or even a whisper. Landon didn't know as he headed back to the cabin, as he passed the time to lunch, as he put together a puzzle in the afternoon.

But little by little, Landon discovered that the answer to his question had already been received. Months ago, he'd felt like he needed a change. Needed to leave Montana. Needed a place to own, to train horses, to belong.

And that hadn't changed. Megan notwithstanding, that hadn't changed.

With a heart laden with gravity, he drove down the mountain on Wednesday night to buy replenishing supplies. As he came back to civilization and gained cell service, his phone chirped and chimed.

He left it until he passed the horseshoe-shaped falls in Gold Valley. He had several missed calls—only one from Megan, but five from Shelly.

"Shelly?" He pulled over and checked the number to make sure he'd seen it correctly. "The realtor from Brush Creek." His heart stalled and he didn't dare to hope for much more than a misdial. But she wouldn't do that five times.

He called into his voicemail, his heart blipping at the sound of his girlfriend's voice. She was kind, as always, but

Landon would've had to be deaf not to hear the undercurrent of concern in her voice.

Shelly's first message sent Landon's heart into a frenzy. "Landon, give me a call. The sellers at Brush Creek are interested in renegotiating your offer."

By the time she'd left her third message, he was ready to call her back, visions of horse ranches galloping through his head. She'd called twice more but hadn't left messages. The last call had been yesterday evening.

"Landon?" she answered.

"Shelly," he said, relief pouring through him. "I was up at my cabin. No cell service. Sorry I missed your calls."

"Did you get my messages?"

"Yeah, I listened to them. The family will take my counteroffer?"

"If it's still cash."

"It's still cash."

"Then let's make a deal."

A thread of disquiet pulled through Landon. He opened his mouth to say something, but he didn't know what. He'd just spent three days trying to find the answers he needed. And he had.

"I'd like to come see the place again," he finally said. "Is that all right?"

"Sure, of course. We'll need to meet to do some paperwork anyway."

"When works for you?"

"Anytime that works for you." She wore a smile in her voice, and Landon wondered if he could get the sellers to come down in price again. It had only been a couple of months since his visit to Brush Creek. They must not have any others interested, or they really wanted to unload the ranch.

"Landon?"

"I—" He swallowed. It wasn't a matter of when *he* would be ready to return to Utah. When *he* would be ready to move to Brush Creek.

But when *Megan* would be ready to go with him.

"How about this weekend?" he asked. His memories of Brush Creek were fond, and while he did want to see the place again for some reason, he also knew he'd buy it if he could get it for the right price.

"This weekend works great. See you Saturday?"

"Saturday," he confirmed. He hung up, his emotions on a pulley system. With every thought of Brush Creek, joy tugged a little harder. But with every thought of Megan, despair yanked back.

———

Time passed in Megan's world, but she felt caged off from the rest of the world, almost like she was living her life behind a layer of plastic wrap. She wasn't sure when she'd become so dependent on seeing Landon, hearing his voice, smelling his cologne. But when he'd called—and she hadn't answered because Belle had just asked her if she'd moved past Eric—and told her he wouldn't be back until Thursday, her days had turned long.

Quiet and long.

Boring and long.

Lonely and long.

She'd tried to fill her time with Belle, but her friend lived out on the ranch now and had responsibilities of her own. So Megan had turned her attention to her father, and then her gospel studies. But there were only so many hours she could talk about faith, and forgiveness, and she found she didn't enjoy her father's company as much as she had before she'd started dating Landon.

Because her dad questioned her mercilessly. From "Do you love him?" to "Will you move out to Horseshoe Home Ranch if you get married?" to "Are you even ready for marriage?" set her teeth on edge.

She'd been dating Landon for six weeks—as she pointed out to her father—and if Megan knew one thing, it was that if she wanted to scare off a man, she'd start talking about their wedding before they'd even kissed.

Her father had asked about that too. Megan had never felt so much like a preacher's daughter than during that conversation. Her face burned just thinking about it, and she'd never missed her mother so much.

If there was one person besides Belle Megan wanted to confide in, it was her mother. Over the past few days while she'd been alone, she'd taken to driving to the falls and strolling along the boardwalks, a whispered conversation with her mother streaming under her breath.

She'd leaned against the railings on the bridges, her face north toward Bear Mountain, her thoughts on Landon. She wasn't sure why he'd escaped town, but Belle had mentioned that Jace had said Landon was in a foul mood on Monday.

Hearsay, she told herself as she walked over to the waffle truck parked at the park closest to her house. She reasoned she could eat a waffle for lunch because she hadn't actually been awake to eat breakfast.

She took her dessert waffle, laden with strawberries, raspberries, and whipped cream, to a bench in the shade. The smell of yeast and sugar made her mouth water, and the way her knife had to break the crisp of the waffle told her she was really going to enjoy her lunch.

And she did, but she wished she wasn't eating alone, on this perfect summer day. She rubbed her arms as a chill ran across her skin. Though she'd just eaten, her stomach felt like an endless pit, and the urge to get another waffle dove through her.

Because surely more carbs would erase this nervous twitch tumbling through her.

Intellectually, she knew carbs wouldn't help anything. In fact, she knew nothing would rid her of this feeling—except Landon.

She checked her phone as a breeze picked up the hem of her skirt and tried to take it through the trees. Pressing one hand to her knees, Megan willed a message to appear on her cell. A call to come through.

The device remained silent. A sigh traveled from the tips of her toes, up through her body, and out of her mouth. She couldn't face the church today, not with the gaping hole in the balcony. Didn't want to see her father after the question-fest of yesterday.

"Can't sit in the park forever," she muttered as she gained her feet.

Landon didn't call or text that afternoon. Megan kept her phone face-up as she heated a frozen pizza in the oven. When the apartment filled with smoke because she wandered down the hall for too long, her phone clutched in her hand, she threw the burnt pizza in the trash and ran out to grab a salad from the corner market.

With every step, she came up with a new reason why Landon hadn't called. Maybe he decided to stay up at his cabin for another day.

Maybe he'd returned to the ranch and been caught away in a whirlwind of work.

Maybe he'd been in a terrible accident on the way down the mountain.

After the last one, she shut her mind off from thinking about Landon. She couldn't stand the thought of him injured. Or on the ranch without a way to reach her. Or still on the mountain.

No, better not to muse about why he hadn't called.

She ate, she watched a movie, she settled down in bed to study her scriptures. Midnight came and went, and Thursday became Friday without a peep from Landon.

Megan thought sure she wouldn't be able to sleep at all that night. But she woke sometime later, her lamp still burning, her Bible still open though lying down on her stomach.

She blinked against the light, trying to figure out what time it was. She finally located her phone and saw the time: four-fifteen a.m. After padding to the bathroom and back to bed, Megan turned off the lamp and snuggled into her pillows. Her mind ran in circles, with Landon at the center. The more she thought about him, the wider the hole stretched. The more that hole filled with hurt.

Stop it, she commanded herself. He'd said himself that he wasn't Eric.

And he's not.

He's not Eric.

He's not Eric.

She repeated the mantra until sleep claimed her again.

CHAPTER 16

Megan startled at a noise outside her subconscious. Outside her dreams.

"Phone," she blurted out. Her phone was ringing. And ringing. Her fingers scrambled for it and knocked it to the floor, where it made the most sickening shattering sound she'd ever heard.

A moan started deep in her chest as her feet met the floor and the call silenced. Time slowed as she reached for her phone. She paused before touching it and sent up a prayer that it would be whole.

Several pieces of glass actually fell from the front of the phone when she lifted it. Definitely not whole.

Or even operational, as the screen sat in darkness. "No," she said. "No, no, please no." She pressed the power button and held it down, but nothing happened. She didn't even know who had called. And she didn't know what time it was.

She hurried into the kitchen and checked the microwave. Only seven forty-five in the morning. "Definitely Landon." No one else would call her this early. Panic seized her lungs, and she gasped at the air. It felt like water, too thick and nowhere near satisfying her need for oxygen.

Megan did the only thing she could think of: She got in the shower and got ready for the day. She headed over to the church, fully expecting to see Landon's big truck in the parking lot. When she found only a handful of sedans, her spirits fell again. If they got any lower, they'd be underground.

She put on a strong, happy face and entered the church. Landon was not there. She heard classical music filtering down the hall, coming from her father's office. She turned toward the chapel instead, making her way inside and taking a seat in one of the back pews. The stained glass window peered down on her, making her feel like her problems were insignificant. Or at the very least, fleeting.

Megan loved sitting in the chapel, especially when the choir sang. She always felt like the very angels themselves added their voices to the song. The acoustics made the sound fly to the rafters and back.

At the same time, the chapel was also an excellent place to listen, to get answers. And if there was something Megan needed right now, it was answers.

She closed her eyes, hoping to quiet her rising anxiety. She didn't articulate her thoughts though, because they didn't come together into coherence. All she could come up with was, *Help.*

Go get a new phone, came into her mind. Without thinking too hard about what she should do, or when, she sprang to her feet and headed out the door.

After all, she needed to get a new phone as soon as possible.

Landon wasn't one for sitting around on a beautiful summer day. He'd already packed for his trip to Utah and now that he had some spare time on his hands, all he could do was pace in his cabin.

He hated that Megan hadn't answered his call that morning. Hated that she hadn't phoned him back. Hated himself for not calling her yesterday—"On Thursday,"—like he'd said he would.

But he'd bought replacement supplies on Wednesday night, and talked to Jace, and slept late, which for Landon meant six-thirty instead of five-thirty, and then he'd returned to Bear Mountain and the cabin. By the time he'd returned to Gold Valley, evening had fallen and his exhaustion won out over stopping by Megan's.

He changed his mind every time he changed his direction.

Go to town and find her.

Leave her alone. You called.

Maybe just try the church real quick.

You left a message. She'll call when she wakes up.

But it was almost noon, and she hadn't called. Sure,

Megan liked to sleep late, what with her nocturnal studying, but he'd never known her to sleep past mid-day. Of course, he'd only known her for a short time as it was.

From his time at the cabin he knew finding a more permanent place of his own was the right thing for him to do. Was he greedy and ungrateful if he wanted Megan too?

"Ah, but it's not about what *you* want anymore, is it?" Landon shook his head. He wanted to be on the path *God* wanted him on, and he'd told the Lord he'd do whatever he was instructed.

But what if Megan wasn't on the same path he was? What then?

Landon wasn't sure he had enough faith to leave her behind. He'd asked her to call him back, that he had news about Brush Creek in Utah, that he needed to leave town again soon, but he just had to see her before he went.

He wanted to see her in person to invite her to come away with him again. Wanted to hear her laugh. Wanted to smell her essential oils. Wanted to taste the sweetness of her lips.

With his mind made up, he swiped his keys from the front table and headed out the door. *Thirty minutes,* he coached himself. He could wait thirty more minutes to see Megan.

He tried the church first, but she wasn't there. Landon poked his head into the pastor's office. "Hey, have you seen Megan?"

He looked up from his desk, the soft sound of classical music framing him. "She hasn't been in today."

Landon tipped his hat and returned to his truck. Her apartment was only ten minutes from the church. He could wait ten more minutes. He flexed his fingers as he waited at a stoplight, his patience near the snapping point.

He took the stairs to her second-floor apartment two at a time and practically beat down her door.

She didn't answer. He pulled his phone from his back pocket and tried calling her again. Frustration surged with his impatience, making everything inside his body tight, tight, tight.

Defeated, with nowhere else to try, he sat down on the top step in her stairwell to wait for her.

He could wait. "You can," he told himself. He'd already told himself to give her the time she needed to get over her ex-boyfriend. He didn't believe someone could heal after only eight months, but he also realized not every relationship was the same, and that everyone dealt with things in different ways.

She certainly seemed ready to move forward in a new relationship. She'd never said she wasn't. And *she* had kissed *him* that first time.

After what seemed like hours, someone came up the steps. By the delicate clicking sounds, Landon hoped it would be Megan. He stood as she came into view. "There you are."

She stalled, her face placid as she appraised him. After she'd scanned him from boot to head and back again, a smile bloomed on her face. "What are you doing here?"

"I called you this morning. Left you a message. You

never called back." He shrugged, suddenly self-conscious inside his own skin. "I wanted to see you."

She curtsied and he noticed the bag she held. "So now you see me."

"Did you get a new phone?" He nodded to the bag.

She glanced at it and then held it up. "Oh, yeah. Mine shattered this morning. That's why I didn't get your call, or your message, or call you back. I didn't actually know you'd called." She came up the steps toward him, all the way into his arms, pressing closer and closer. "It's so good to see you."

He leaned down to claim her waiting mouth, everything inside him softening with her touch. He kissed her until she pulled back, and that happened too soon for his liking.

"How was the cabin?"

"Great," he said, wrapping his arms around her to keep her close. "You should come next time."

"I'd come if you invited me."

He detected a cool note in her voice. "Sometimes I crave the solitude and tranquility of Bear Mountain."

She rocked in his arms, as if she wanted to be there and nowhere else. "So if I go with you, there won't be that solitude."

"I like being with you," Landon said, speaking the truth. "I like that you give me the time and space to like being with myself."

"I'm not even sure what that means." Megan giggled, the vibration of her voice sending shockwaves through him.

"It means I'm going to Utah tomorrow, and I want you to come with me again."

She stepped out of his arms, her dark eyes searching his face. "Utah? Tomorrow?"

"The owners of Brush Creek want to renegotiate the price. It's mine if I want it. I said I wanted to come see it again."

She moved to her apartment door and unlocked it. "I thought you said it was too far from civilization." Megan didn't wait for him before disappearing into her apartment.

He followed, his heart tapping out a frantic rhythm. "It's a bit far from a major city, yes. But it's gorgeous country, and the ranch itself is in pristine condition."

Megan threw her purse and bag on the couch and faced him. "It sounds like you've made up your mind."

With her arms folded like that and her tone so full of acid, Landon wanted to deny it. He shrugged instead, thinking if he said he had made up his mind to purchase Brush Creek, he'd lose her.

"I don't see the point in paying for an airplane ticket to go see a ranch you already know you're going to buy." She blinked rapidly, a slight wobble in her chin.

"Megan." He strode toward her, desperate to make her understand. He brushed his lips across her forehead and wove his fingers through hers. "Just come with me. See how you feel while you're there."

"I don't—"

"I love you," he blurted. His blood pounded through his veins with the strength of hurricane-force winds. What had he just said? Was it true?

"It's not my ranch," Megan said, completely ignoring his

declaration. "I don't need to know how I'd feel there." She gently released his fingers. "But you have a good trip. Call me when you get back."

She turned her back on him, effectively ending the conversation. Landon stood there for a few moments, trying to understand. He backed up one step, then another. "I'll call you when I get back."

Megan lifted one hand in a good-bye wave, but she didn't turn around. Her shoulders and head bent forward, and Landon ached to comfort her, assure her that he did in fact love her. But she was unreachable, so he turned and left, every step tearing out a little piece of his heart. He left the bits behind, hoping they'd be the breadcrumbs he needed to find his way back to her.

CHAPTER 17

$\mathcal{B}$rush Creek was every bit as amazing as Landon remembered. Too bad he felt like he'd left a vital part of his life in Montana.

"Stay as long as you like." Shelly dropped a key into Landon's hand. "Let me know what you decide." She climbed into her car and left him standing on the horse ranch of his dreams.

He exhaled as he tipped his head back. "Is this where I'm supposed to be?" he asked the sky. "You know the nearest city of any size is an hour away, right? The town of Brush Creek is maybe five thousand people."

He'd taken more time in the town that morning. Yes, there was a grocery store where he could get food and household supplies. They had a section in the back with feed and basic farm equipment, but Landon would definitely need a bigger supply store to outfit a horse ranch—and some horses.

He was planning to start small. Him and maybe one other horseman. A couple of horses. Tom had mentioned a breeder he knew who'd set up her stables in Texas after retiring from the rodeo. He could start with some of her horses, some of his contacts in the rodeo....

A smile crossed his face as he imagined what kind of life he could have here at Brush Creek. He flipped the key around in his hand. He didn't need to go back inside the house to know how he felt about this ranch.

"I want it." His voice echoed in the country stillness surrounding him. He cast his eyes around, wishing Megan were here with him. Because he wanted her too, right here beside him.

He pulled out his phone and called her, unsurprised when she didn't pick up. She'd said to call, but he had—three times now—and she hadn't answered once. He'd left messages the first two times, but this time he just hung up. She had eyes and a brand new phone; she could see that he'd called.

He drove down into town—only about ten minutes—and picked up lunch at the gas station in the form of a hot dog and a soda. He found a bakery and a diner, so he wouldn't starve despite his limited sandwich skills in the kitchen. The city center had a town hall, a large park with tennis and basketball courts, along with the post office and a couple more shops.

After he'd seen all there was to see in Brush Creek, he began the long drive back to the airport. He'd flown out of

Montana on Saturday morning, and he wanted to be back on Sunday night.

He'd call the realtor in the morning and confirm the offer. She could fax papers. As the miles rolled by under his tires, he wondered when he'd move to Utah permanently.

"Maybe you won't," he said to himself. He knew people had summer homes and winter homes and even holiday homes. Heck, at least half of the cabins up the east side of the mountain in Gold Valley sat empty most of the time, only inhabited when their owners came for vacation. Even Sterling Maughan, whose family owned just such a summer vacation home, had bought a house in the valley instead of living up in the cabin community full time.

So Landon could have a summer home in Utah if he wanted to. Lots of rodeo stars did. At the same time, he knew he didn't want to live in Utah part-time. He wanted to call it home, train horses during his work hours, and relax in that hot tub at night, maybe with a dog at his side.

Yes, at Brush Creek, he could get the dog he wanted. But no matter what, a four-legged furry friend was a poor substitute for Megan. Instinctively, he pressed harder on the gas pedal. He needed to see her, talk to her, as soon as possible. They needed to figure things out, because he wasn't quite ready to give up on her yet.

He'd have to wait a little longer. Hours, at least. He had a layover that would delay him, and his flight wasn't landing in Missoula until almost midnight. He'd planned to stay in a hotel until morning and make the nearly-two-hour drive before anyone else woke. Certainly before Megan did.

The urge to call her while he waited for his flight almost consumed him. He stared at his phone, but didn't make the call. Proud of himself for his resilience, he boarded the plane and turned off his phone. By the time he touched down in Montana and checked into his hotel, it was too late to call.

Or was it? Megan stayed up late. Maybe he *could* call, and she wouldn't have any excuse not to answer.

But he was tired, and he didn't want to fathom how he'd feel if she chose not to answer for a fourth time. So he set his phone face-down on the nightstand and hit the hay.

The next morning, he went straight to Megan's apartment once he arrived in Gold Valley. The clock on his stereo system barely read eight o'clock, and nerves paraded through Landon. Should he wait? Call first? Go barreling up there and pound on the door until she dragged herself out of bed?

He waited, his anxiety and frustration building until he wasn't sure he was even thinking rationally. He got out of his truck and took a deep breath of the air he loved so much. He took his time glancing around before heading toward the stairwell.

Another man approached at the same time Landon did, and Landon waved for the dark-haired man to go first. Unshaven, the man had a wild look in his eye though he smiled and said, "Thanks."

Landon followed him, surprise shooting to his brain when the man stepped toward Megan's apartment. "Oh, you're going to 2C also?"

"Yes." The man twisted back toward Landon as he leaned into the doorbell. "My girlfriend lives here."

Landon stumbled backward like he'd been punched. "Your girlfriend?" He glanced over the railing like maybe he'd gotten the wrong building. "Megan Palmer lives here, right?"

"Right."

Pieces clicked around in Landon's brain. This man's girlfriend was…Megan?

This man is Eric.

Landon's fists curled as shock and anger traveled through him in the powerful waves of a tsunami.

"How do you know Megan?" Eric pounded on the door. "Come on, Megs. Wake up!" He turned back to Landon expectantly.

"Oh, I…." Landon waved his hand toward nothing and everything at the same time. "I work with her at the church. Been doing the remodeling."

"Oh, that's nice." Eric faced the door again and lifted his fist, but the door swung inward before he could strike.

"I said not to come until ten," Megan said in a groggy voice. "You're—" She cut into silence when her eyes landed on Landon.

He couldn't wrench his eyes away from her lovely face. Even without makeup, even with her hair spilling wildly over her shoulders, even wearing a tank top and pajama shorts, Landon found her intoxicating and beautiful. So beautiful, his heart hurt.

Was this really happening? She knew Eric was coming?

She'd spoken to him about coming to her apartment at a specific time?

Memories of Lauren's lies, of finding Lauren and Jerry together, of watching Lauren sneak off to meet that other man, flooded Landon's mind. He'd done a great job keeping them boxed up, taped closed, stapled down, never to be opened again. But he couldn't control them now, staring at Megan and seeing the absolute horror on her face.

The absolute horror tinged with guilt.

He'd seen that look before. Hated that look.

He couldn't think. But he still acted by lifting his phone. "I called you several times," he said, his voice almost robotic. "I thought *I* was your boyfriend."

The scraping of Eric's shoes on the ground alerted Landon to his continued presence. His face heated, and he wanted nothing more than to get away from her apartment, get away from *her*.

"I'll see you at the church when you can get there." Landon turned and fled, his feet barely hitting the ground before moving again. He forced himself to walk to his truck, hoping Megan would call for him to come back.

When she didn't, he locked himself in his truck and refused to look up to her balcony. He kept his eyes trained away as he drove out of the parking lot. Then he wouldn't have to torture himself with the knowledge that Eric had entered her apartment. Eric had touched her. Eric was now her boyfriend.

Megan stared after Landon, her muscles frozen and her vocal cords numb. The roar of his truck's engine finally thawed everything. She smacked Eric in the chest. "What are you doing here?" Her voice came out as a growl.

"You told me to bring you your money."

"At ten."

"Well, that guy was here to see you too." He hooked his thumb over his shoulder. "Who's he?"

Megan tossed her curls over her shoulder. "He's who I was telling you about yesterday."

"Oh, *that* boyfriend." Eric rolled his eyes. "Too bad he left so fast."

Megan squinted at him, her ears detecting something in the lower registers of Eric's voice. "What did you say to him?" It certainly wasn't like Landon to run from anything, and flashes of what he'd said about his previous girlfriend stole through Megan's mind.

"I think he probably figured a woman couldn't have two boyfriends." Eric started to swagger toward her living room, but Megan pushed him back.

"You told him you were my boyfriend?"

"I may have used that word." He smirked at her, a familiar gesture Megan used to find sexy. Now she wanted to smack it from his lips.

"I am not your girlfriend, Eric. I don't even want to see you, or talk to you, or anything, ever again. I made that very clear last night." She stretched up on her toes. "Didn't I?"

He lifted his hands as if a cop had just shouted, "Hands

up!" His grin turned sheepish. "You did, yes, Megs. I just… miss you."

Megan laughed, the sound cold and harsh. "Right. You miss me. You miss me picking up dinner and paying for everything. You don't miss *me*." She retreated to her apartment. "Where's my money?"

He pulled an envelope from his back pocket and extended it toward her. She yanked it from his fingers. "And now we're done. You were leaving town right after this, remember?"

"I remember."

"Good." She gripped the door, her teeth aching from how hard she was clenching her jaw. Eric really knew the exact right way to mess up her life. Again. "I never want to see you again." She started to close the door, but paused. "And don't call me Megs." She slammed the door in Eric's face and hurried to lock it.

Once safe, she ran to her bedroom to collect her phone. She'd noticed Landon's calls, two of which had come while she was in meetings with community members. The third had come yesterday about four seconds after Eric had shown up on her doorstep. She'd been so flustered by his reappearance in her life, she hadn't answered. Hadn't called back.

And of course, Landon had shown up on her doorstep the very next morning. The man was as unpredictable as he was steady. *And strong,* her mind added. *And sexy.*

She tapped to get to his name, muttering while the line rang. He didn't pick up. "Landon," she said. "Please answer the phone. I can explain everything if you'll just come back to my apartment. Or I'll meet you somewhere. Wherever you want." She half-exhaled, half-sighed. "I'm going to call you again. Please, please answer."

Megan hung up and looked at her phone. Maybe he was driving. Maybe his phone was off after traveling. Maybe, maybe, maybe.

She hated maybe. She just wanted Landon to come back.

Go get him, she thought, and she flew into action. He'd come for her. She could go to him too—he said he'd be at the church. She could go to the church.

She threw on the first clothes she found and flew down the steps into her car. The ten-minute drive to the church seemed to take hours, and her parking job looked like a ten-year-old had done it. She hurried into the church, realizing his truck wasn't in the parking lot. "Landon!" she called anyway.

No one was there, and that classical music wafting from her father's office only pushed her nerves further into despair.

"Dad." She skidded to a stop in his doorway.

He glanced up. "Sweetie, good morning."

"Hey." Her gaze swung around wildly, searching for something she knew wasn't there.

"Megan, are you okay? You sound—"

Tears leaked out of Megan's eyes. "No, Dad, I'm not okay. I need to go find Landon."

"He was just here at the church."

Hope leapt into her mind, clouding her reasoning for a

few seconds. Finally, she was able to say, "Is he still here somewhere?"

"No, he just came in and looked at the chapel. I asked him if he needed anything, and he shook his head and left." Her father exhaled. "Megan, he seemed fine."

She shook her head. "Did he say where he was going?"

"He didn't say anything."

She turned to leave. "Thanks."

"Megan—"

"Dad, I don't want to talk about it right now."

The wheels on his chair scraped as he slid backward. "Megan, wait."

Her shoulders rose and fell as she inhaled. Her dad joined her in the hall, stepped right in front of her, and lifted her chin so she had to look at him. "Megan, just remember that you've always had great faith. And that means you can take steps into darkness. Steps you don't see."

Megan didn't want one of her father's adages right now, but she nodded anyway. He stepped aside and she hurried back to her car. She wasn't one-hundred percent sure where Landon would go when he was upset, but she was going to start in the one place he loved most: Horseshoe Home Ranch.

CHAPTER 18

"And the only thing I could think to do was come out here." Megan finished her story as Belle leaned forward and set her coffee mug on the table. "I know he's here, Belle. His truck is in front of his cabin." The hope and relief Megan had felt when she'd pulled up and seen the giant, gray truck had been astronomical. Now, though, she simply needed to find him, talk to him, help him understand everything.

"I haven't seen him," Belle said. "But Jace might have." She reached for her phone and thumbed out a message. "We'll see if he responds. If he's out working, he doesn't always take his phone."

Megan's fingers rolled around and around each other. Her stomach swooped from one side of her body to the other, and she felt sure she was about to be sick. Minutes ticked by while Belle tried to distract her with small talk from the town.

It felt like a lifetime had passed, but when Megan checked her phone, only ten minutes had gone by. "Belle, what—?"

"He hasn't answered." She stood, a long sigh hissing from her lips. She placed one hand on her belly and took slow, careful steps. "The cowboys carry radios when they go out. Let's go over to the administration lodge and find him."

"Find Landon," Megan corrected.

"We'll find them both." Belle gave her a warm smile, one that usually calmed Megan. But she didn't think anything or anyone could help her right now—except maybe Landon.

"So you really like my brother, huh?" As they walked down the stairs, Belle bumped into Megan's side, her elbow linking with Megan's, a giggle floating on the air between them.

Megan scanned the area around them, hoping Landon would emerge from the landscape and come straight to her. He didn't. In fact, she didn't see any cowboys right now. Only trees surrounding the homestead. The bright, blue sky. The burning, yellow sun, which seemed much too bright.

"Yeah," she said. "Yeah, I really like your brother." A sob wrenched free from her throat. "I think I may have messed up too badly."

"Because your ex came into town? Nah." Belle's boots kicked up dust as they scuffed their way toward the administration lodge. "Landon will understand. You just need to talk to him."

Megan nodded and fell a step behind Belle as they

entered the lodge. She expected to see the place crammed with men wearing cowboy hats, but the building was practically empty. Only one man sat at a desk near the door.

"Hey, Caleb," Belle said to the blue-eyed cowboy. "Is Jace in his office?"

"No, ma'am. He and some of the boys are out in the hay barn, putting up the fresh load from the north fields."

Belle leaned against his desk. "He take a radio?"

"Always, Miss Belle." He lifted the one on the corner of his desk. "Want me to call him?"

Belle flicked her gaze to Megan, and a skitter ran over her shoulders when Caleb's eyes found hers. "We're actually looking for Landon. Can you call him?"

"I think he went to the hay barn too." Caleb put the radio to his mouth. "Landon, come back. Come back, Landon."

Excruciating seconds passed. The radio didn't so much as crackle. Megan spun away from Caleb's inquisitive gaze, her heart squeezing, squeezing, squeezing.

"Landon here." His voice shot life right into Megan's body and soul. She pressed her eyes closed in a silent prayer before turning to face Caleb.

"Landon, there's someone here to—"

Megan waved her hands to cut him off at the same time Belle said, "Tell him *I* need him. Me, Caleb. *I* need him to come back in."

Caleb's wild eyes flew from Belle to Megan and back. "Uh, Belle needs you for a minute."

"Put 'er on."

"No, uh." Caleb pulled his cowboy hat off to reveal his

sandy brown hair, which he ran his free hand through. "She needs you to come into the admin—"

"My house," Belle hissed.

"Uh—she needs you to come on over to her place for a minute."

Dead air came through the radio. Megan thought sure Caleb would resend his request, but he just stood there, the silent radio in his hand and something akin to panic riding in his eyes.

"Megan Palmer is there, isn't she?" Landon finally asked.

Caleb lifted his eyebrows at the same time Belle's chin dropped to her chest.

"Are you Megan Palmer?" Caleb asked. "The preacher's daughter?"

Megan nodded, that label burying itself under her skin and burning.

Caleb sealed her fate by saying, "Yeah, Megan Palmer's here," into the radio.

"I'm not comin' in," Landon said almost immediately. "I'm working."

"What should—?"

"Tell her whatever you want, Caleb," Landon said. "I'm not comin' in."

Caleb set the radio back in the corner of her desk. "I'm afraid he's pretty much the most stubborn man on the planet."

"Actually, that's Jace." Belle flashed a smile toward Megan, but it withered.

"He won't come in," Caleb said.

"Well, you live with him," Belle said. "What should we do?"

"He won't come in," Caleb said again, his voice thoughtful. "But he wouldn't abandon his work either. He's in the hay barn. It's a free country." Caleb shrugged as he sat back down behind his desk.

Megan glanced at her ballet flats. Definitely not the best footwear for tromping around a ranch. She had no idea what horrors a hay barn held. "Maybe you could just point in the general direction of the hay barn," she said, employing some of that faith her father said she had.

———

Landon pushed his gloves tighter onto his hands and reached for another bale of hay. He warred with himself constantly. Had been since he'd left Megan's place. He'd wanted to turn around and go back. Turn around and go back and fight for her, for them. Turn around and go back and tell her what he'd gone there to tell her.

He hadn't. He'd stopped by the church to see if Carlos had finished the demolition on the balcony. He had. With that done, Landon had maybe two weeks of work left to finish on the church. Maybe two weeks to get everything packed that he needed for Utah. Those same two weeks to get his rodeo contacts on the phone, find some horses to buy, get everything delivered to Brush Creek for both himself and his animals.

He'd then come straight to the ranch, where he found

Jace and reported for work. His best friend had looked at him with questions in his eyes, but Landon had said, "I just want to work, Boss," and Jace had put him to work.

They'd talk later. Jace had a way of getting everything out of Landon, whether he wanted to share or not. But for now, Landon didn't want to talk—which made Megan's sudden appearance at the ranch all the more troublesome.

And Belle…. Landon's frown deepened and his frustration for his meddling sister increased. If it wasn't for Belle, Landon wouldn't be in this mess. He wouldn't have fallen in love with Megan, wouldn't have gotten hurt again.

Bitterness surged, coated his tongue, made breathing difficult. Just like with Lauren. He swallowed, cleared his throat, reached for another bale of hay. Half a dozen men worked on the load, but Landon was alone at the bottom of this side of the hay barn, the only one pulling bales from this stack to send up to the loft.

He bent, grabbed, lifted, tossed the bales onto the conveyor belt to be delivered to the top, where another man would pull them off and pass them along for stacking. The work made his muscles scream, but at least he didn't have to think too hard about it.

That was one thing he loved about ranching. It was good, honest work. It was dirty, and difficult, and downright exhausting. But Landon loved it.

"There you are." Megan's voice cut into his labor, first kicking his heart into another gear, then making his muscles sag in defeat, and then producing a sneer of anger on his face.

"I don't want to talk to you," he said.

"Fine." Megan sat on a hay bale several paces away. She wore a flowery top that had no business being seen on a working ranch, a pair of denim shorts, and the flimsiest shoes Landon had ever seen. The fact that she hadn't tripped over twine or punctured her foot on a nail was just plain miraculous. "I'll talk," she said.

"Whatever you want," he said. "But my mind's made up."

"It is?"

"Yeah." He faced her, his heart and body and soul all firing on different cylinders. None of them lined up, and it left him feeling dizzy and drunk. "I bought Brush Creek. I'm moving to Utah in four weeks." He stared at her as she winced, as pain came into her eyes, as she straightened her shoulders and composed herself.

He wasn't sure what to make of her reaction. The pain... did she care about him?

"Four weeks," she said. "Wow."

"Two to finish the church. Two to tie things up here. Four weeks." He reached for another hay bale.

"You're still going to finish the church?"

"I don't leave a job undone." He cast her a glare. "What are you doin' here?"

"I called, but you didn't answer."

"Well, then, we're even." Landon wished his words weren't quite so poisonous.

"Eric tracked me down to pay back some money he'd stolen." A mirthless laugh escaped her mouth. "Money I hadn't even known he'd taken."

Landon glanced up and found her studying her hands, her countenance completely broken. Oh, how he wanted to bridge this distance between them, cross to her and comfort her. He bit back the desire.

"Apparently it's part of his parole."

"So he's not in jail?"

"Got out by testifying against a bigger fish," Megan said. "And promising to right his wrongs, which is why he showed up in Gold Valley yesterday afternoon."

"And you all just picked up right where you left off." Landon wasn't asking. He'd seen the look on Eric's face that morning. He was still interested in Megan.

"Of course not," Megan said. "Do you really give me no credit?"

Landon threw the bale on the belt. "No, Megan. This isn't about you at all. It's about me, all right?" His chest heaved and he wasn't quite sure what he wanted to say. "I'm —I thought I was ready to move on, but maybe I'm not. I don't think you're anywhere ready to move on, despite what you say and how you act." He took a deep breath. "But I know one thing: I don't want to be the other man. I don't want to get hurt again. I don't. I can't. So it's best if I just don't date right now."

Her chin trembled. "Landon—"

"I'm sorry." He turned away, unsure of how *he'd* ended up apologizing to *her*. "I shouldn't have started anything with you in the first place. I thought I was ready to fall in love again. I was wrong."

"No, you weren't." Her footsteps came closer and her

arms snaked around his midsection. The distinct scent of lemons came with her, something new to add to his misery every time he smelled it. "You were ready to fall in love again. You told me you loved me. Was that a lie?" Her heated breath seeped through the cloth of his shirt.

He shook his head. "No." He twisted in her arms. "But I'm not like you, Megan. I just barely came back to church a couple of years ago. I don't have the faith you do. I don't even know *how* to have it. I know horses, and I know ranching, and I know God wants me in Utah." He brushed a curl from her face, almost unable to look into the depths of her dark eyes and see so much pain.

"I don't know what happened with Eric—"

"Absolutely nothing happened with Eric." At the sincerity and force of her words, a song floated through Landon's soul.

"I believe you," he whispered. "But I still don't think we're…." He stepped away from her touch and looked up to the loft, where Ty stood watching and listening to everything.

"You're not ready," Landon concluded, reaching for another hay bale. "And I have to get back to work."

Megan stepped back as he lifted the bale and set it on the conveyor. "And that's it. You won't give me any more time to get ready? We've only had a couple of months."

"I'm leaving in four weeks," he said.

"But once, you said you didn't have to go right away. That you could wait a year, or however long you wanted."

"I want to wait four weeks."

"Well, Landon." Megan's voice broke on his name, and the shards of sound sliced right through his heart. "I don't think I'll be ready in four weeks." Her pinched, high voice made him wince.

He couldn't look at her when he said, "I know, sweetheart. That's why I said I shouldn't have started anything with you. I've always known I wouldn't be staying in Montana for much longer."

He bent, grabbed, lifted, tossed another bale. And another. And another.

"What if I said I loved you too? Would you take me to Utah with you?"

Another bale landed on the belt. "We both know you're not a liar, Megan." She didn't love him, and he wouldn't take her to Utah just because she said she did. He wanted her there. Wanted it more than anything. But not under false pretenses.

"I didn't answer when you called because I was in meetings, and then Eric had just shown up on my doorstep," Megan said. "I'm not mad about you buying Brush Creek."

"That's nice to know." Landon tried to make his voice as gentle as possible.

"I've never once thought of you as anything less than me because you only came back to church two years ago. In fact." Megan got between him and the conveyor belt, pausing him in his work. "I think you have more faith than you know." Her dark eyes glinted like black diamonds, and Landon almost lost the inner battle he was waging.

"I'll see you at the church tomorrow," he forced through

his dry throat. "I aim to have that balcony done in less than two weeks."

"I'll be there," Megan said before turning and marching out of the hay barn. Landon wasn't sure if she meant her words as a promise or a threat. He dropped the hay bale and collapsed onto it.

"What am I doing?" he moaned. Her explanations made sense. He believed her when she said nothing had happened with Eric. Why hadn't he swept her into his arms and kissed her in that moment?

"What *should* I be doing?" he asked, hoping his whispered question would fall into God's ears, and that Landon would get a definitive answer in the next instant.

Okay, the next…or the next.

But he didn't.

"You don't need another answer," Landon chastised himself. "You've asked this question, and it's been answered." He was meant to be at Brush Creek. He knew it. "But what about Megan? Where should she be?"

But the Lord didn't give Landon that answer, and Landon had a distinct feeling it was because it wasn't his answer to get. Megan would have to work that one out on her own.

CHAPTER 19

*L*andon's heart pumped like it might explode out of his chest, and he hadn't even gotten out of his truck yet. The beautiful carved doors of the church seemed to mock him. He refused to search the parking lot for her car, prolonging the moment of disappointment or euphoria.

Landon sighed, slid out of the truck, and shoved his phone in his pocket. He settled his cowboy hat lower on his head and kept his eyes on the ground as he strode toward the doors. Once inside, he knew Megan wasn't there. The very air would be perfumed with jasmine and lemons, and it simply smelled normal.

His muscles released and he dropped his tools to the floor. Carlos and his crew came through the doors, the ends of their laughter coming with them. Landon wished he had a reason to so much as smile these days.

"I'll need some help unloading the lumber," he said, stuffing his personal troubles to the bottoms of his boots.

The rest of the week followed the same pattern. He showed up at the church, nervous as a cat on hot bricks until he discovered Megan wasn't there. He worked the day away, trying to get the project completed quickly. He spoke with Tom in the evenings, got the number for the horse breeder in Texas, started making business plans and lists of what he'd need to start training horses into rodeo champions.

He skipped church on Sunday, unable to bring himself to go, even when Belle told him he was being a big baby about the whole "Megan thing."

Landon had ignored her texts after that, ignored Jace's pounding on his cabin door, ignored Caleb when he asked, "This about Megan Palmer?"

Of course it was about Megan Palmer. The woman had dominated his thoughts since that moment in Jace's cabin when she'd kissed his cheek. Once Caleb left for church, Landon hung his head and wondered how on earth he could possibly survive without Megan in his life. He lifted his eyes and ran his fingers through his hair. He could do it—he'd done it after Lauren left. Somehow picked the pieces of himself up and moved on.

Going to church had helped so much, and Landon desperately wanted that comfort and peace in his life. He'd lost Megan; he wouldn't lose his faith too.

Determined, he grabbed his hat and marched out to his truck. The same anxiety from the past week assaulted him, but he soldiered on. He had to park in the outer lot and walk and when he finally entered the chapel he realized the need for a functioning balcony. The hymn was still being sung, and no one seemed to notice him standing on the fringes.

He swallowed, the urge to turn and leave burning through him with the power of bright red coals. He couldn't help scanning the backs of people's heads, looking for that dark, curly hair. He didn't find it before Caleb hissed at him and scooted over on the bench to make room.

Landon took the seat with a muttered, "Thanks," and slumped against the bench. When Pastor Palmer got up to speak, Landon pretended not to notice. It had taken him months to develop the diligence to listen to an entire sermon. How to clear his mind of his own pain and troubles for long enough to allow something better inside.

Today, Pastor Palmer started his sermon with the words Landon needed to hear most: "My friends, the Lord loves you."

Everything inside Landon released, sighed, relaxed, softened. Maybe Megan had been right. Maybe he had more faith than he realized.

———

If there was anything more excruciating than watching Landon come and go from church without being able to speak with him, snuggle into his side, Megan didn't ever want to experience it.

Megan had been reliving the things Landon had said—and the things he hadn't. He hadn't invited her to come to Brush Creek with him. She hadn't anticipated the hurt that would cause. She smiled and shook hands with the patrons, half of her mind lingering with Landon.

"How are you?" Belle drew her into a hug, and Megan melted into her friend's embrace.

"Good enough."

"Landon wouldn't come."

"He was here." Megan drew back and peered into Belle's confused face. "He sat in the back with Caleb."

She looked at Jace, who shrugged one shoulder. Belle gave her a small smile, linked her arm through Jace's, and left.

"Dad, I have to go." She flashed a smile at an elderly woman as she passed and then dashed down the steps after Belle and Jace.

"Hey, can I catch a ride out to the ranch?"

Belle and Jace paused to exchange a glance.

"He'll probably be angry," Megan said, remembering the dark look in his emerald eyes when she'd shown up in the hay barn. "But if I only have three weeks left with him, I don't want to waste them."

Belle squealed, and Megan couldn't read Jace's expression. But he allowed her to get in the truck and pepper his wife with questions about Landon for the next thirty minutes.

Once on the ranch, though, all of Megan's confidence evaporated. She wasn't entirely sure what to say to Landon that wouldn't drive him further away. And she couldn't lie and say she loved him. She felt certain she *could* love him, could live a very happy life with him, if she only had more time.

And she wasn't sure three weeks was enough, even if she spent every waking moment with Landon. She simply needed more time to figure out her own life, make sure her father had everything in hand to retire, discover who she was without Eric.

"Good luck," Belle called over her shoulder as she and Jace went up the steps to their front porch. Jace opened the door and waited for Belle to enter first, a look of complete adoration on his face. Megan watched as he put his hand on the small of her back, as his lips curved upward ever so slightly, as he breathed in the scent of her as she passed him.

Megan wanted that love. She faced Landon's cabin, with his imposing gray truck out front. She wanted that chance at love with Landon. Feeling strong and determined, she strode toward his cabin. He came out the front door before she'd gained the first step, and she came to a halt.

"Megan." He exhaled and gazed into the distance beyond his front porch. "What are you doin' here?"

"When are you going to stop asking me that?"

He leaned against the pillar at the top of the steps. "You don't make any sense. So I guess I'll keep asking until I can figure you out."

She smiled and tucked her hands into her skirt pockets. "Good luck with that. I can't even figure myself out." She took a deep breath and released it. "Which is why I'm here, I guess." She started up the steps slowly, giving Landon plenty of time to back away if he wanted to.

He maintained his position, his hat obscuring his face as he lowered his chin to maintain eye contact with her.

She slid her hands around his waist, every cell in her body sighing with relief at the allowed contact. "I don't want to spend the next three weeks avoiding you. I did it for a few days, and I was miserable."

His arms came around her, accepting her as she was, and gratitude filled her. "I've been doing a lot of soul-searching, and thinking, and praying the past week or so. I don't have everything figured out. Heck, there's a ton I don't know how to fix about myself. But I'm trying, and I realized this week that I don't want to do it alone."

The brim of his cowboy hat bumped her shoulder as he lowered his mouth to her jaw. "I'm still moving in three weeks."

"Utah's not that far," she whispered, her skin itching to be touched by him, kissed by him. "And we both have phones and computers."

"Long distance?"

"For a few months. Until my dad is retired and settled. Until…." But she couldn't finish the sentence. She didn't want to admit out loud that she didn't love him, and she wasn't quite sure how she could fall in love with him when he was so far away.

"I don't know, Megan."

"How happy have you been this week?" she asked.

"I'm miserable." He chuckled, the sad sound vibrating

through his chest and into hers. "But I know what God wants me to do, and I know I'll be happy if I do that."

"And you can't wait?"

"Maybe long distance would work." He released her and stepped back, stuffing his hands in his pockets and shuffling his feet along the wood of the porch.

"I don't understand why you can't wait just a few months to move," she said, her frustration frothing and boiling over. "Before, you said you wanted to see if there could be something between us. You said you didn't have to move right away."

"Megan—"

"Don't," she said. "Don't be all sad and make your voice sound like that." She shook her head.

"Sound like what?"

"Like you really want to do what I'm suggesting. You don't. If you did, you'd wait." She turned and stomped down the steps. "I don't know why I came out here. You said your mind was made up." She stopped at the bottom of the steps and peered up at him. "I guess I just can't know if what you say is true or not." She spun and marched away. Where she was going, she didn't know. She didn't have a car. In her head, she'd imagined them making up, and she'd spend the afternoon in his arms, and he'd drive her home near midnight.

"Hey," he called after her, his boots making a ruckus on the steps as he flew after her. "That's not fair."

"Not fair?" She turned back to him, feeling dangerous and wild. "What's not fair is claiming you love me in one breath and insisting you're going to move in three weeks in the next. *That's* not fair." Tears threatened to tumble from her eyes, but she blinked them back. She did not want to cry in front of Landon. Not right now.

His eyes blazed and he threw his hands in the air. "I don't know what to do!"

"That makes two of us."

"What do you want from me, Megan?"

"Time," she practically yelled. She inhaled slowly. "Landon, I want more time with you." The fight left her body as quickly as it had come. Her chin wobbled. A tear fell. "Please don't move in three weeks."

CHAPTER 20

Megan couldn't believe she was standing on the ranch, begging Landon Edmunds not to leave. She'd had a crush on the man for as long as she could remember. She'd promised herself she'd never beg to be with him.

And he still hadn't said anything. His jaw worked against itself and his fingers kept curling into a fist and then releasing. They seemed locked in a battle of silence. Megan knew she didn't want to be the first to speak. She didn't trust herself not to say something that would push him further from her.

Her stomach growled, and the horizon blurred. "I need to go," she said.

"I'll drive you back," he said.

She shook her head, her mouth pressed into a thin line. "Landon, I don't want you to be nice to me. It…." She sucked in a shuddering breath. "It actually hurts more than you just cutting me loose."

He took a step toward her. "Do you want me to cut you loose?"

"You know what I want. I just told you." She fell back a step, then another, in the direction of Belle's cabin. "Maybe you should figure out what *you* want, Landon." She turned, making her steps sure and strong—and commanding herself to not look back at him—until she made it all the way to Belle's front door.

Even then, she kept her attention forward. Jace opened the door and stepped back. "Megan." He looked over her shoulder, and Megan didn't know what he found. She hadn't heard Landon move, but the man had many and varied talents.

"I was hoping I could join you for lunch," Megan said, lifting her chin a fraction of an inch.

Belle's fingers wrapped around the door and pulled it further open. "Megan. Of course you can join us for lunch."

Megan gave her a grateful smile, stepped past an unyielding Jace, only daring to glance back the way she'd come once she was safely in the house.

She didn't see Landon.

———

Landon rode Crossfire hard, getting as far from the ranch epicenter, from Jace's questioning glare, from Megan, as possible. He wasn't sure why he'd thought Megan would let him simply walk out of her life.

She'd always pushed him. Always questioned him. Made him admit things he usually didn't. Sure, she'd stayed away from the church for four days while he worked. But he should've known she wouldn't just let him walk out of her life.

Part of him absolutely adored that about her. Felt special that she'd come and fought for him, for them. That she'd kissed him first. That she seemed to know so clearly what she wanted, just not how to get it.

With a start, he pulled up the horse. Both of their sides heaved, and Landon's hip ached from the hard ride. She knew what she wanted. She just wasn't sure how to get it.

She wanted more time with him.

She wanted *him*.

And what did he want? When she'd asked him, he thought he'd be able to answer easily. But watching her walk away had muted his thoughts. Without her, he was miserable. He'd spoken true on that. But without her, he also thought more clearly.

Crossfire snuffled and tossed his head. Landon moved him into a walk, letting the horse go where he wanted to.

Clop, clop, clop.

He wanted Megan.

Clop, clop, clop.

He wanted Utah.

Clop, clop, clop.

How could he have both?

Wait.

He could wait. He'd done it before. Loads of times.

But he was tired of waiting. He was thirty years old, ready to start his own life, his own ranch, get going on his own path.

"So will six more months really set you back that much?"

He knew it wouldn't. He turned the horse around and set him into a canter. He needed to get back before Megan left the ranch. Just to make sure she would still be there when he got back, he pulled out his phone and texted his sister.

Don't take Megan back to Gold Valley. I want to drive her into town.

It took a few minutes, but when her reply came back, it made Landon's heart stop trying to outpace the horse. *We just sat down to lunch. You should come on in when you get back. Pork ribs...your favorite!*

His mouth watered just thinking about the food—and the woman he'd be able to share it with.

By the time he got Crossfire taken care of, and his hands washed, Landon thought sure lunch had ended. He went to Jace's anyway, satisfied that his truck still sat out front. He knocked at the same time he opened the door, just as he had when Jace had summoned him to the cabin to meet Megan.

"Hey," he said, stepping inside and shutting the scorching heat out. He found the three of them still seated at the dining room table. "Oh, good, I didn't miss lunch. I'm starving." He could at least pretend like the awkwardness between him and Megan didn't exist. But, by the way everyone already at the table exchanged glances, Landon couldn't truly ignore it.

"Okay," he said, pulling out a chair and tucking himself under the table. "So I acted like an idiot. Can we just eat and not talk about it?"

"We've already been eatin'," Belle said. "*Someone* ran off on their horse."

"*Someone* needed a few minutes to think." Landon picked up the spoon for the mashed potatoes and dolloped a healthy serving onto his plate.

"*Someone's* been gone for more than a few minutes."

"Crossfire likes to run." Landon shot his sister a glare that said, *Stop it, Belle.*

She stopped. Landon's eyes flitted to Megan, staying long enough to assess whether she'd been crying or not. Didn't look like it.

"Church looked good today," Jace commented, and both Megan and Landon swung their attention to him. He glanced between them, his eyes ping-ponging back and forth several times. "I mean, uh." He cleared his throat. "Belle just got a new account at the community college. Tell 'em about it, honey."

Once Belle started talking—especially about design—she could carry the conversation by herself. Thankfully.

Landon knew the meal would eventually end. He'd have to face Megan again. They'd have to talk through everything, make decisions. He wished his weren't so colored by his feelings—especially when she didn't quite reciprocate those feelings. He coached himself to *wait. Hold your horses, and just wait.*

The idiom had never hit so close to home before. He literally had to hold his horses if he wanted to hold onto the woman he loved.

He sighed like he was dining alone, and every eye traveled to him. "What?" he asked.

"You just made a noise like you have the worst life on the planet," Belle said.

"I'm just breathin'."

"Let the man breathe," Jace said when Belle opened her mouth to retort. Landon wished Megan would say something. He caught her eye, but she remained quiet. Apparently, she knew how to wait for important things too.

———

Megan finally excused herself after chocolate cake and two cups of coffee. She had more patience than him, and when she stood and said she should be getting home, he almost knocked the table over in his haste to leap up. "I'll drive you," he said after the silverware had stopped clattering against the plates.

"That would be great." She gave him an easy smile. The conversation had turned to lighter topics once the dessert came out, something Landon had been grateful for.

He hurried to the front door and opened it for Megan, taking a deep drag of her floral scent as she passed. "I've noticed you've added lemon to your perfume," he said as he closed the door behind him.

She turned at the top of the stairs. "I love the citrus oils. They're energetic. They revive me when I don't feel well."

"You haven't been feeling well?" He approached her, almost desperate to say the right things, in the right order.

"Duh." She leaned into him. "Remember how I said I'd been avoiding you? I didn't like it."

He tucked his hand in hers and went with her down the steps. "I'm sorry about…me."

"You don't need to be sorry." She waited until he'd helped her up into his truck. "Did you figure out what you wanted?" She smoothed her skirt so it lay properly over her knees.

Landon tore his gaze from her now-covered skin. "Sort of. I'll explain on the drive into town." He joined her in the cab and started up the truck. "I want Utah," he said as he backed out and straightened onto the gravel road that led to the highway. "But I want you, too."

She scooted over on the bench seat until her leg pressed against his. She laid her cheek against his bicep. "So do I get more than three more weeks with you?"

"Yes." His voice came out rough, like old rust on a dead tractor. "Yes," he said again, stronger. "I was right when I said I didn't have to move to Utah right away." He turned onto the paved highway. "Just gonna have to exercise some of that faith you seem to think I have."

She laughed and snuggled closer. "Good, because I have a lot of meetings at the church this week."

Landon fought against the question he wanted to ask. But if he was going to see if this could go somewhere, he should be able to ask her anything. "Megan, why are you trying so hard to set up all the community groups?"

"I like doing it."

"Why?"

She squirmed next to him. "I like creating…."

He gave her a few moments to finish her thought, but she remained silent.

"You like creating…?"

"Are you always this pushy?"

He chuckled. "I learned from the best, because no. Not usually."

"Remember how I don't talk about things I don't want to?"

"I do remember that." He shifted in his seat. "I think you should get over that."

"Okay." She took a deep breath. "I like creating a sense of community. A place for people to belong." She put an inch between them. "I like taking care of other people."

Landon nodded, wishing he could pull her back into place next to him. "So follow-up question…Are you taking care of yourself?"

Her silence said it all. He dropped one hand from the steering wheel and put it on her knee. "I think you should do that."

"What if I don't know how?"

"Like I don't know how to use my faith? We'll figure it out, I think."

"But we get more than three weeks to figure it out." She curled both of her hands around his.

"Right," he confirmed again. "We get more than three weeks to figure it out."

CHAPTER 21

*L*andon finished the church by the end of the next week, every day punctuated with being able to see Megan, smell her essential oils, speak with her, and kiss her in the privacy of the new balcony.

"Landon," she whispered on Friday afternoon after his crew had left.

"Hmm?" He traced his lips along her collarbone, his pulse galloping like a herd of wild horses. How he'd thought he could go to Utah without her was a mystery to him. He pressed his lips to the hollow of her neck, then the spot just below her ear. She usually arched into him and slid her fingers through his hair when he did that.

His cowboy hat had been knocked off long ago, and her nails along his scalp sent shivers down his back. He claimed her mouth, deepening the kiss until he thought sure she'd push him away.

He crossed the line where she usually did, and still she

kissed him back. Encouraged by her reaction, he tightened his hold on her waist and slid his hands up her back.

She put a breath of space between them, because that was all he'd give her. "Landon."

He enjoyed the breathless quality of his name in her voice. Wanted to hear her say it like that all the time, every time he kissed her good-morning and each time he kissed her good-night.

"You have somethin' to say, sweetheart?" He lighted kisses on her forehead, her cheekbones, her lips. Seconds passed before she resisted him again.

"Your phone keeps ringing."

"So?" He dipped his head to kiss her again.

"It might be important." She kept her eyes closed as he kissed each of her eyelids. "It's been going off for a long time."

"Don't care." He tried to kiss her again.

She giggled and pressed herself into a hug. "Will you just check it and then take me to dinner?" Her breath ticked his earlobe, and he'd do anything she asked if she'd whisper it like that.

He stepped back and pulled his phone from his front pocket. He'd missed eight calls and had just as many texts. All from the same person: Shelly.

His stomach dropped through the floor and landed near the entrance of the church, a full story below. "It's Shelly." He glanced up at Megan, his voice sounding haunted as it echoed around them. "The realtor for Brush Creek."

He moved further from Megan as he tapped to dial Shelly. When she answered, he said, "What's goin' on?"

"Did you read any of my texts or listen to my messages?"

Landon ran his hand up the back of his head. "No, I just saw that you'd called." He glanced at Megan. "I was busy, and—I just called right back."

"The house at Brush Creek has flooded. I think it probably happened yesterday, from what I can tell. It was just dumb luck that I came up at all. I wanted to leave you a housewarming present—non-perishable, of course—and I noticed a distinct chlorine smell."

Landon's heart had left his body, but somehow it was pulsing in his temples. "Well, I—"

"I called a restoration company, but they need a credit card for a deposit."

"Of course, of course." Landon headed for the stairs. "Let me get to my truck. My wallet's there."

"Landon, I know you said you weren't going to move here for a couple more weeks, but I think you should come now. The restoration guys will need you to confirm what you want done."

Landon's boots smacked against the polished wood of the stairs, and he jogged to his truck, his mind spinning. He managed to give Shelly his credit card information, get the phone number of the restoration company she'd hired, and say good-bye before he leaned against his truck, all thoughts of dinner with Megan and then more kissing completely gone.

"Megan," he moaned, and he rushed back to the church,

where she waited in the doorway. It framed her perfectly, and his heart ached. "My house at Brush Creek flooded." He gestured over his shoulder like the house was just right there and she could see all the water damage. "I don't know how bad it is. The real estate agent just happened to be there, but she thinks it happened yesterday. I—"

Megan put her finger on his lips, silencing him. "Landon." She smiled at him lazily, like they'd taken an evening hike and she wanted him to kiss her before they left the waterfall, the way they'd done last night after work. "Go. Call me when you get there."

"The chapel's done," he said weakly. "Come with me."

She shook her head, her smile turning down in the corners. "I can't come."

"Why not?" He swept into her personal space, his mind operating on very little at the moment. Instinct. Desire. Emotion, not rationality.

"I have my community groups to oversee and my Sunday School class to teach."

Landon recognized a flimsy excuse when he heard one, and with so much teeming in his mind, he let it go. "Okay, well, dinner, then?"

She grinned and it seemed pretty genuine. "Go book your flight and pack your bags. Again, call me when you get there." She stretched up and pressed her lips to his. He hung onto her hungrily, hoping to infuse his desire for her to come with him to Utah into his touch.

"I'll call you," he promised.

Megan watched Landon hurry to his truck, get in, and drive off. She had the distinct feeling it would be the last time she'd see him in Gold Valley.

"Ridiculous," she scoffed as she turned back to the church so she could get her purse, go get her dinner for one. She stopped by her father's place, unwilling to grab something and go home alone.

"Dad," she called as she entered her childhood home. Strong memories stared at her from the walls. Her and her younger sister wearing Mickey and Minnie Mouse ears. The only family vacation to Disneyland they'd ever taken.

Her high school graduation, with Carrie's right beside it. Family pictures over the years she never wanted Landon to see. Her life had changed when cosmetic companies started making anti-frizz products.

"Megan." Her father appeared at the mouth of the hallway.

"Want to go to dinner?"

He tried to see around her. "Where's Landon?"

"His house in Utah flooded. He's in emergency mode." She did a little curtsy. "Just me tonight." Her voice almost cracked on the last word, so she pasted on a smile. "Where do you want to go?"

Her father smiled. "It's Friday night."

"Ah, so the all-you-can-eat buffet."

"It's seafood night."

Megan tipped her head back and laughed. "Seafood night. I've never been tempted less."

"You can still get your rabbit food." Her father grabbed his wallet and gestured toward his garage. "I'll drive."

"That would be great," Megan said.

He ushered her into the garage and locked the door behind her. Once they'd settled into the car and he was backing out of his driveway, he asked, "How are things with Landon?"

"Dad, I don't want to play Twenty Questions tonight."

"Okay, okay. I just know you didn't come into the church at all last week. Canceled all your meetings."

"We worked things out." She watched the houses go by, wondering if she should just tell her father about Eric. Come clean and tell him everything.

He doesn't need to know, she told herself. She'd only brought Eric home a handful of times, and claiming they broke up without further explanation had been hard enough.

"I'm glad to see you with him," her dad said. "He's a good man."

"He is," Megan agreed.

"How are you feeling about things with him?"

"Dad."

He took both hands off the wheel in a sign of acquiescence. "Sorry. I just want you to be happy."

"I'm working on it."

He glanced at her, concern etched in the lines around his eyes. "You're not happy?"

"You asked me to come back to Gold Valley for two years before I did."

A frown settled between his eyes. "But you seem so happy here."

"I've been throwing myself into the community groups. That brings me happiness."

"You fixed up the church. It's beautiful."

She sighed and leaned back in her seat. "Yes, it is." She patted his hand and gave him a smile. "That makes me happy."

"But you're not inherently happy here." He wasn't asking, and she shouldn't claim that she was. She was trying to stuff her life with purpose, living each day with faith that one day she'd be able to achieve that inherent happiness.

The truth was, she still needed to figure out how to get over her own humiliation. Get over her fear that she couldn't choose the right man. Get over her whole self, basically.

"I'm working on it," she said again, wondering what about Landon made her distrust herself to make an intelligent decision regarding him. She certainly liked how she felt when she was with him. She absolutely liked kissing him. She definitely wanted to tell him everything about herself.

He'd never given her a reason to feel anything but safe with him. Anything but loved. Why then, did she feel like she needed to slow things down between them? Really take her time to learn who she was before she figured out who she was *with him.*

She got herself a big salad at the buffet, with a side of macaroni and cheese. Her dad eyed her dietary choices and grinned. "You've always loved that mac and cheese."

She took a delicious bite. "I totally have." Megan smiled when she realized there were some parts of herself Eric hadn't touched. She'd been doing great before he showed up two weeks ago. Seeing him had brought back everything she'd been trying to forget.

Forget, not get over.

Forget, not move past.

Forget, not forgive.

Sitting there with her father, with Landon preparing for yet another trip to Utah, Megan realized she need to forgive Eric before she would be ready to move forward with Landon.

CHAPTER 22

*L*andon called the next morning, right after Megan had stepped out of the shower. "It's after ten," he said by way of hello. "I didn't wake you, did I?"

"No." She collapsed onto her bed at the sound of his voice. "Where are you?"

"Just landed in Salt Lake City."

"I did like that city."

He sighed. "There's something magical about the mountains here."

"I've always loved the mountains. It's one of the reasons I lived in Jackson Hole. The Tetons were only minutes away, constantly looming over you."

"Brush Creek isn't quite like that," he said. "Though it is in the mountains."

"Tell me about it."

He talked, and for a man who usually finished a story after three sentences, he spoke for several long minutes.

"You nervous?" she asked him.

"Yeah," he admitted. "Water damage isn't cheap to repair, and I just got the place. I don't even live in it yet."

She wondered how much of his savings he'd spent on the ranch, and how much was left. He'd never seemed worried about money before. "I believe it will work out," she said. "Listen, I hate to cut this call short, but the gardening club is expecting me today."

He burst into laughter. "So you're ditching me to go hang out with a bunch of geriatrics who are worried about their rose bushes?"

"Your dad is the chairperson of the group."

"I know that. That's how I know they're talking about the diseases their bushes are susceptible to at this time of year."

Megan sniffed. "Yes, well, the leaves on our rose bushes along the back of the church have this powdery stuff on them."

"Right. Powdery mildew."

Exasperation shot through her. "How do you know that?"

"My dad is a *horticulturalist,*" he said. "And he never stops talking about it. I've known about powdery mildew and Dutch elm disease since I was born."

"He is the perfect candidate for our garden club, then."

Landon laughed again. "I think you made the right call there, for sure."

"Well, I really do have to get dressed and get to the meeting."

"You're not dressed?" The interest in his voice couldn't be mistaken for something else.

Megan grinned. "You caught me just as I got out of the shower." She gripped her towel tighter with her free hand, like he might burst through the door.

"Hmm."

A flush rose through her neck, though he was miles and miles away. "Call me once you know the extent of the damage." She hung up, got dressed, and walked to the church, her thoughts always circulating around Landon.

Is this what it feels like to be in love? she wondered as she approached his father and the other members of the garden club. They'd clustered around the rose bushes she'd mentioned, and she finally forced Landon from her mind as she joined the ring peering at the white dust on the bush's leaves.

———

Landon kept the music loud in the rental car. He didn't want his mind to have the ability to wander, to speculate, to obsess over what he might find at Brush Creek. The car seemed like a box, much too small for his tall frame. Or maybe it just couldn't contain his anxiety.

He drove slowly through town, not only to obey the speed limit, but to see what a Saturday afternoon in Brush Creek might look like. People walked down the street pushing strollers and walking dogs. The park's picnic tables were full of families eating. The grocery store parking lot held dozens of cars, as did the diner and the barber shop. Landon noticed more streets branching east and west than he'd noticed before, and he liked the small-town atmosphere of Brush Creek.

He turned at the north end of town and headed up to the horse ranch. He found Shelly's red convertible there, along with a van that read RIVERSIDE RESTORATION on the side and had multiple hoses spilling out the back.

After parking next to Shelly, he took a few seconds to whisper a prayer. "Please, if it be Thy will, let this be a quick and fairly inexpensive restoration." He opened his eyes and got out of the car, his boots crunching over the gravel until it met sidewalk and grass.

He almost paused at the front door and knocked, then he remembered that he owned this place. Still, he wasn't sure if he could just start traipsing around the place, so he retraced his steps to the garage, where all the hoses led.

"Hello?" he called into the three-car garage.

Shelly poked her head out of the entrance that led into the mudroom. "Landon, you made it."

"I sure did." He met her in the middle of the garage. "You wanna show me around?"

Her face didn't change. No smile. No sympathy. She gave a quick jerk of her head toward the backyard. "Let's start with the swimming pool."

"Starting" with the scene of the crime—the swimming pool—had seemed like a good idea. But all it did was alert Landon to the fact that he didn't know the first thing about maintaining a swimming pool. Or a hot tub.

The lawn he could handle. The exterior of the house, everything inside. He reminded himself that it was just a swimming pool, and surely there'd be instructions somewhere online to help him keep it algae-free.

Oh, and fix the pump that had broken underground, causing the leak into the house.

"So the flooring will need to be redone," Shelly said as she stepped into the open dining room from the back patio. The sound of several industrial fans made the house feel like an airplane hangar.

"The restoration company very nearly has everything dried out." She scuffed her toe along the warped wood. "But this was hardwood, and well, wood and water don't mix that well."

Landon swept his eyes along the bottom of the cabinets —it was obvious how high the water had reached. About three inches up was all, but it was enough to leave stains.

"They'll dry out the walls, do the mildew treatments, replace the baseboards, and restore the cabinets." The more Shelly spoke, the more money Landon bled. He nodded, and kept nodding, until she finally fell silent.

"Carpet?" he asked.

She inhaled and took him into the living room. "The carpet probably saved the rest of the house, because it absorbed the water. It was wet all through here and all the way down the hall."

"So a new floor in the whole house."

"Not upstairs," she said. "And the master down here was completely spared. So you have somewhere to sleep that isn't filled with fans and chemicals. I brought you an air mattress."

Landon managed a smile before he stepped down the hall and into his master suite. Without any furniture, it just seemed like a great big empty room.

At least it wasn't wet.

———

He put off calling Megan for as long as he dared. Sure, he knew she'd still be awake, but he was functioning on his last pod of energy, and if he didn't call her now, he wouldn't until morning. And she wouldn't like that.

But she wouldn't like what he needed to tell her either.

He dialed anyway. Either she was meant to be his, or she wasn't. They'd worked through some hard things the past couple of weeks. He had faith they could get through this too.

"Hey," she said, sounding chipper and more awake than he'd felt all day.

"Hey." He wiped his hand down his face. "It's not good news, sweetheart."

"Oh, no." She moaned. "How bad?"

"Swimming pool malfunction. Water in the house. All the floors need to be replaced. The walls have to have holes drilled in them and fans blowing air inside for three days. Then they have to do a mildew treatment, and then come back and test to make sure everything is dry and clean." He exhaled, his heart suddenly pulsing against his lungs. "They've got dehumidifiers going like crazy. And the fans. It's a good thing I like white noise, because they're *loud*."

"Well, look at it like this. You can redo the floors however you want."

"Silver lining," he said. "I like that. And Megan, here's the thing…."

She waited on the other end of the line, and he wanted her to say something. What, he didn't know. Maybe he wanted her to tell him that maybe he should stay until everything was done. He didn't want to be the first to say it.

"What's the thing?" she asked.

"I feel like I need to be here until the restoration is done. The guy shot questions at me for a half an hour today." When she remained silent, he added, "And I kinda want to put in the floors myself. You know, find some reclaimed wood or something. Fix it up nice. Lay it throughout the living room, kitchen, and dining room." His fingers twitched with the need to hammer something, to get outside of these walls. But he had no jobs here in Brush Creek, no horse to ride.

Just this empty house, the distinct smell of chlorine, and the deafening sound of all those fans.

"Megan?"

"So you're going to stay at Brush Creek?"

"For a few weeks," he said, making his voice light. He didn't quite pull it off. "Actually, Megan, I think I'm just going to stay here permanently. I can pay a moving company to pack my stuff and drive it down here. I have—"

He cut himself off from saying he didn't have anything in Montana keeping him from moving.

Megan was in Montana. And only five days ago, he'd told her he'd wait for her. Wait for her to work through things. Wait for her in Montana.

"I have plenty to do here," he finished lamely, hoping she hadn't heard his unspoken words.

"Okay, Landon." Her voice sounded calm and quiet. He almost wanted her to get frustrated like she had when she'd come out to Horseshoe Home and confronted him in the hay barn. This acceptance unsettled him. "I'll talk to you later." She hung up before he could respond.

He pulled the phone from his ear and looked at it. Definitely disconnected. He dropped the phone, his head drooping toward his chest. Would his decision to stay at Brush Creek end his relationship with Megan?

It certainly felt like it, though she hadn't said as much. He felt it deep down inside himself, but he couldn't bring himself to go back. His life was here now, and he needed to be at Brush Creek.

He didn't offer up a prayer. He'd made his choice, and he knew God wouldn't change Megan.

Only she could do that.

CHAPTER 23

*L*andon put in long hours at his new home. He drove to Salt Lake and bought furniture, an expense he'd planned on because the only thing he owned in his cowboy cabin was his clothes.

He hired a moving company to pack up his belongings—including his truck—in Montana and drive everything to Brush Creek.

He pruned trees, and learned swimming pool care, and spoke with the horse breeder in Texas. Brynn Bowman was a champion barrel racer. He'd known her while he was riding bulls and winning championships himself. He hadn't realized she'd retired from the rodeo circuit, had gotten married, and now lived in Texas. But she had.

Landon called Megan every morning around ten. She'd only answered once the first week, and she claimed he was calling too early. So he moved his call time to eleven. It had only been two days, but she hadn't answered yet.

Whenever he thought about her, which was all the time, a blip of anxiety would steal through him, infecting him, sickening his stomach. His jaw clenched and he'd have to take a deep breath to center himself.

Working helped keep his mind from running rampant. And with a trip to Texas in the immediate future, getting a horse would help calm him too. The morning of his flight to Amarillo, he worked up the courage to call Megan.

Surprise drenched him when she said, "Hey, Landon," as if they'd been carrying on long conversations for the past ten days.

"Megan," he said, the simple sound of her voice soothing him. "How are you?"

"I'm fine."

"I just haven't—" He leaned against the wall that separated the yard from the pool area. "It's good to hear your voice."

She didn't say anything, and Landon wracked his brain for something else to say. "I'm going to buy a horse today."

"Oh yeah?"

"Yeah, flying to Amarillo in a few hours."

"What's the stable called?"

"This place called Bowman's Breeds."

"Huh."

"Are you okay?"

"Just peachy."

But she wasn't. Landon knew she wasn't, but he didn't know how to fix things with her unless he went back to Montana. And the very thought of doing that made his skin itch like he'd taken Crossfire through a patch of poison ivy.

"I'm—" he started, but she said, "So you have time to go to Amarillo? The house must be finished."

His pulse paused, skipped, stalled, popped. "It's dry now, yes."

"And if I know you, and I think I do, you've been workin' on it nonstop for the past ten days."

"Except to call you," he said, not quite sure where the acidic bite in his tone had come from. So what if he worked eighteen hours a day? He didn't have anything else to do.

"I've been busy at the church," she said.

"Last time we talked, you said I was callin' too early."

"You were."

"You have a phone. You could've called me back when you got a free moment."

"I don't have a lot of those. In fact, I need to go."

"Megan, wait."

She didn't speak, but she didn't hang up either.

"Come down here," he said.

"I can't."

"I love you, and I want you to come to Brush Creek."

Her voice hitched when she said, "I'm sorry, Landon. I can't right now." She hung up, leaving Landon to admire the brilliant, blue sky and the mountains that cut into it. He didn't really see the gorgeous landscape though, because he knew that when Megan said, "I can't right now," she meant, "Please stop calling. I can't *be with you* right now."

He didn't want to do what she wanted, but he thought it

selfish and unfair to keep calling her, keeping trying for something she obviously didn't want.

———

Megan wiped the tears that seemed to be permanently streaming from her eyes. These days, at least. Had she just broken up with Landon? Felt like it, though the past ten days had felt like that too.

She gathered her curls off her neck and bound them in a ponytail. She had been attending all the clubs and classes at the church, not because she needed to or even wanted to. But simply to have something to do with herself. Without Landon working around the church and Belle out on the ranch, Megan didn't have a whole lot of people to talk to.

Everything in her ached, and not just because she'd started attending the Zumba class. Her heart didn't seem to know it could keep beating without Landon.

Funny, she thought. *I didn't feel like this when everything ended with Eric.*

And she hadn't. No, if Megan had to choose one emotion to describe how she'd felt when she'd found out about Eric, it would be relief. Okay, and a lot of anger. And some humiliation. But mostly relief.

But when Landon had said he was staying in Brush Creek, Megan had only felt devastated. Heartbroken. Lost. And nothing was getting better.

Someone knocked on her door, startling Megan from her thoughts. Her grip on her phone slipped, and it fell to the floor. She stooped to pick it up and moved to open the door. Belle stood there, all made up and beautiful, a six-month baby bump pushing against her shirt.

"Hey," she said brightly. "You haven't eaten yet, have you?"

Megan shook her head, her misery almost a tangible weight pushing, pressing, pulsing against her lungs.

"I thought not." Belle waved her out of the apartment. "Come on. Let's go get that Chinese you like."

The mention of Pan's made Megan wince. The last time she'd been there was with Landon. Would she ever be able to enjoy the string bean chicken without thinking of him? Smelling his aftershave? Wishing he'd kiss her later?

Megan went through the motions of walking, ordering her food, sipping her soda. Belle finally reached across the table and put her hand on Megan's. "When are you going to Utah?"

The few swallows of cola she'd had surged up her throat. She swallowed them back and shook her head. "I'm not going to Utah."

Belle sat back in her chair like Megan had punched her. "Why not?"

I love you, and I want you to come to Brush Creek.

Megan shrugged. "I have things to finish here."

"Name one."

Megan opened her mouth to speak, but her mind came up blank. "My church classes," she finally said.

"They're running great," Belle said. "You don't have to do anything."

"Well—"

"True or not true?" Belle asked. "You being present doesn't actually have any bearing on whether the classes and clubs are successful."

Megan glared, then sighed. "True." She pinned Belle with a look. "My father needs me."

"He does? For what?"

"I'm teaching the Sunday School class."

Belle snorted. "No offense, Megan, but anyone can do that."

Grasping at anything she could come up with, Megan said, "I just moved here. I don't want to move again."

Belle took her time answering. Megan knew she wouldn't like it, because Belle wouldn't look directly at her. She picked something invisible from her blouse, then glanced up as their food was delivered to their table. She unwrapped her chopsticks and picked up a piece of shrimp.

"Do you love him?" she finally asked.

"I—" Megan had never told Landon she loved him. She'd been trying to examine her feelings, but she hadn't come to a decision yet.

"Okay," Belle said. "Don't answer that. But think about this." She leaned into her elbows, her green eyes blazing with emerald fire. "Someone as miserable as you are feels something. Something bigger than themselves, and sometimes that something is hard to label and scary to define."

Megan blinked at her. "Okay."

"So how do you feel?"

"You just said I was miserable."

"Are you?"

"Yes," Megan clipped out.

"What would make you happier?"

"If Landon came back."

"Aha!" Belle pointed her chopsticks at Megan. "And you say you don't love him."

"I never said I didn't love him." But she never said she did either.

"Your entire happiness depends on him being with you. That sounds like love to me."

"He's not coming back."

"Nope," Belle said. "And I don't want him to, because I love him. He's my brother, and I want him to be happy. He's wanted a horse ranch his whole life. He finally got it. I'm happy for him."

Megan stuffed her mouth with chicken and rice so she could digest Belle's words. She didn't want him to come back because she loved him.

With a jolt, she realized the Landon she knew, the Landon who'd left Montana, hadn't been happy.

"He's spent a lot of time making other people happy," Belle said. "That's all I'm saying."

"I doubt that's all you'll say."

"You're right." Belle laughed. "So let me lay it out. I think you're in love with him and you just haven't admitted it to yourself yet. You have nothing tying you to Gold Valley, so why are you still here, especially when the person you love is somewhere else?" She took a bite of her beef. "*Now* that's all I'm saying." And true to her word, she let Megan contemplate what she'd said, and they finished their food in silence.

Megan thought as she chewed, the food barely having any taste at all. She wanted Landon to be happy, and the horse ranch at Brush Creek did that. She wanted to be happy herself, and being with Landon did that.

Because she was in love with him.

"Belle," she yelped. "I'm in love with him."

Belle squealed and laughed, jumping up from the table so fast, she almost upended their drinks. "I know you are, Megs." She hugged Megan, whose smile took several long seconds to cross her face.

She stepped back and held Megan by the shoulders. "So when are you going to Utah?"

"Tonight," Megan said, her insides shaking with the force of an earthquake. "Tonight."

Megan felt like a whirlwind, rushing here and there and everywhere. Since her lunch with Belle, she'd been firing on all cylinders, first packing, then driving to the airport, then finding out that the plane to Amarillo had just left.

She slept in the airport hotel, but it wasn't true sleep. Nerves kept dancing through her bloodstream, keeping her close to consciousness. Every other second, she'd change her mind. *Call him. Tell him you're coming.*

Don't call. Show up as a surprise! That's romantic.

She boarded the plane without calling him. Got a rental

in Texas without calling him. Drove into the middle of nowhere without calling him. Seeing as how she'd never been there, Belle had performed her Google magic and then texted Megan a pin of the boarding stable out at Three Rivers Ranch.

With every passing mile, her restlessness grew. At the same time, she recognized and acknowledged things about herself. She had felt a great drive to make the church a hub of activity, a centerpiece of the community. But not because it fulfilled something inside her.

Her father didn't need her to do all she'd done.

The people didn't need her to set up clubs and classes.

She'd done those things to try to find her own sense of belonging. And she hadn't found it. The only place she'd felt safe, and loved, and like she fit, was in Landon's arms. And she wanted so badly to tell him that.

Finally, she pulled onto a dirt road. The sign she'd passed a quarter mile ago had read *Three Rivers Ranch*, *Courage Reins*, and *Bowman's Breeds*. As she bumped along, Megan hoped to find Landon here. If he wasn't, she wasn't sure where to look, and she'd be forced to call him.

She parked next to a fence—and another car that looked suspiciously like a rental—outside the barn that boasted the *Bowman's Breeds* sign. Her sandaled feet drank up the dust as she walked through the gate and stepped into the barn.

The air in July in Texas seemed so heavy, so silent. Megan could barely inhale it. Yet something about Three Rivers felt cleansing too, almost like she could shed her skin and become the person God really wanted her to be.

"Can I help you?"

A blonde woman who looked near full-term with a baby approached. She wore a smile, a pair of jeans, and a billowing blue blouse that couldn't hide the fact that she was usually thin and petite.

"Maybe," Megan said. "I'm looking for…." She cleared her throat. "I'm looking for my boyfriend. He said he was coming here to buy a horse. Landon Edmunds?"

She cocked her head, her expression growing curious. "Sure, he's in the sheltering barn. Come on, I'll take you." She moved with the grace of a woman who wasn't nine months pregnant, and Megan hurried to follow her.

"Name's Brynn," she said as they left the main barn.

"I'm Megan."

"Right. Landon's mentioned you a time or two."

"He has?"

Brynn gave her a smile, though the eager look in her blue eyes didn't diminish. "Of course, what with you bein' his girlfriend and all."

"Oh, right." A blush worked its way into Megan's face. "I didn't realize you guys talked all that much."

"Oh, he's been here all day." She waved her hand as if swatting at a fly. "First he likes Million Dollar Man, then he wants to see Thaddeus again. The man can't make a decision to save his life."

Megan tossed her curls and laughed. "He really can't."

Brynn's chuckle made Megan think they could be good friends. "Well, he's right through here." She entered the second barn first, and Megan heard Landon's low voice from somewhere deeper inside.

"Landon," Brynn called. His voice cut off. "Your girlfriend's here."

"I don't have a girlfriend," he called back.

Brynn's bright eyes found Megan's. "Huh. Well, she seems to think you do." She patted Megan's shoulder as she exited the barn, leaving Megan to peer down the shady hallway. Leaving Megan to face Landon alone.

CHAPTER 24

Megan straightened her shoulders, having long given up smoothing her hair as a way to release her anxiety. She stepped with confidence toward the direction Landon's voice had come from. After only a few steps, she saw his body framed in the doorway, the sunlight streaming in from outside behind him, bathing his face in shadows.

"Hey," she said when she thought sure he'd seen her. "So is Brush Creek as far from civilization as Three Rivers?"

"Farther."

A pit opened in Megan's stomach, a hole she hoped she could keep from infusing her voice.

"What are you doin' here?"

"I came because…." She took another step closer to him, straining to see his face against the shadows. He watched her straight-faced, his fingers curled around the reins of a horse that lingered just beyond the door.

"I came because I'm in love with you." Her feet shuffled, almost urging her to run. "And I wanted to tell you, and you told me to come to Brush Creek, but I knew you weren't there, so I had Belle look up this place, and I flew to Amarillo this morning." She took a breath, ready to start in again.

But Landon dropped the reins and swept her into his arms, his cowboy hat falling to the ground as he brought his mouth to hers. "I love you, too," he murmured just before kissing her. She pressed into him, that safety and warmth she felt whenever she stood in his embrace descending on her. With absolute certainty, she knew she'd made the right decision. Knew that God had guided her to this man, even if the timing was inconvenient, even if it meant she had to move again.

She was ready to move on, and that was worth packing up everything she owned and carting it to a remote horse ranch in Utah.

He kept his strong hands on the small of her back as he broke their kiss and moved his lips to her earlobe. "It's so good to see you." He took a deep breath of her, and Megan smiled, the strength of happiness running through her a direct contrast to the misery she'd been experiencing for the past several days.

"We have a lot to work out," she whispered, holding onto his broad shoulders and tracing her fingers through his hair.

"Mm." He seemed keen to keep kissing her, and if Megan were being honest, she didn't mind a bit.

The emotions coursing through Landon sparked and popped. Megan had left Montana. Megan loved him. Megan was coming to Brush Creek with him.

The horse he'd been working with—Thaddeus, a year-old gelding who showed great promise—nickered, a chastisement for Landon's affections. He pulled away from kissing Megan and gazed down on her. "I can't believe you're here."

"I love you."

Landon couldn't believe she did, but at the same time, the love was right there, shining in her eyes, pulling her lips into a smile, streaming with sincerity in her voice.

"But I can't really move in with you at Brush Creek. In fact, I don't even have a flight out of Texas yet. And I need to take care of—"

He started laughing. "We can do one thing at a time," he said. "Brynn gave me the name of the hotel where I'm staying. We'll call and get you a room too. Then we can go to dinner."

Megan laid her cheek against Landon's pulse. "Dinner would be great."

"I brought my computer." He stroked her hair, inhaled her jasmine scent. "We'll get you on the flight I'm on. It leaves tomorrow afternoon."

"What about your horse?"

He twisted toward Thaddeus. "I think I'm gonna get

him," he said. "There was another I liked, but Thaddeus has something special about him."

"Just one? Maybe you can get them both."

With the price tag the purebred horses carried, Landon hesitated. He could afford them, sure. He just wasn't sure he wanted more money streaming from his savings. He felt like he'd been bleeding dollars for the past couple of weeks.

Still, if he trained the horses to be champions, carrying their riders to victory in barrel racing or team roping, he'd more than triple his investment.

"Maybe I will get them both."

"Can you rename a horse?" Megan extracted herself from his arms and slipped her fingers into his.

"I suppose," he said. "Why?"

"I don't like the name Million Dollar Man. Seems like a lot of pressure." She peered up at him. "A lot to live up to. Don't you think?"

He blinked at her, trying to decide if she was kidding or not. A smirk played with her lips, and Landon chuckled. "It certainly does."

Later that night, with Megan's rental car returned and her luggage in a nearby hotel room, Landon felt like he could conquer the world. "And...done." He pushed away from the desk. "Your flight is confirmed. We fly out at three." He leaned back. "That'll put us back at Brush Creek close to dark, but you'll still be able to get the general idea of the place. Especially the house."

"And you don't think it's improper for me to stay with

you?" Megan sat in the armchair in the corner, her legs tucked under her body. "There isn't a hotel in town?"

"I didn't see one." He'd driven around the whole town and hadn't noticed a hotel. "But, you know, Flaming Gorge is only an hour away. There will be lots of places to stay there, if you feel weird about it." He stood, his stomach growling. "But my bedroom is on the main level, and I have a full basement. Different floors. Doors that lock. Just like here." He extended his hand toward her. "Let's go eat."

Megan unleashed her questions after they'd been seated in a busy restaurant. She wanted to know who he'd hired to move his things, when he expected them to come, if she could find somewhere to rent in town. She didn't ask him the one thing his mind couldn't seem to release.

She didn't ask him when they'd get married.

Finally, after the steak and seafood, the baked potatoes and almond green beans, after the waiter set a single piece of chocolate mud pie between them, Landon glanced at her. "So when do you want to marry me?"

She froze with her fork halfway to her mouth, her eyes widening. Lowering her fork, she asked, "Is that a proposal?"

He shrugged. "Well, I love you and you love me, and you're moving to Brush Creek. Seems sort of ridiculous for you to find an apartment when I have that big old house up the canyon."

"Ridiculous, huh?"

"So how long will it take you to plan a wedding?"

"Not that long." She took her bite of pie, licked her lips

and swirled her fork through the chocolate sauce on the plate. "I'd been planning this big to-do with Eric. But I don't want to do anything I'd thought of then. I just want—" She looked up at him, and he cocked his head to the side, waiting, listening.

"I just want to be married in my father's church, with that beautiful stained glass window you cleaned."

A smile burst onto his face. "I think we can do that."

"When can you come back to Montana?"

"You tell me when, and I'll be there." He enjoyed his own bite of chocolate and cookies and whipped cream. "And anything I can do to help, I will." He cleared his throat. "You know, paying for anything, or whatever." He honestly didn't know what one would have to pay for to pull off a wedding, but flowers and refreshments came to mind. Maybe a photographer, announcements, a cake. He forced back a measure of panic. What had he just offered?

"I'm going to go simple," she said. "White roses. A simple, plain cake." She leaned forward. "How about you take care of the honeymoon? I expect to be surprised, and there's nothing I love more than a good beach."

He grinned at her, stole the piece of cake she was about to scoop onto her fork, and said, "Noted."

*L*andon wasn't sure when his red blood cells had grown barbs and started jabbing into him. Maybe somewhere over the Rocky Mountains.

He turned to Megan, sitting next to him in the rental he'd been using since his arrival in Utah. They'd landed an hour ago, and still had an hour to go until they reached Brush Creek. "What if you don't like Brush Creek?"

And just like the last three times he'd asked her, she smiled and said, "Of course I'm going to like Brush Creek. Stop worrying."

But he didn't stop worrying. By the time they reached the town, Landon half-wished she'd suddenly go blind. "So this is the town," he said. "Population: Six thousand and thirty-three. I've met a few people."

"There's a store," she said. "Gas station. Post office. Library. Look at that park." She turned to him, her dark eyes alight with surprise and wonder. "There's plenty here. It's wonderful."

Relief cascaded through him, but the turnoff to the ranch sat just ahead. Would she be okay living ten minutes from the store, the gas station, and the library? Horseshoe Home was different than Brush Creek. That ranch—as well as Three Rivers—functioned as their own mini-communities. The cowhands lived there full-time. The administration building had a kitchen, a common area. They had entertainment in the summers, and the ranch owner's wife brought lunch and dinner to the cowhands regularly.

Landon hadn't wanted to leave that sense of family; that wasn't the source of his unrest in Montana. But the fact remained that Brush Creek didn't offer that.

But it could, he thought as he made the turn. He'd purchased the additional land surrounding the horse ranch, and he could build cowboy cabins, get a staff, expand his training facilities beyond the two or three horses he could work with. The idea grew, puffing into a full-fledged reality as he made his way up the canyon to Brush Creek Ranch.

With the windows down, the sound of gravel crunching under the tires signaled their arrival to the property. "It's just beyond that rise."

He crested the small hill and the house came into view. He loved the log cabin feel of the home and thought of it as more of a luxury lodge than a rustic cabin in the woods. "Oh," he said. "And we can go visit Montana anytime you want. I still have my cabin on Bear Mountain."

"Of course you do," she said, her eyes fixed on the house,

the yard, or the land beyond. "Landon, this place is beautiful." She turned toward him, that sense of childlike wonder almost intoxicating. "It's like a quaint little log cabin."

"It ain't that little," he muttered, causing her to laugh. He opened the garage, entered, and came to a stop. "Okay, so—"

She leapt from the car before he could qualify that he still needed to repair the walls, and he quickly followed her. "It's locked," he said as she tried to muscle her way into the house. "Eager little thing, aren't you?" He stepped next to her, one hand sweeping around her waist and pulling her close.

"I want to see the house that took you from me." She smiled up at him though the words sliced into him.

"Megan, the house didn't take me from you."

"I know," she said, her smile faltering. "God did that."

"And then He brought you back." He pressed his lips to hers in a momentary kiss. "I'm glad you weren't so mad at me that you couldn't listen to Him."

"Me too." She glanced at the door. "Are you going to make me wait forever?"

He chuckled as he unlocked the door, grinned as she pranced over his new reclaimed wood floors, sighed as she exclaimed over and over how beautiful the house was, the yard, the pool, the barns, the land, all of it.

But as perfect and gorgeous it all was, none of it compared to Megan.

———

"Okay, so Alli is bringing the flowers in the morning." On the kitchen table in front of her, Megan had a checklist a mile long. Four weeks to plan a wedding bordered on insane, but the only thing that had taken that long was getting a proper picture of her and Landon for their announcements.

He'd taken her to Salt Lake the day after they'd arrived back in Utah and bought her an engagement ring. She'd found a dress the day she flew home to Montana. And since then, she called him every evening after she knew he'd be in from the barns, and he called her every morning after he knew she'd be awake.

She'd ordered flowers from a childhood friend, a wedding cake from Natalie Ringold, who was teaching cooking classes at the church, and booked the church for Labor Day weekend. Landon had flown into town the previous evening, and he was staying with his parents until the wedding tomorrow.

"And Natalie said the cake will be ready tonight," Belle said, looking at the checklist when Megan got up to pace in her living room. "Your dress is hanging in the closet. I brought in all the trays from Gloria and Rose. The women from church will have the cookies and milk ready for the reception...." Her eyes raked down the paper.

"Megan, I think you're ready to get married." A warm smile accompanied the words, and the same feeling infused Megan's muscles.

"Has he mentioned at all where he's taking me on our honeymoon?"

Belle turned away and took another sandwich cookie from the package lying open on the kitchen counter. "I'm not the one who talks to him twice a day."

"You know where we're going."

"I do not."

"Belle."

"You're going to love it." Belle finally faced her. "I should've married a rich man." After a moment of stunned silence, they both burst into laughter.

The next morning, Megan woke early but stayed in bed. She allowed herself several minutes to severely miss her mother. As most little girls did, Megan had dreamt of her wedding day, and in those fantasies, her mother had always been there to straighten the skirts of her dress, tuck her curls behind her ear, and beam at her from the front pew.

Landon's mother would be there. Karen had taken Megan under her wing the past few weeks, given much needed advice and love and acceptance.

"And she'll be here in half an hour," Megan told herself as she sat up in bed. If she couldn't have her own mother, she definitely wanted Landon's family surrounding her.

She'd barely had time to shower and pull on under-clothes before she heard her front door open. "Megan," Belle called. "It's me and Mom."

"I'm in the bedroom."

Belle appeared in the doorway, having snagged the wedding dress from the hall closet where it had been waiting for a couple of weeks. "Time to get married."

Megan turned so Belle could zip her party dress, then

took the dress bag from her friend. "Let's get over to the church, then."

Once in the safety of the locked bride's room, Megan let them help her into her dress, roll and pile her hair on top of her head, apply the layers of makeup. Finally, Karen embraced Megan and handed her a small bouquet containing three white roses among the green foliage.

"You are beautiful." Karen wiped her eyes. "Landon is the luckiest man on Earth."

"Be sure to tell him that," Megan joked.

"Oh, I have."

Belle turned from the crack in the door, where she'd been stationed for the past ten minutes. She bent and gathered Megan's skirts. "Let's go. Landon is in position."

The drone of the organ met Megan's ears as she stepped into the hall. Since her father was performing the ceremony and would already be at the head of the chapel, Megan slipped her hand into Landon's father's elbow.

"I am so happy for you," he said as Belle and Karen slipped down the hall to the side door so they could take their seats inside.

"How's Landon?"

"Awake at four this morning, wondering why we couldn't get over here and get this done." He chuckled. "He's never been that good at waiting."

Megan nudged him with her shoulder. "Now you tell me."

The doors opened, and Megan cut off the giggle but kept

the smile hitched in place as the organ switched to the wedding march.

It seemed as though every person in Gold Valley had come out for the wedding. Smiling faces and wet eyes looked back at her. Megan had grown in the summer she'd been home. She'd helped the church members as well as the community.

She saw the weathered lines on Gertrude Brooks's face, saw the love shining in the woman's eyes. She felt her mother's presence nearby, taking every step with her until she arrived at Landon's side. Then his father sat, and her mother's spirit faded, and Megan looked at the man who was about to become her husband.

Nothing but adoration streamed from his eyes. He bent close, the brim of his fashionable cowboy hat bumping against her forehead. "Hey, beautiful girl."

"Hey, cowboy."

He wore a deep black tuxedo, the white shirt absolutely pristine. His bowtie shone like freshly fallen snow, and he somehow made a tuxedo and a cowboy hat seem perfectly reasonable together. She took a deep breath of his woodsy smell, a sense of peace infusing her with the nearness of Landon.

Her father started speaking, and Megan tightened her fingers on Landon's as she listened to her father talk about love and family, hard times ahead and never-ending joy. She wanted all of that with Landon—the good, the bad, the hard, the easy. Because she knew that if they were together, there was nothing they couldn't overcome.

"Yes," she said when it was her turn, and she waited without breathing until Landon said it too.

Then her father said, "I now pronounce you husband and wife. You may kiss the bride."

Landon pulled her close with his free hand, pausing for a heartbeat before kissing her completely. Shouts and applause sounded behind them, and Megan started laughing as she broke the kiss and faced the crowd.

She lifted her bouquet to another rousing round of applause and went with Landon as he moved down the aisle. Behind her, her father announced the couple's reception later that evening, but Megan escaped the chapel with her new husband.

He helped her into his truck, which had been decorated with the white words JUST MARRIED across the tailgate, and leaned into the door. "You still want to go up to Bear Mountain?"

"You said we could get there and back before the reception."

"We can."

"Then, yes. I want to go see my summer home." She'd been teasing him about having a summer home, a winter home, and a holiday home.

"Oh, jeez."

"And I want to know where we're going on our honeymoon!" she called as he closed the door. He shrugged, a devilish look in his eye as he went around to the driver's side of the truck.

He climbed in and set the truck northwest, as if heading

out to Horseshoe Home Ranch. He bypassed the road that would've taken them up to the ranch, and kept going straight. About an hour later, he turned onto another road.

The lace along Megan's collar had started to itch a while ago, and she couldn't wait to change out of it. They bumped over the gravel road until he finally turned and a cabin suddenly appeared out of the woods.

"Here we are." He sat in the idling truck, watching the cabin.

She nudged him. "Well, let's go in. I want to get out of this dress."

"I want that too," he said, sliding her a heated look.

She laughed. "You have to get out first."

He did, waiting for her, offering his hand to help her down. He twisted the doorknob and let the front door of the cabin settle open. "After you."

She stepped into his cabin, not quite sure what to expect. A tall vase of white and red roses sat on the coffee table immediately in front of her, with a giant envelope stuck among the blooms.

"That has my name on it." She glanced at Landon.

"That's because it's yours." He nodded toward it. "Go on then. Open it."

Her fingers fumbled over the glued down flap, and when she pulled out the cards, she realized what they were. Airplane tickets. Her eyes moved rapidly then, trying to find their destination.

"This is what you're looking for." Landon waved a brochure in front of her face, obviously enjoying her confusion a little too much. "You didn't even see it fall to the floor."

She took the paper from him. "Turks and Caicos," she read across the top. "A luxury resort…." Her eyes ran down the picture of the beautiful white sand, the impossibly deep blue water. "In the Caribbean."

He grinned and her, and her heart swelled with love for him. "It's perfect."

"And I've booked this place for January, when it's supposed to be frigid in Utah." He handed her a brochure for a gorgeous beach in—

"Brazil?"

"You got your passport, right?"

"I did."

Landon took the brochures and airplane tickets from her. "Perfect. Now I believe you said something about getting out of that dress…."

Megan laughed and threw herself into her husband's arms. "I love you, Landon Edmunds."

"I will love you forever," he whispered, and Megan felt his joy, love, and adoration for her from the top of her head to the very tips of her feet. "Megan *Edmunds*."

———

Read on for a sneak peek at **THE COWBOY AND THE NANNY**, the next book in the Horseshoe Home Ranch Romance series.

The barn door banged open as Gil, one of the male counselors, burst through it. "Owen, there's a fight we need your help with." He didn't wait to see if Owen would come. He did. Owen Carr had the most experience with the troubled boys at Silver Creek, having worked with the at-risk boys for the past seven years, since he'd been at the part therapeutic riding center, part rehabilitation center.

He left the saddles where they were on the bench, left the horses in the stall, left everything, and followed Gil at a run. "Is it one of my boys?" he called after the other man.

"Stanley! He has a weapon."

Owen's heart sped at the same time he groaned. He increased his speed, leaving behind the horse barn and stalls, the cabin where he used to live, and the hay barn. He tore around the corner of the building to find a crowd of boys circling two others.

"Move," he called. "Now, boys. Move aside." No one dared disobey Owen when he spoke, whether it was in his normal quiet way or in the intense bark he used now. The boys parted to reveal Stanley holding a homemade knife.

"Stanley," Owen said. "Drop it right now." The stick looked to have a piece of metal from a belt or a saddle strap attached to the end of it. And it glinted sharply in the September sun.

Stanley glanced from the other boy to Owen. "Mister Carr—" He swallowed.

Owen strode forward, his nerves already preparing to be hurt. They fired on all cylinders as he got closer and closer to Stanley. He really didn't have time for this. He'd been fifteen minutes away from finishing his work in the barn and leaving. He had an appointment to keep.

"Give me the knife, Stanley." Owen stopped five feet from the teen, whose dark eyes seemed wild and scared. "This doesn't end well if someone gets hurt. You can come over to the cabin and tell me what happened." Owen met the other boy's eyes, and he didn't look nearly as afraid as Stanley did. Owen settled his weight on his back foot. "What's goin' on?"

"He said he knew my sister," Stanley said, and Owen cringed. Stanley was fiercely protective of his family, and he hasn't yet grasped that it didn't matter what anyone else said about them. "Said she was easy, said all his friends had kissed her."

"So you thought you'd make 'im bleed over somethin' that ain't true?" Owen kept the sigh he wanted to add from escaping. "Give me the knife, Stanley. This boy isn't worth it." He glared at the other boy now, who wore a smirk. He'd gotten exactly what he wanted, and Owen hoped Stanley wouldn't suffer too much because of it.

Stanley inched toward Owen until Owen could wrap his fingers around the boy's wrist. He did, as tight as he dared, and Stanley dropped the knife. Owen stomped on it, kept his grip on his boy, and turned to the crowd. "Go on, now. Get back to your chores." He twisted toward the other boy. "You're comin' with me."

"You're not my counselor."

Owen growled and took two steps toward the boy, who flinched away. Satisfied, Owen pushed his cowboy hat lower over his eyes. "Come on." He spied Dr. Richards hurrying across the lawn, and he held his ground as the crowd dispersed.

"Owen," Dr. Richards panted. "What's happened?"

"Stanley was gettin' teased and he fashioned some weapon." He moved his boot to reveal the makeshift knife. "To teach this other boy a lesson. I'll let you handle him."

Dr. Richards turned his gaze on the other boy and frowned. "Gerard." His eyes blazed with anger. "You have to stop this." He turned and headed back toward his office, the other boy in tow.

"My cabin," Owen said, nudging Stanley in that direction.

"I thought you moved out."

"I did." Owen had lived there so long, he'd always think of it as his. Dr. Richards hadn't given it to anyone else, because Owen still oversaw the horses, still worked with the at-risk boys. His hours were the same, and Dr. Richards simply assigned the at-risk boys to his on-call counselors for after-hours emergencies.

Because Marie had changed everything.

The fight left Owen's body and he gave that sigh he'd held back earlier. "You know, you're makin' me late, Stanley." He redirected him toward the barn. "So you get to do the clean-up chores in the barn."

"I'm sorry, Owen." Stanley sounded remorseful too. He always did, once he actually calmed down enough to think rationally.

"It's Mister Carr. And you need to work on your impulse control," Owen said as he released the boy into the barn. "Oil the saddles and hang them up. All the reins go up there too. And both those horses need to be fed and brushed down."

Owen leaned against the doorframe while Stanley got to work. It would take the boy twice as long as it took Owen, and he'd be even later. But he couldn't abandon Stanley—he wouldn't. Not when he barely had anyone to hang on to.

"What're you gonna be late for, Mister Carr?"

Owen pushed away from the wall and reached for the reins as Stanley finished the last saddle. "Remember how I have my niece living with me now?"

"Marie, sure."

"Well, because I'm here with you guys so much, I need help takin' care of her." Everything in him twisted and wound tight. He'd always loved Marie, the daughter of his only sister. He'd agreed to be her guardian if anything happened to her sister and her husband. He'd just never expected anything to actually happen to them.

Owen's life had changed a lot in the past six months. He'd become a father and an only child because of an ice storm and a horrible, horrible car accident.

He pushed away the memories that threatened to drown him every time he let his mind linger on them too long. "I'm hirin' a nanny to help out." He checked his watch. "And I'm supposed to meet with her in ten minutes."

Because an eight-year-old girl couldn't live fifteen yards from half a dozen troubled boys who had landed at Silver Creek because of their tendencies to mix weapons with drugs, Owen had found a cottage in a nice neighborhood—fifteen minutes from Silver Creek. No matter how he sliced it, he was going to be late.

He'd gotten Marie a simple cell phone the very first day she'd come to live with him. He called her and told her he'd be several minutes late. "Is that okay, Marie? Maybe you can ask the lady a few questions." He smiled despite himself, despite the fact that he had very little in his life to smile about. No matter what, Marie did bring a smile to his face. So blonde her hair was almost white, with deep blue eyes like his sister's. Like his.

"I can do it, Owen."

"I shouldn't be too long." He turned when Stanley walked Ole Red past him. Only one horse remained, and if Owen helped, he could be on the road in under ten minutes. He hung up with Marie and grabbed a curry comb.

"Now, Stanley, you got any other weapons?"

"No, sir."

"I'm gonna have to search your things. You know that, right?"

"Yes, sir." Regret laced his words. "I really am sorry, Owen."

Owen didn't correct him this time. He didn't mind being more casual with his boys. He wanted—needed—them to trust him. They finished in the barn, and Owen searched Stanley's belongings. He filed the incident paperwork, and asked Dr. Richards if he could meet with him in the morning, that he needed to get home to Marie.

Dr. Richard's waved him out of the office, and Owen hurried to his truck. A pang of longing for his old life reared up as he left the parking lot. Before Marie, after a day like today, Owen would retreat to his cabin and make himself a sandwich. Then he'd sit on the front porch with his guitar and sing until all his boys came and sat on the steps with him.

He'd talk to them, and they'd listen, and the bond between them would strengthen until incidents like this didn't happen anymore. He'd lost that when he'd moved out. He didn't need to play on the porch every night—though he usually did. But after days like today, he did—which was why he needed a nanny for Marie.

A black sedan sat in his driveway, so he parked on the street. He hadn't yet gotten out of his truck when Marie squealed. She appeared around the side of the house, a huge smile on her face. Owen's dog followed, his tongue lagging out of his mouth.

Owen smiled at the two of them as Tar Baby overtook Marie and knocked her to the ground. They wrestled amidst Marie's laughter as a tall, slim woman came from the backyard as well.

She moved with the grace of someone who knew exactly where to put their feet. Her long, dark hair was streaked with blonde, and her hazel eyes glinted with happiness as she watched the girl and dog in front of her.

Owen's heart skipped several beats and he seemed frozen to the seat. This woman's beauty exceeded any he'd met before, and she seemed vaguely familiar.

He managed to slide out of the truck and start to cross the lawn. "Hey," he called, his voice finally thawing. It sounded semi-normal too, thank goodness. He hadn't had the best of luck in the dating department, not that he'd tried that hard—especially after his return to Gold Valley several years ago.

He'd ruined everything with his high school girlfriend when he'd left town the day after their graduation, and then he'd had his heart broken by a woman in Nashville. So no, he hadn't tried that hard at all since coming home and starting at Silver Creek.

"C'mon Tar Baby." The black cocker spaniel leapt away from a still-giggling Marie. "Hey, sweetheart." He bent over and picked up the little girl, hugging her tight. His momma had told him to show Marie how much he loved her, that he was glad to have her living with him. He tried to tell her he loved her, and he gave her as much affection as he could muster. "Did you interview the nice lady?" He cut the woman a glance. "Sorry I'm late."

The woman's eyes had flecks of gold in them, and they hooked Owen and held him fast. "Do I know you?"

"Of course you do, Owen." She gave a nervous laugh. "I'm Natalie Lower."

The name reverberated through his head, and old wounds opened, hurt, and bled. He shook his head real slow. "No. No, you said your name was Natalie Ringold."

"Well, it is." She looked like she'd been doused with ice water. "I got married nine years ago."

The internal injuries widened, and the pain knifing through Owen felt as hot as fire. "Married?"

"Lasted less than a year, Owen. Honestly, don't you know any of the town gossip?" She smiled, but it was full of nerves and lasted only a moment.

"Only been back for the last seven years." His voice sounded like he was speaking into a tin can. "And no, I've only actually lived in town for six months." He set Marie on her feet. "Go play with Tar Baby, sweetheart. Go on, Tar Baby." The girl ran off with the dog, leaving Owen to talk with the high school sweetheart he'd left twelve years ago.

All he could do was pray, and he didn't even know for what. Only that he'd definitely need the help of the Lord to make it through the next few minutes.

———

Natalie stared at Owen, the same Owen Carr she'd fallen in love with all those years ago. So much of him was the same —that fire in those navy eyes. That black cowboy hat. Those wide shoulders, the day-old scruff on his chin, the cowboy boots he had to have specially made because his feet were so large.

The only thing missing was his guitar.

"I kept up with you," she said, her voice on the edge of shaking. "They played your songs all over the country."

His expression stormed and his teeth clenched. "That's over now." He stepped past her toward the front steps.

She scrambled after him, her stomach quaking. "You had a record deal, Owen. You got what you wanted. What you left—" She cut herself off before she could finish the sentence. He heard what she'd say anyway. *You got what you wanted when you left me here to pursue your own dreams.*

He'd promised her he'd come back. Promised he'd come back and take her to Nashville with him. And he might have, but she'd gotten married about the same time his first single hit the country music charts. She'd known while dating Jeremiah that she shouldn't, but she'd accepted his diamond and gone through the whole charade of a wedding anyway.

Why, she wasn't sure. But now, following Owen into his house, she knew why. She'd been so lonely, so empty, without Owen. She'd simply wanted someone, and it didn't seem to matter who.

She was older now. While she still felt lonely most days, and empty even after she ate, she didn't turn to a handsome face to fill her life. She'd turned to serving the community on the library board, teaching cooking classes through the church's community program, and finishing her dance degree. She taught ballet to little boys and girls, and she loved it. But she needed more. Thus, why she'd applied for this job, though she'd known exactly who Owen Carr was and how he came to need a nanny. She'd been back in Gold Valley for two years, and she knew all the gossip.

"Marie's great," she said once she'd closed the door behind her. "I'd love to help you with her."

He kept his back to her as he moved into the kitchen and opened the fridge. "Want somethin' to drink?" He pulled out two bottles of water.

She nodded and accepted the water. "I can help in the mornings, like you said. I can be here after school. She can come over to the dance studio with me. I teach ballet there, and you can pick her up whenever you're done."

"She doesn't dance."

"Well, maybe she'd like to." Natalie tucked her hair behind her ear, suddenly aware of the weight of his gaze. That hadn't changed either. The way his muscles rippled under his skin certainly had, as well as the way he collected his emotions close and kept his temper in check. "I teach from four to seven on Mondays and Tuesdays. The other afternoons, I can just pick her up from school and bring her home, make dinner." She waved her hand. "Whatever else you need around here."

He didn't seem to need much, but dirty dishes did wait

in the sink, and dust seemed to have taken up permanent residence on the shelves.

He regarded her with those gorgeous eyes. The very same ones that had drank her up when they'd sat next to each other at a swim meet, which she'd attended to watch her brother. He'd come to support one of his friends. Though they'd grown up together in Gold Valley, she'd never *seen* him until that meet. They started spending a lot of time together after that, and by their senior year, she'd fallen in love with him.

He'd always talked about going to Nashville and becoming a country star. His voice was smooth and even and beautiful, and the man could play a guitar like he was born to do exactly that. The fact that he'd achieved his dreams, even if it was only one record, one single that went to the top of the charts, didn't matter. He'd done it.

"Natalie—" he started.

"I need this job, Owen." She wrung her hands until she realized she was doing it. She rubbed her palms along her thighs. "Marie likes me. Ask her."

He blinked at her. Drained his water, never taking his eyes from hers. "Fine. I will." He tossed the empty water bottle in the sink and moved toward the back door, a perfect storm of Owen Carr that made Natalie want to soothe him, the way she often had. Kiss him, the way she often had. Whisper to him that she loved him, the way she often had.

He'd soothed her too. Kissed her. Told her he loved her. But in the end, none of that had been enough. He'd still left.

She followed him as far as the deck on the back of the house, watched while he scrubbed behind his dog's ears and spoke to Marie. The little girl brightened and nodded, and Owen's shoulders fell. A surge of satisfaction moved through Natalie.

She'd wondered how she could reinsert herself into Owen's life. She'd seen him from a distance since she'd come back to Gold Valley. Seen him at church. Heard about his work at Silver Creek. And everyone had rallied around him when his sister died. His parents still lived in town, but Tasha's will had specified Owen as Marie's legal guardian, and he'd done what was necessary.

When she'd seen his ad for a nanny, she'd applied, beyond hopeful. *Please let this be our second chance*, she prayed as he turned back to her. She couldn't read his expression under his cowboy hat from this distance, but as he stalked closer, she saw the indecision, the anger, the pain.

"She likes you," he clipped out as he passed.

"So can I have the job?" She hated seeing his retreating back as he marched into the house and around the corner into the kitchen. She'd seen enough of him walking away from her to last a lifetime.

"I'll let you know," he said. "I have other interviews still to do."

She entered the kitchen to find him peering into the freezer. "I teach cooking classes at the church," she said. "I can make dinner. Give you a sample of what a meal might taste like when you get home from work."

"That's not necessary."

Desperation darted through Natalie. "Owen—"

"I'm real sorry," he blurted. "Okay? I'm sorry I left and never came back."

His apology brought warmth to her soul. "It's over," she said. "The past. Something that happened twelve years ago."

He closed the freezer and looked right at her. He'd always been able to see past what she said to get to the root of how she really felt. "Are you over it?"

"I—"

"Because I'm not." Agony shone in his eyes for one, two, three seconds before he erased it. "But I do want you to know I'm sorry."

She touched his arm, and lightning sparked at the skin-to-skin contact, causing her to jerk back. "I am too, Owen."

"Nothin' for you to be sorry about." He backed into the living room. "I'll let you know about the job."

"When?"

"Soon."

"How many more interviews do you have?"

"Three."

He'd resorted to one-word answers, so she nodded, ducked her head, and slipped out the front door.

SNEAK PEEK! THE COWBOY AND THE NANNY CHAPTER TWO

Natalie exhaled as she pulled into her own driveway, only a five-minute drive from Owen's. Had she known, she would've taken two lefts to drive by his place more often. She dismissed the thought. No, she wouldn't have. She wasn't so hung up on him that she'd stalk him.

In fact, though she needed the job, she wasn't sure she actually wanted it. Sure, she thought Owen was as handsome as ever. He radiated strength and warmth from his very person. And the thought of kissing him again sent excitement through her in the form of tremors. On some level, she still loved him. She wondered if she always would, he being her first love and all.

But she didn't like the trapped feelings she'd felt in every relationship since. She didn't like wondering what mood her boyfriend or husband would be in when she walked through the door. With Jeremiah, he saved his worst self for her, it seemed.

He couldn't treat his co-workers badly, but he could his wife. He took so much time off work, he bounced from job to job. He was a good person, constantly thinking of others and doing little things to make their lives brighter. He wrote kind cards and bought gifts—for everyone except her. She'd felt neglected and overlooked from the very first time they'd gone out.

And she'd never known who or what was waiting behind the closed door of their home on the north end of town. She knew the sick feeling deep in the gut of not wanting to go home. And she'd vowed that she'd never endure that kind of anxiety again.

Natalie liked knowing that behind her closed door sat her cat, Cranberry, her dirty cereal bowl from that morning, and the running shoes she'd worn to the gym that morning lying by the front door.

She got out of the car and stretched her back in the waning autumn light. She had liked Marie, and that was who this job was all about. She climbed the front steps to her house and entered the unlocked door. Sure enough, Cranberry mewed as she wound through Natalie's legs and her eyes fell on the shoes by the door.

She took a deep breath and released it, none of the anxiety she'd experienced previously inside her. After her failed marriage, Natalie had finished her dance degree and taken every culinary course the local vocational school offered. In her two-bedroom house, she was able to do the two things she loved most: dancing and cooking. They both kept the thoughts of failure, the ever-looming loneliness, at bay.

She pulled the flank steak from the fridge and set about sharpening her knife. Twenty minutes later, she had razor-thin slices of beef marinating in soy and ginger and garlic. She set her hands to chopping peppers, onions, and broccoli as her mind whirred through her upcoming pie classes at the church.

She needed to meet with the new activity director and make sure she had the budget to do pecan pie. She missed Megan, the previous director. Natalie had made Megan's wedding cake, and the whole affair was only two weeks old. She and her new husband—a cowhand from Horseshoe Home Ranch—had flown off to a tropical destination, and then they were moving to Utah.

Natalie needed to confirm times for the classes. Her cooking lessons were some of the more popular ones offered at the church, and she often did mid-day classes for the older generations and evening times were reserved for working people.

She set the broccoli to steam and reached for her phone. "Maureen," she said when the activity director for the church answered. "When can I come talk to you about the upcoming cooking classes?"

"What does tomorrow look like for you?"

Tomorrow was wide open for Natalie—a real problem if

she wanted to keep eating flank steak and paying her mortgage. She'd been scraping by for years, teaching dance and doing freelance web design. But she hated the online work—didn't quite have the discipline needed to set her own hours and work from home.

With an appointment set for ten a.m., Natalie finished putting together her beef and broccoli dish and sat down at her eat-in kitchen table. She turned on her Internet radio and enjoyed her meal for one. Well, she enjoyed it as much as she could alone. Her traitorous thoughts kept drifting to Owen, and if he'd even fit at the only other chair at the table. She had her doubts.

"Get over him," she muttered to herself as she moved down the hall and changed into a leotard. While lacing her ballet shoes, a memory she'd long abandoned slammed into her head.

Her senior year, she'd danced the part of the Sugar Plum Fairy in her studio's production of The Nutcracker. Owen had come—he always attended her concerts—and brought her a nutcracker and a single red rose.

She crossed the hall to her bedroom, where that nutcracker sat on her dresser. She'd dried the rose, but she wasn't sure where it was now. Jeremiah had asked her about the nutcracker several times, and she'd said it had sentimental value. She'd passed it several times everyday, and yet she hadn't seized onto the memory of where it had come from.

Now, she ran her fingertips along the base and up the

legs. The nutcracker wore a festive green suit coat, and a smile stole across her face. Owen had said, "I would never wear that color, but he looks nice, don't you think?"

She'd taken the gift and embraced the boy she loved.

He's not a boy anymore, she thought as she turned abruptly away from the nutcracker. She went back into her dance studio and moved to the barre. By concentrating on each muscle in her leg, in each slow, precise movement ballet required, she was able to drive Owen from her mind.

At least for an hour.

———

Owen pulled the turkey steaks off the heat and set the pan on the granite cutting board. "Marie," he called. "Time to eat."

The girl came down the hall from her room, a pencil in her hand.

"Got your homework done?" he asked as he got two plates out of the cupboard. "Mashed potatoes tonight." He grinned at her, though he didn't feel an ounce of joy in his body. "Your favorite."

"Did you make gravy?"

He scoffed. "Did I make gravy." He put the pan next to the turkey steaks. "Of course I made gravy." He leaned against the counter, the early hour at which he woke catching up to him. "You know, your mom loved gravy. She used to put it on everything. I even saw her ladle it over spaghetti once."

Marie smiled, and she didn't look like quite as washed out. "I know, Uncle Owen. You told me last time we had turkey steaks."

"Oh. Well." He busied himself getting out silverware and pulling the canned beans from the microwave. "Let's eat, and then I'll look at your homework." He stifled a yawn and served Marie. He'd learned to listen to her talk if she wanted to, but he didn't press her to. He asked her about school, her teacher, the neighbor he'd been using as a nanny since school had started a couple of weeks ago.

She wandered down the hall after dinner, leaving Owen to himself. With shorter days approaching, he felt tired earlier than normal. Or maybe that was just because of the reappearance of Natalie Lower in his life.

He'd always, always regretted cutting her out of his life in the first place. He had few regrets in his life, but that one topped the list. No matter the success he'd enjoyed in Nashville, he shouldn't have left her the way he did. At least he'd been able to apologize, finally.

Her golden eyes played tricks on his heart all night, making him toss and turn until visions of his once-relationship with Nat drove him from bed at five a.m. He arrived at Silver Creek by five-forty-five in time to wake his boys for their six o'clock equine chores. His at-risk boys took exclusive care of the horses, something he'd insisted on from the day he'd started at the center.

He knew the healing power of horses, something he'd experienced on a deeply personal level at a horse ranch in Nashville before he'd returned to Gold Valley. Before waking the boys, he opened the barn and walked down the aisle. His favored horse was Ole Red, and Owen only allowed certain boys to work with her.

A sorrel-colored horse, Ole Red had a black tail and mane that Owen ran his fingers through as the horse nosed his shoulder. "Mornin'," Owen said in the soft voice he reserved just for his animals and his boys. He wasn't soft-spoken, but he didn't need to bluster and yell to get his way. His height had always helped establish his power with the boys, and his no-nonsense attitude achieved the rest.

He thought of the tired eyes of his neighbor when he'd knocked on the door that morning to deposit a sleepy Marie on her couch. It would be so much better to have someone come to his house so Marie could sleep properly until it was time to go to school. He'd had an additional interview the previous evening, but Marie had said, "She smells like that oil you rub into your boots." She'd wrinkled her nose, and Owen had crossed the woman off his list.

He had two more interviews that evening, but he wondered if maybe he should just call Nat and ask her to pick Marie up from school. She'd have dinner ready when he got home....

His mind played tug-of-war with itself as he unlocked and entered the boy's cabin. "Time to get up, boys," he called, clanging the rod through the triangle that served as an alarm clock. Groans and moans met his ears, but his boys got themselves up and in line.

"Trevor and Marcos, you're on feed," Owen said, moving

down the line. "Stanley, saddles and tack. Guy and Cory, hay barn. Jesus, the last three stalls on the north end need to be shoveled out and fresh straw put down." He looked down the line, a rush of admiration for these boys pulling through him. "Breakfast at seven, right back here. I don't want to smell horse on you while we're eating."

"No, sir," they chanted.

"Go on then."

His boys set about getting dressed and heading out to their chores. Owen waited until they'd all exited the building, then he joined them in the barn, where Stanley had switched on the radio. Owen made them listen to the morning news and talk radio while they worked, claiming they needed to know a world still existed beyond Silver Creek. A world they were expected to return to, live in, contribute to.

He went around and spoke to each boy, asking them specific questions about their lives, their struggles. They saw a professional psychiatrist, but they bonded with Owen and he often got more out of them than the doctors did.

"Heard from your dad yet?" he asked Trevor when he got to the boy.

"Yeah, he's coming next week. Doctor Richards said we can go to the football game." Trevor flashed him a grin. "Thanks for setting it up, Owen."

Owen clapped Trevor on the shoulder. "You're a great kid, Trevor. Happy to do it."

Owen wished he had someone to tell him he was great

when he'd failed. When he'd tried to claw his way back to the surface. He'd achieved great success in Nashville, he knew. For every record made, there were probably fifty artists turned away.

One hit wonder, ran through his head. He'd loved every song on his first album. He'd written every one right from his heart. Thankfully, one of them other people had connected to. He shouldn't have asked for more. Shouldn't have expected more.

But he had, and those unrealized dreams tainted the success he'd enjoyed down south. That combined with Clarissa's quick exit from his life, and Owen had a hard time remembering anything good associated with his five years in Nashville.

Taking a chance, the way he did with his boys, the way he had when he'd packed a single bag of clothes and all the money he'd saved from mowing lawns in high school and headed a thousand miles across the country, Owen pulled out his phone. Instead of calling, he sent a text to Natalie.

Can you get Marie after school today? Maybe we can do a trial day.

He shoved his phone back in his pocket and checked on Guy and Cory in the hay barn. The boys over there tended to go back to sleep or make a mess of the hay if Owen didn't make it a habit to stick his head in and make sure they were working.

His phone buzzed before he'd taken more than two steps. Natalie had answered already, and Owen was impressed she was up this early. She'd never been a morning person that he remembered.

"She's not the same person you knew at all," he muttered as he read her text.

Sure! She's at Lincoln Elementary, right? That's what she said last night. She's done at 3:15?

Right, he typed. *Lincoln Elementary at 3:15. I should be home about 5.* His thumb hovered over the send button before he pressed it. He added, *Thanks, Nat,* and sent that too.

No problem.

Relief washed through him as he sent a message to his neighbor that she didn't need to go down the block to the bus stop to get Marie. He asked her to please tell Marie that Natalie would be picking her up after school, much happier with the day's situation than anything else he'd arranged for the girl.

No one's called me Nat since high school. Natalie's text burned his retinas—another reminder of how much she'd changed.

Sorry. I didn't know.

Just another reminder of what he didn't know about her, and a creeping thought settled in his mind. He wanted to know all about the new Natalie Ringold.

It's fine. She inserted a smiley face and then said, *See you tonight.*

For the first time since Tasha's death, since Marie came to live with him, since Owen had been forced to leave his cabin, he felt a measure of peace slip into his system. He realized he had something worthwhile to look forward to, and he was a bit shocked, scared, spooked that he felt that way because of Natalie.

———

Read THE COWBOY AND THE NANNY today! A country music star, his nanny for his niece, and their second chance at true love and family…

Scan the QR code below to get it!

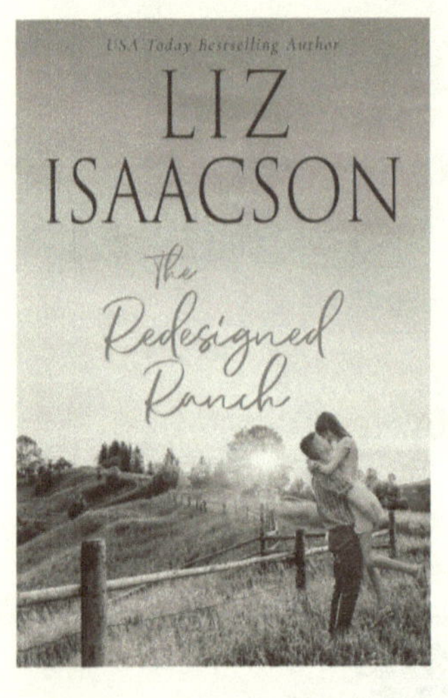

The Redesigned Ranch (Book 1): Jace Lovell, still nursing a wounded heart after being jilted at the altar, has dedicated himself to becoming the best foreman at Horseshoe Home Ranch. When he decides to hire an interior designer to please the ranch owner's wife, he didn't expect to be faced with a familiar face from his past. **Can Belle's patience and faith help Jace find the path to forgiveness and lead them to discover their own slice of happily-ever-after?**

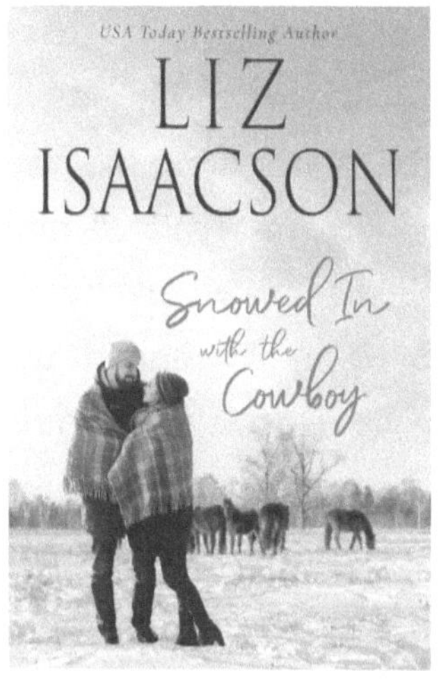

Snowed in with the Cowboy (Book 2): Sterling Maughan, once a renowned snowboarder, is in self-imposed exile at his family cabin after a tragic accident stole his career. Lost and without purpose, solitude is his only companion until an unexpected visitor disrupts his isolation. **Can Norah trust Sterling enough to let him into her life and give their unexpected and forbidden love a chance?**

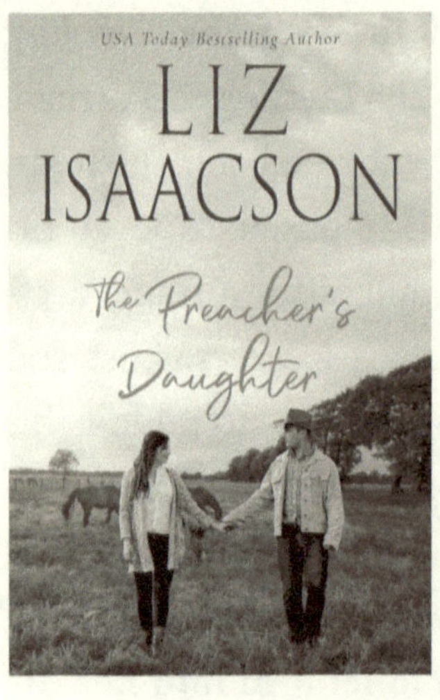

The Preacher's Daughter (Book 3): Landon Edmunds, a cowboy born and bred, has had his rodeo dreams realized and then dashed by a career-ending injury. Back in his hometown working at Horseshoe Home Ranch, he yearns for a new beginning with a ranch of his own. His sights are set on buying a horse ranch to train rodeo horses, but his plans take a detour when his high school best friend, Megan Palmer, steps back into his life. **Will they choose to follow their hearts, or will they let true love slip through their fingers again?**

Be sure to check out the spinoff series, the Brush Creek Cowboys romances after you read THE PREACHER'S DAUGHTER. Start with BRUSH CREEK COWBOY.

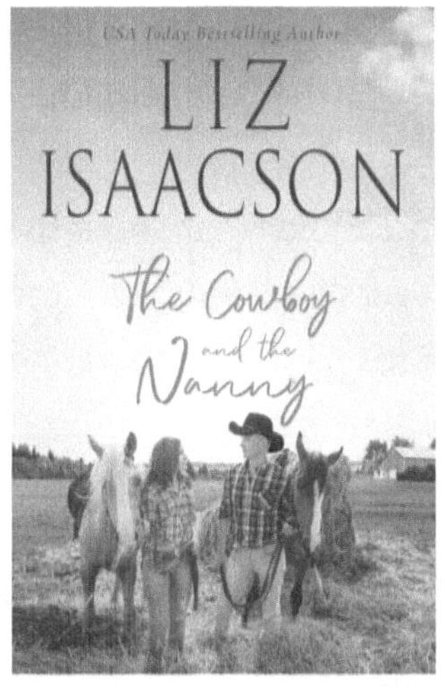

The Cowboy and the Nanny (Book 4): Twelve years ago, Owen Carr traded his roots and his sweetheart in Gold Valley for the bright lights of Nashville, where he found fame as a country music star. But when a tragic accident leaves him single-handedly raising his eight-year-old niece, Marie, he's forced to return home. Overwhelmed and out of his depth, Owen finds a lifeline in a most unexpected place. **As they mend bridges and explore the sparks that still sizzle between them, will they open their hearts to a second chance at love?**

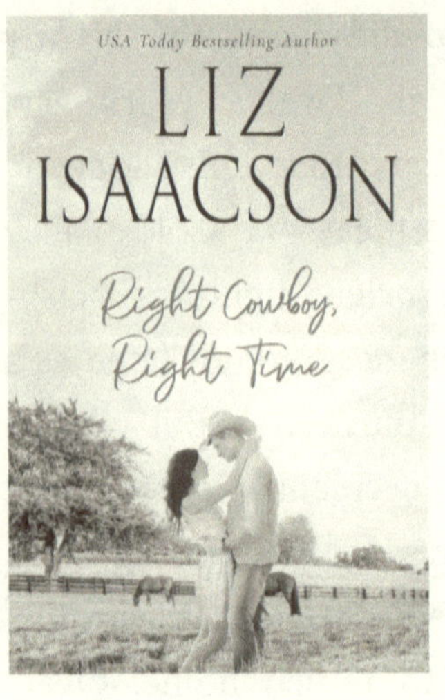

Right Cowboy, Right Time (Book 5): Caleb Chamberlain, a fun-loving cowboy at Horseshoe Home Ranch, has spent the last five years wrestling with the ghosts of his past—a devastating breakup, alcoholism, and a near-fatal accident. Now, he's finally found solace in laughter and the rhythmic simplicity of ranch life. But a chance encounter with a familiar face threatens to upheave his newfound peace. **Can they navigate the shadows of the past to find their happily-ever-after?**

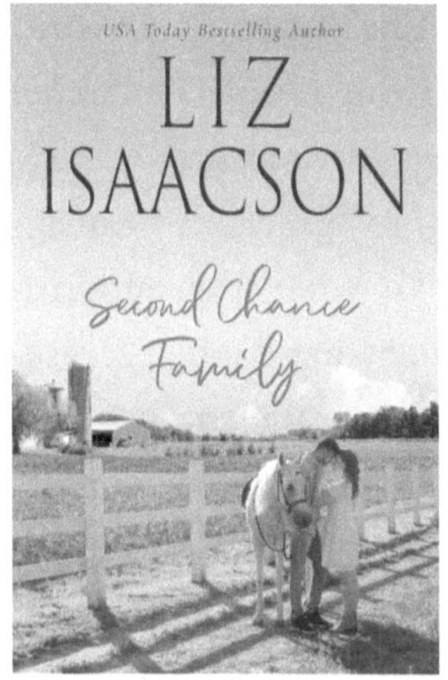

Second Chance Family (Book 6): Ty Barker has been living a carefree existence for the last thirty years. As friends around him found love and started families, Ty filled his time by giving horseback riding lessons and serving on a community service committee. But beneath the jovial surface, he's starting to feel the sting of loneliness. **He knows he wants River Lee in his life—but the question is, can he navigate the delicate steps needed to make her stay with him?**

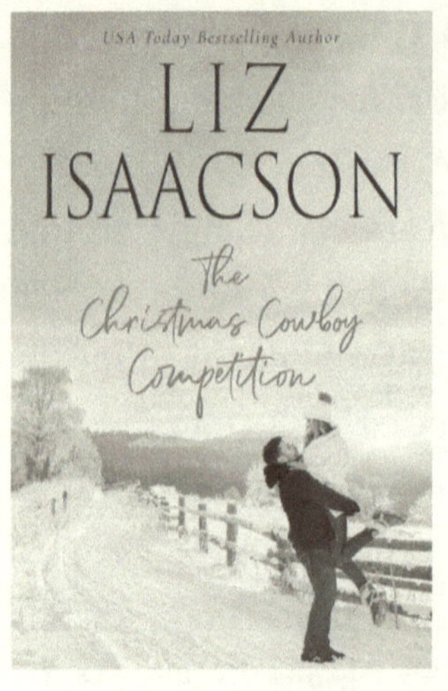

The Christmas Cowboy Competition (Book 7): Archer Bailey has already had to yield one job to Emersyn "Emery" Enders. So when the opportunity of a cowhand job at Horseshoe Home Ranch presents itself, he keeps it to himself. Emery, whose temporary job is ending but whose responsibilities towards her physically disabled sister aren't, is left in the dark.

As the festive season unfolds, **will Emery and Archer navigate the complexities of the ranch, their close living arrangements, and their personal challenges to discover the love building between them? Or will their rivalry rob them of the greatest Christmas gift of all—true love?**

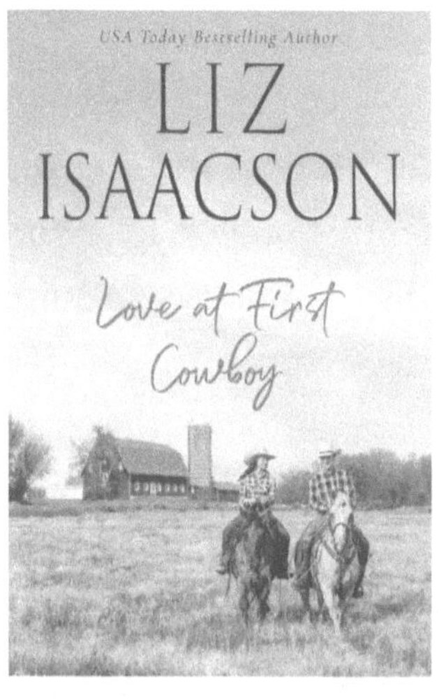

Love at First Cowboy (Book 8): Elliott Hawthorne, a career cowboy, has just witnessed his best friend and cabinmate forsake bachelorhood for matrimony. He'd be joyous if he weren't so green with envy. When a call about a family accident demands his presence, Elliott finds himself rushing from the ranch to his parents' house to see what's going on with his daddy, where he encounters the most stunning woman he's ever laid eyes on. **But as they encounter the complex dynamics of family responsibilities and personal desires, can their love-at-first-sight grow strong enough withstand the test of time?**

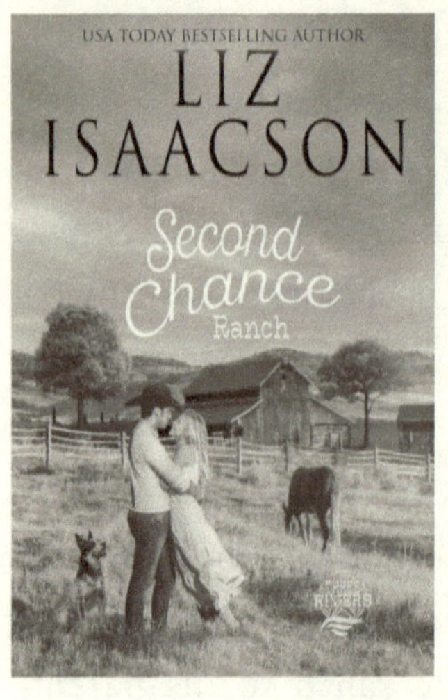

Second Chance Ranch: A Three Rivers Ranch Romance™ (Book 1): After his deployment, injured and discharged Major Squire Ackerman returns to Three Rivers Ranch, wanting to forgive Kelly for ignoring him a decade ago. He'd like to provide the stable life she needs, but with old wounds opening and a ranch on the brink of financial collapse, it will take patience and faith to make their second chance possible.

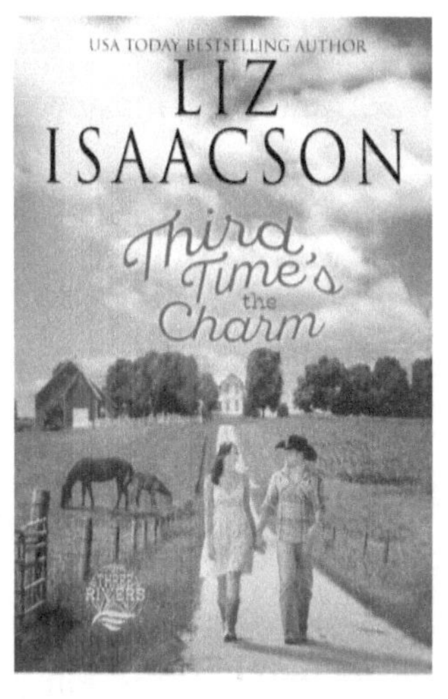 **Third Time's the Charm: A Three Rivers Ranch Romance™ (Book 2):** First Lieutenant Peter Marshall has a truckload of debt and no way to provide for a family, but Chelsea helps him see past all the obstacles, all the scars. With so many unknowns, can Pete and Chelsea develop the love, acceptance, and faith needed to find their happily ever after?

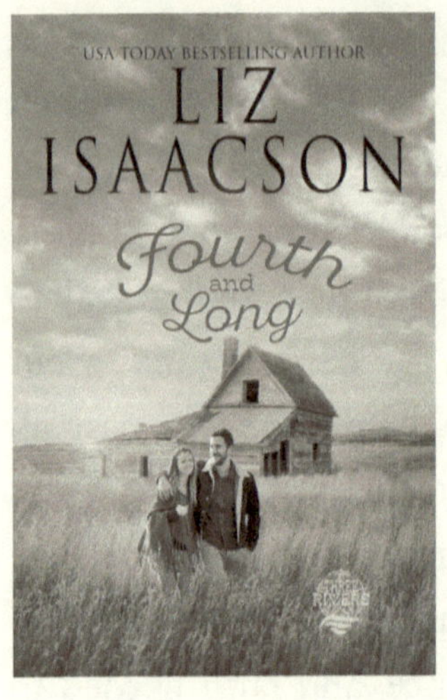

Fourth and Long: A Three Rivers Ranch Romance™ (Book 3): Commander Brett Murphy goes to Three Rivers Ranch to find some rest and relaxation with his Army buddies. Having his ex-wife show up with a seven-year-old she claims is his son is anything but the R&R he craves. Kate needs to make amends, and Brett needs to find forgiveness, but are they too late to find their happily ever after?

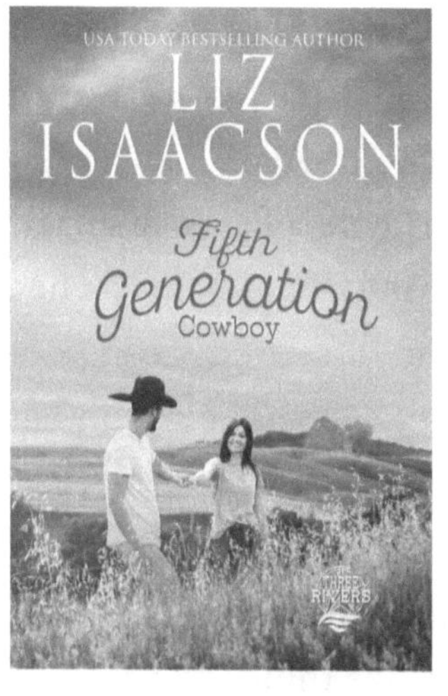

Fifth Generation Cowboy: A Three Rivers Ranch Romance™ (Book 4): Tom Lovell has watched his friends find their true happiness on Three Rivers Ranch, but everywhere he looks, he only sees friends. Rose Reyes has been bringing her daughter out to the ranch for equine therapy for months, but it doesn't seem to be working. Her challenges with Mari are just as frustrating as ever. Could Tom be exactly what Rose needs? Can he remove his friendship blinders and find love with someone who's been right in front of him all this time?

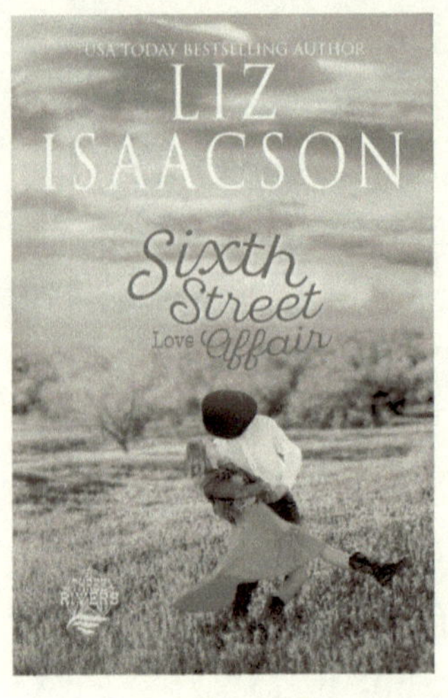

Sixth Street Love Affair: A Three Rivers Ranch Romance™ (Book 5): After losing his wife a few years back, Garth Ahlstrom thinks he's ready for a second chance at love. But Juliette Thompson has a secret that could destroy their budding relationship. Can they find the strength, patience, and faith to make things work?

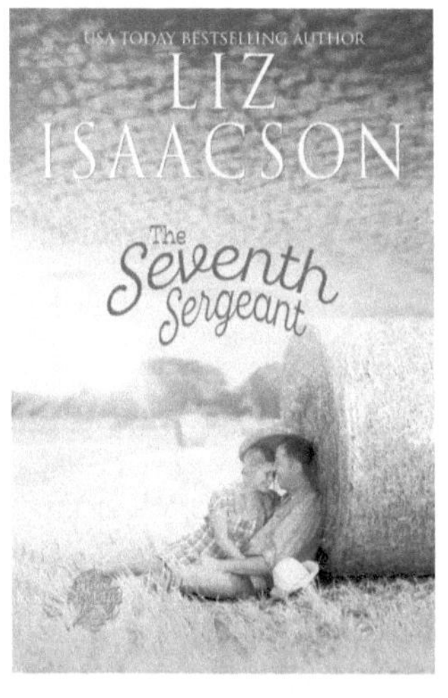

The Seventh Sergeant: A Three Rivers Ranch Romance™ (Book 6): Life has finally started to settle down for Sergeant Reese Sanders after his devastating injury overseas. Discharged from the Army and now with a good job at Courage Reins, he's finally found happiness—until a horrific fall puts him right back where he was years ago: Injured and depressed. Carly Watters, Reese's new veteran care coordinator, dislikes small towns almost as much as she loathes cowboys. But she finds herself faced with both when she gets assigned to Reese's case. Do they have the humility and faith to make their relationship more than professional?

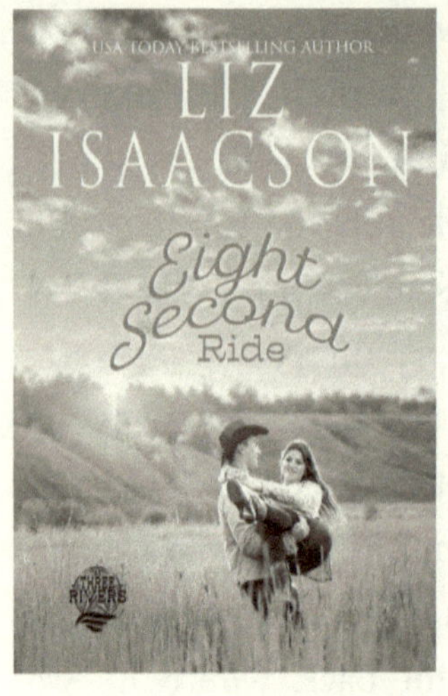

Eight Second Ride: A Three Rivers Ranch Romance™ (Book 7): Ethan Greene loves his work at Three Rivers Ranch, but he can't seem to find the right woman to settle down with. When sassy yet vulnerable Brynn Bowman shows up at the ranch to recruit him back to the rodeo circuit, he takes a different approach with the barrel racing champion. His patience and newfound faith pay off when a friendship--and more--starts with Brynn. But she wants out of the rodeo circuit right when Ethan wants to rejoin. Can they find the path God wants them to take and still stay together?

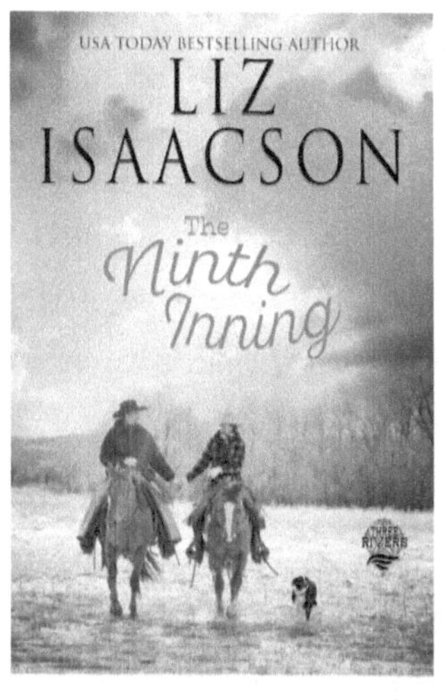

The Ninth Inning: A Three Rivers Ranch Romance™ (Book 8): The Christmas season has never felt like such a burden to boutique owner Andrea Larsen. But with Mama gone and the holidays upon her, Andy finds herself wishing she hadn't been so quick to judge her former boyfriend, cowboy Lawrence Collins. Well, Lawrence hasn't forgotten about Andy either, and he devises a plan to get her out to the ranch so they can reconnect. Do they have the faith and humility to patch things up and start a new relationship?

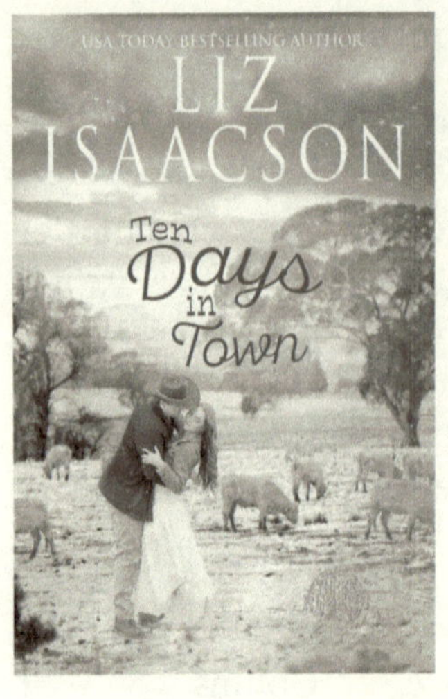

Ten Days in Town: A Three Rivers Ranch Romance™ (Book 9): Sandy Keller is tired of the dating scene in Three Rivers. Though she owns the pancake house, she's looking for a fresh start, which means an escape from the town where she grew up. When her older brother's best friend, Tad Jorgensen, comes to town for the holidays, it is a balm to his weary soul. A helicopter tour guide who experienced a near-death experience, he's looking to start over too--but in Three Rivers. Can Sandy and Tad navigate their troubles to find the path God wants them to take--and discover true love--in only ten days?

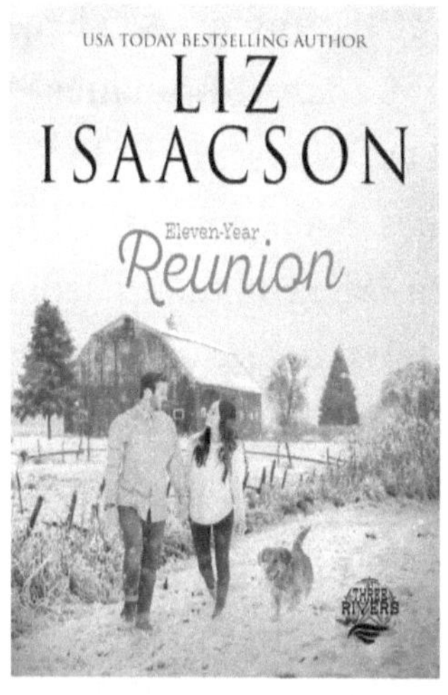

Eleven Year Reunion: A Three Rivers Ranch Romance™ (Book 10): Pastry chef extraordinaire, Grace Lewis has moved to Three Rivers to help Heidi Ackerman open a bakery in Three Rivers. Grace relishes the idea of starting over in a town where no one knows about her failed cupcakery. She doesn't expect to run into her old high school boyfriend, Jonathan Carver. A carpenter working at Three Rivers Ranch, Jon's in town against his will. But with Grace now on the scene, Jon's thinking life in Three Rivers is suddenly looking up. But with her focus on baking and his disdain for small towns, can they make their eleven year reunion stick?

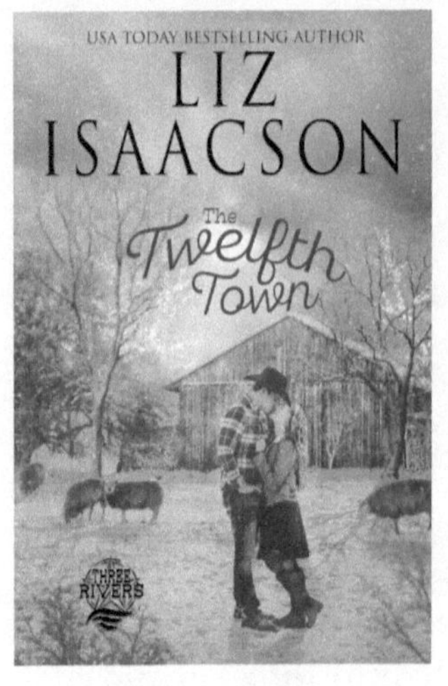

The Twelfth Town: A Three Rivers Ranch Romance™ (Book 11): Newscaster Taryn Tucker has had enough of life on-screen. She's bounced from town to town before arriving in Three Rivers, completely alone and completely anonymous-- just the way she now likes it. She takes a job cleaning at Three Rivers Ranch, hoping for a chance to figure out who she is and where God wants her. When she meets happy-go-lucky cowhand Kenny Stockton, she doesn't expect sparks to fly. Kenny's always been "the best friend" for his female friends, but the pull between him and Taryn can't be denied. Will they have the courage and faith necessary to make their opposite worlds mesh?

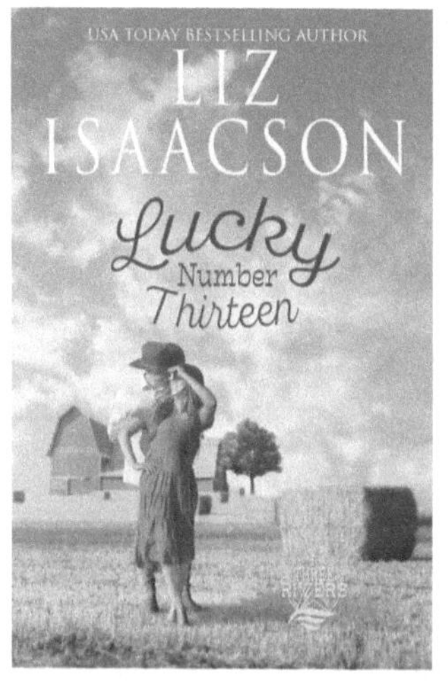

Lucky Number Thirteen: A Three Rivers Ranch Romance™ (Book 12): Tanner Wolf, a rodeo champion ten times over, is excited to be riding in Three Rivers for the first time since he left his philandering ways and found religion. Seeing his old friends Ethan and Brynn is therapuetic--until a terrible accident lands him in the hospital. With his rodeo career over, Tanner thinks maybe he'll stay in town--and it's not just because his nurse, Summer Hamblin, is the prettiest woman he's ever met. But Summer's the queen of first dates, and as she looks for a way to make a relationship with the transient rodeo star work Summer's not sure she has the fortitude to go on a second date. Can they find love among the tragedy?

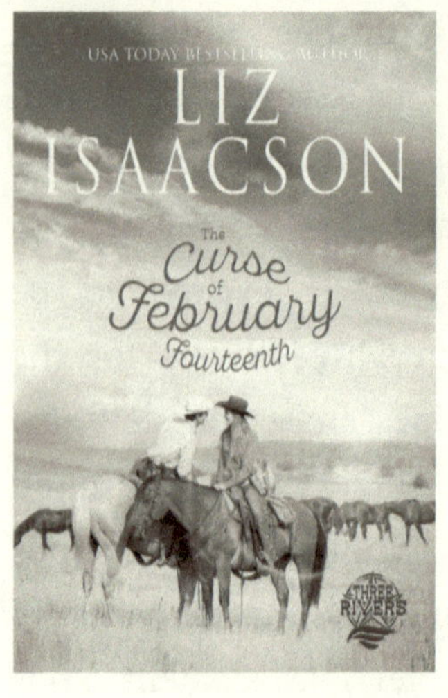 **The Curse of February Fourteenth: A Three Rivers Ranch Romance™ (Book 13):** Cal Hodgkins, cowboy veterinarian at Bowman's Breeds, isn't planning to meet anyone at the masked dance in small-town Three Rivers. He just wants to get his bachelor friends off his back and sit on the sidelines to drink his punch. But when he sees a woman dressed in gorgeous butterfly wings and cowgirl boots with blue stitching, he's smitten. Too bad she runs away from the dance before he can get her name, leaving only her boot behind...

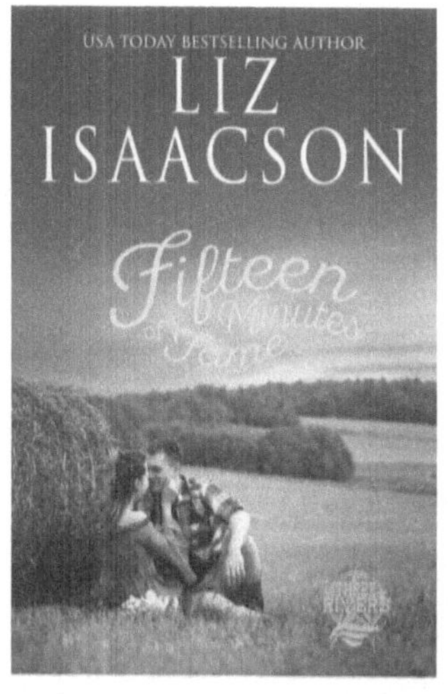

Fifteen Minutes of Fame: A Three Rivers Ranch Romance™ (Book 14): Navy Richards is thirty-five years of tired—tired of dating the same men, working a demanding job, and getting her heart broken over and over again. Her aunt has always spoken highly of the matchmaker in Three Rivers, Texas, so she takes a six-month sabbatical from her high-stress job as a pediatric nurse, hops on a bus, and meets with the matchmaker. Then she meets Gavin Redd. He's handsome, he's hardworking, and he's a cowboy. But is he an Aquarius too? Navy's not making a move until she knows for sure…

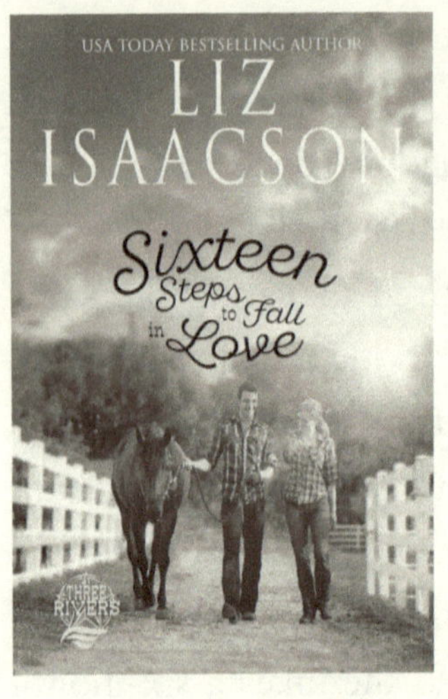

Sixteen Steps to Fall in Love: A Three Rivers Ranch Romance™ (Book 15): A chance encounter at a dog park sheds new light on the tall, talented Boone that Nicole can't ignore. As they get to know each other better and start to dig into each other's past, Nicole is the one who wants to run. This time from her growing admiration and attachment to Boone. From her aging parents. From herself.

But Boone feels the attraction between them too, and he decides he's tired of running and ready to make Three Rivers his permanent home. **Can Boone and Nicole use their faith to overcome their differences and find a happily-ever-after together?**

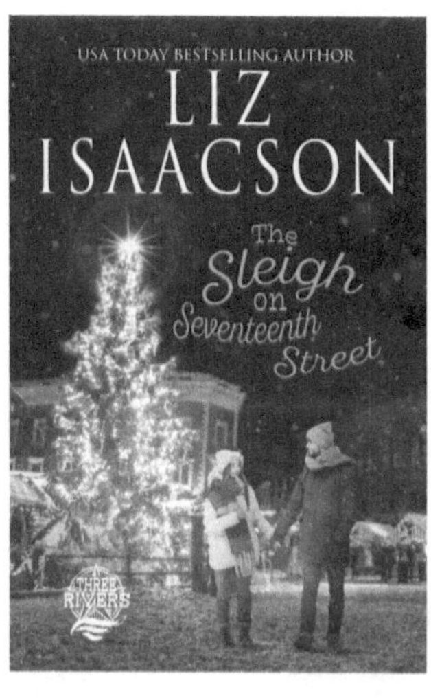

The Sleigh on Seventeenth Street: A Three Rivers Ranch Romance™ (Book 16): A cowboy with skills as an electrician tries a relationship with a down-on-her luck plumber. Can Dylan and Camila make water and electricity play nicely together this Christmas season? Or will they get shocked as they try to make their relationship work?

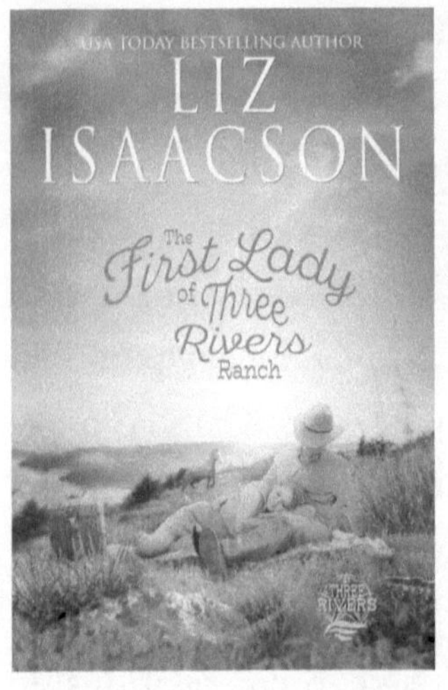

The First Lady of Three Rivers Ranch: A Three Rivers Ranch Romance™ (Book 17): Heidi Duffin has been dreaming about opening her own bakery since she was thirteen years old. She scrimped and saved for years to afford baking and pastry school in San Francisco. And now she only has one year left before she's a certified pastry chef. Frank Ackerman's father has recently retired, and he's taken over the largest cattle ranch in the Texas Panhandle. A horseman through and through, he's also nearing thirty-one and looking for someone to bring love and joy to a homestead that's been dominated by men for a decade. But when he convinces Heidi to come clean the cowboy cabins, she changes all that. But the siren's call of a bakery is still loud in Heidi's ears, even if she's also seeing a future with Frank. Can she rely on her faith in ways she's never had to before or will their relationship end when summer does?

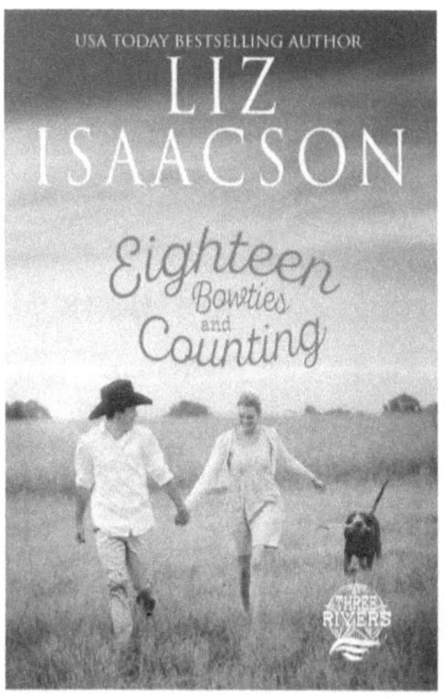

Eighteen Bowties and Counting: A Three Rivers Ranch Romance™ (Book 18): He's her older brother's best friend and completely off-limits. She's got a way with horses...and a heart condition. Can Beau and Charlotte navigate close quarters to find their happily-ever-after?

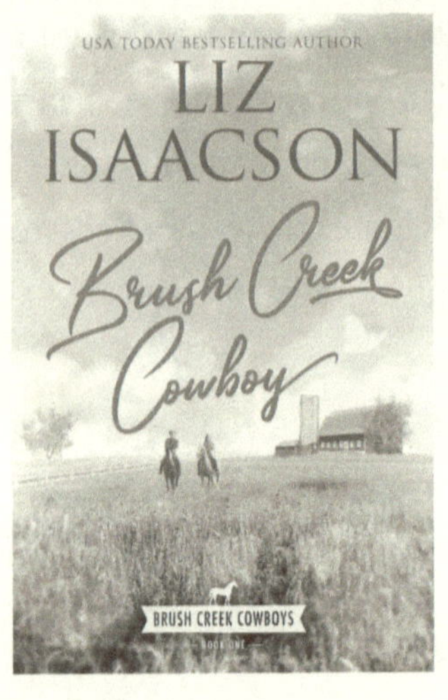

Brush Creek Cowboy (Book 1): Former rodeo champion and cowboy Walker Thompson trains horses at Brush Creek Horse Ranch, where he lives a simple life in his cabin with his ten-year-old son. A widower of six years, he's worked with Tess Wagner, a widow who came to Brush Creek to escape the turmoil of her life to give her seven-year-old son a slower pace of life. But Tess's breast cancer is back...

Walker will have to decide if he'd rather spend even a short time with Tess than not have her in his life at all. Tess wants to feel God's love and power, but can she discover and accept God's will in order to find her happy ending?

The Cowboy's Challenge (Book 2): Cowboy and professional roper Justin Jackman has found solitude at Brush Creek Horse Ranch, preferring his time with the animals he trains over dating. With two failed engagements in his past, he's not really interested in getting his heart stomped on again. But when flirty and fun Renee 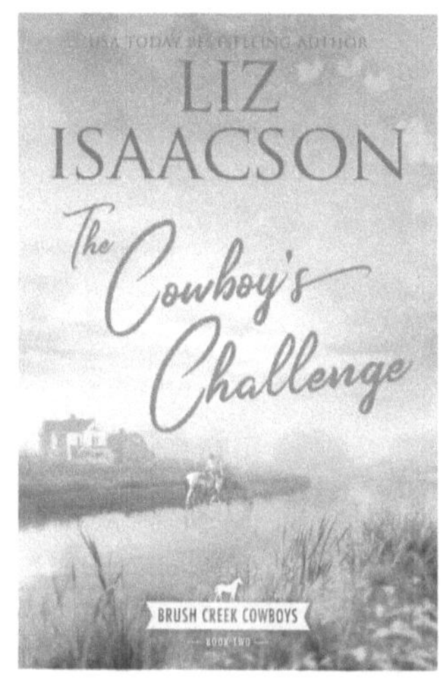 Martin picks him up at a church ice cream bar--on a bet, no less--he finds himself more than just a little interested. His Gen-X attitudes are attractive to her; her Millennial behaviors drive him nuts. Can Justin look past their differences and take a chance on another engagement?

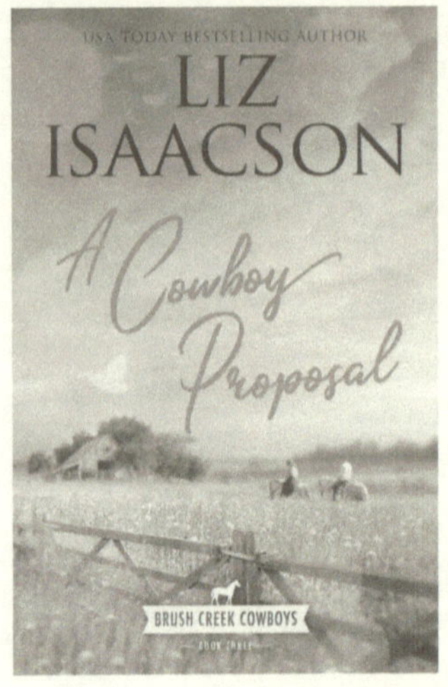

A Cowboy Proposal (Book 3): Ted Caldwell has been a retired bronc rider for years, and he thought he was perfectly happy training horses to buck at Brush Creek Ranch. He was wrong. When he meets April Nox, who comes to the ranch to hide her pregnancy from all her friends back in Jackson Hole, Ted realizes he has a huge family-shaped hole in his life. April is embarrassed, heartbroken, and trying to find her extinguished faith. She's never ridden a horse and wants nothing to do with a cowboy ever again. Can Ted and April create a family of happiness and love from a tragedy?

A New Family for the Cowboy (Book 4): Blake Gibbons oversees all the agriculture at Brush Creek Horse Ranch, sometimes moonlighting as a general contractor. When he meets Erin Shields, new in town, at her aunt's bakery, he's instantly smitten. Erin moved to Brush Creek after a divorce that left her penniless, homeless, and a single mother of three children under age eight. She's nowhere near ready to start dating again, but the longer Blake hangs around the bakery, the more she starts to like him. Can Blake and Erin find a way to blend their lifestyles and become a family?

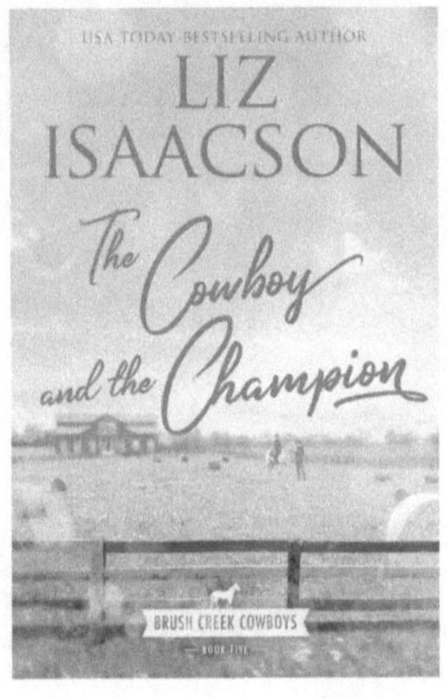

The Cowboy and the Champion (Book 5): Emmett Graves has always had a positive outlook on life. He adores training horses to become barrel racing champions during the day and cuddling with his cat at night. Fresh off her professional rodeo retirement, Molly Brady comes to Brush Creek Horse Ranch as Emmett's protege. He's not thrilled, and she's allergic to cats. Oh, and she'd like to stay cowboy-free, thank you very much. But Emmett's about as cowboy as they come…. Can Emmett and Molly work together without falling in love?

Schooled by the Cowboy (Book 6): Grant Ford spends his days training cattle—when he's not camped out at the elementary school hoping to catch a glimpse of his ex-girlfriend. When principal Shannon Sharpe confronts him and asks him to stay away from the school, the spark between them is instant and hot. Shannon's expecting a transfer very soon, but she also needs a summer outdoor coordinator—and Grant fits the bill. Just because he's handsome and everything Shannon's ever wanted in a cowboy husband means nothing. Will Grant and Shannon be able to survive the summer or will the Utah heat be too much for them to handle?

ABOUT LIZ

Liz Isaacson writes inspirational romance, usually set in Texas, or Wyoming, or anywhere else horses and cowboys exist. She lives in Utah, where she writes full-time, takes her two dogs to the park everyday, and eats a lot of veggies while writing. Find her on her website at feelgoodfiction-books.com

www.ingramcontent.com/pod-product-compliance
Lightning Source LLC
Chambersburg PA
CBHW050517110726
47899CB00005B/1493